When I seduced Tyler Flynn at the beginning of senior year, I never imagined he'd still be sneaking in and out of my bedroom window six months later.

Then again, nothing about our relationship had ever been conventional.

"Shh," I said. "My mom's upstairs."

"She never hears anything," Tyler said with a frustrated grunt.

My window was stuck again. I lay on my stomach on the bed, my eyes on his slim silhouette as he banged his palm against the latch, trying to loosen it. A string of profanity followed each thump. Tyler had zero patience for things that didn't yield easily.

I rolled over and pulled the covers up to my chin. He was right—my mother never heard anything. Not even the strange noises coming from her daughter's basement bedroom in the middle of the night. Just like she never smelled my cigarette smoke or saw the roadmap of red lines that snaked through the whites of my eyes after a particularly wild party. She probably wasn't even aware that my bedroom window opened up to the side of the house where a person could slip in and out, undetected in the darkness.

FAKING PERFECT

REBECCA PHILLIPS

KENSINGTON PUBLISHING CORP.
www.kensingtonbooks.com

KENSINGTON BOOKS are published by

Kensington Publishing Corp.
119 West 40th Street
New York, NY 10018

All Kensington titles, imprints, and distributed lines are available at special quantity discounts for bulk purchases for sales promotions, premiums, fund-raising, educational, or institutional use.

Special book excerpts or customized printings can also be created to fit specific needs. For details, write or phone the office of the Kensington sales manager: Kensington Publishing Corp., 119 West 40th Street, New York, NY 10018, attn: Sales Department; phone 1-800-221-2647.

ISBN-13: 978-1-61773-880-7
ISBN-10: 1-61773-880-8

First Trade Paperback Printing: July 2015

10 9 8 7 6 5 4 3 2 1

Printed in the United States of America

First Electronic Edition: July 2015

ISBN-13: 978-1-61773-881-4
ISBN-10: 1-61773-881-6

Chapter One

When I seduced Tyler Flynn at the beginning of senior year, I never imagined he'd still be sneaking in and out of my bedroom window six months later. Then again, nothing about our relationship had ever been conventional.

"Shh," I said. "My mom's upstairs."

"She never hears anything," Tyler said with a frustrated grunt.

My window was stuck again. I lay on my stomach on the bed, my eyes on his slim silhouette as he banged his palm against the latch, trying to loosen it. A string of profanity followed each thump. Tyler had zero patience for things that didn't yield easily.

I rolled over and pulled the covers up to my chin. He was right—my mother never heard anything. Not even the strange noises coming from her daughter's basement bedroom in the middle of the night. Just like she never smelled my cigarette smoke or saw the roadmap of red lines that snaked through the whites of my eyes after a particularly wild party. She probably wasn't even aware that my bedroom window opened up to the side of the house where a person could slip in and out, undetected in the darkness.

After a few more minutes of abuse, the window finally

creaked open. The faint, crisp scent of winter filtered through the stuffiness in the room. Tyler shoved his feet into his sneakers and turned to the window, bracing his arms on the sill and steeling his body in preparation to boost himself out. Then, changing his mind, he spun back around to face me.

"You really need a new window." He raised his voice as if he was *trying* to alert my mother to his presence. He loved to goad me, see how far he could push me before I got mad and started locking him out. "I can't risk getting stuck in here for the night."

My insides recoiled at the thought of spending the entire night with him. "I'll just grease the hinges again or something. Good night."

"Anxious to get rid of me, Lexi?"

"You're letting all the heat out," I replied.

He reached behind him to shut the window again and returned to the bed, where I was still snuggled up under the multicolored quilt my grandmother had made for me when I was a baby. I wondered what she'd think if she could see me now.

"What are you doing?" I asked when Tyler kicked off his shoes and crawled onto the bed.

He settled on his back on top of the quilt's patterned squares, eyes closed, arms crossed over his chest. "I'm not ready to go yet."

I squinted at his profile. Usually, he was out of here before his heart rate and breathing even had a chance to slow down. He never stayed with me, never lay next to me while my cheeks still burned from his prickly stubble and my own secret shame.

"We're going to get caught, Tyler."

"We're not going to get caught," he said with utmost confidence, like the petty criminal he was. "You said your mom never sets foot in your room."

This was true. She'd avoided my room for years, and not because she respected my privacy. Six years ago, when I brought Trevor home from the pet store, I quickly realized that owning a corn snake came with some unexpected perks. For one, people thought I was weird, which I didn't mind much back in sixth grade. And two, my mother's deathly fear of snakes afforded me hours of uninterrupted alone time in my room, which I didn't mind either.

I wasn't sure why she was so afraid. Trevor (named after a boy I had a crush on at the time) lived in a tank on my dresser and rarely escaped anymore. He spent most of his time either hiding or eating the dead mice I stored in boxes behind a stack of ice trays in the freezer. Mom avoided the freezer too.

"So," Tyler said, wrapping one of my strawberry-blond curls around his index finger. "You wanna do it again?"

"No." I reached down to retrieve my T-shirt and slipped it on under the blankets. Once was enough. Once was always enough to release the pent-up frustration inside me, if only for a little while. Twice wouldn't happen unless I initiated it. I needed to be the one in control, which was why I'd chosen Tyler, Oakfield High's resident badass/burnout/man-whore. His type dodged commitment and never fell in love. He didn't care about being used, and he knew how to be discreet. And even though he was failing most of his classes, he wasn't stupid. He'd never risk the good thing he had going with me. Also, the sneaking around turned him on.

Tyler gave up on trying to tempt me with an encore and lit up a cigarette. He wedged a couple pillows behind his head and took long, lazy puffs as if relaxing in the park.

Annoyed, I sat up and flicked on the lamp.

"Hey," he said, shutting his eyes against the light.

I looked over at him, noticing that his perpetually tousled dark hair was even messier than usual, likely because I'd been running my fingers through it earlier. His shirt was inside out, his zipper half down, his neck mottled with what looked like a bite mark. Was this what he looked like afterward? I'd never actually looked closely at him after the fact. Usually, all I saw was his back and then his legs as he shimmied out my window.

"Why are you still here, Tyler?" I asked, waving away his smoke. "It's one o'clock in the morning. I want to go to sleep."

He smirked. "And have sweet dreams about Mr. Wonderful?"

"Don't push me," I warned.

"Oh right. Sorry, I forgot. It's a Lexi Rule."

I shot him a look. Okay, so I did have a few rules, but nothing unreasonable or difficult to follow. One, he had to avoid me at school. Two, he had to keep his mouth shut about what we did together. And three . . . under no circumstances was he ever allowed to tease me about my friend Ben, who I'd had an unrequited crush on for two years. Ben, with his integrity and values and golden boy looks, did not belong in this room with us. He wasn't like us.

Tyler finished his cigarette and dropped the butt into the half-empty can of 7-Up on my nightstand. As he did this, I heard a cough coming from upstairs and then footsteps plodding across the floor. My mother was walking from her bedroom, where she stayed up late every night watching the Game Show Network, to the kitchen, which was right above my room. Next, she would pour herself a glass of iced tea or white wine if there was any left over from the weekend, and then trudge back to her bedroom and shut the door. *Family Feud, Press Your Luck, Match Game, Password, The Price is Right* . . . she watched them all for hours on end, her expression never changing aside from a raised eyebrow now and again when a contestant was being particularly boneheaded. She gave me the same look sometimes.

"Okay, it's time to go now," I said, elbowing Tyler in the ribs. It freaked me out that he was beside me and not evacuating the house like it was on fire, which had been the case most other nights. Having him here while my mother was awake went way beyond my comfort zone. "I have a math test first period tomorrow. Come *on*." I poked him again, and he finally started to get up.

"Oh yeah, I guess I do, too." He looked down at me and smirked again. "Thanks for helping me study again. I never knew vectors and shit could be so interesting."

"You're welcome," I said, even though we hadn't studied at all. The last time we really studied together was back in late September, when I used our upcoming math quiz as an excuse to get him into my room for the first time. He needed a tutor, I needed an outlet. It was all very practical and casual. Clinical, almost. Devoid of emotion.

Lately, though, I could feel something changing, the way animals can sense when a storm is near. A subtle shift in the air between us. A possessive look burning into my back as I passed him in the hall at school. A touch so gentle it made my breath hitch. And now this, sticking around as long as he dared, not quite ready to leave.

This was bad. It seemed Tyler was on the verge of breaking the one rule I'd left unspoken. Do not get attached.

I needed to squash this problem immediately.

"Let's not do this anymore," I said to his bare back as he took off his shirt and turned it right side out. I kept my eyes on the tattoo on his left shoulder blade—the grim reaper in his black cloak, smiling and holding a scythe. The harvester of souls.

Tyler pulled on his shirt and glanced back at me with a

flickering of a smile. I tried not to let it get to me. All my life, I'd suffered such a weakness for boys like him. In the first grade, I'd had a massive crush on Cody Hatcher, who pushed kids at recess and regularly spit on the teachers. By middle school, I felt myself drawn to the troubled boys with bad home lives who cut class and sneaked cigarettes behind the convenience store. Then, in the tenth grade, when I started cultivating my good girl image and making new friends, I gave up on the bad boys and set my sights on the nice, well-adjusted ones. Like Ben Dorsey, for instance, track star and honors student and way too good to be true. Too good for *me*, anyway, which was why I'd strayed back to the bad boys again.

But nobody could ever know about that.

"Do what?" Tyler said, even though he knew full well what I meant. He'd heard those words from me before.

"This." I gestured to the tangled sheets and my half-nude body and then to him, the ultimate bad boy with his tattoo and cigarettes and close, personal acquaintance with the entire Oakfield police department.

"This," he repeated, leaning over the bed toward me, his hands sinking into the mattress. I pulled away from him, but not before I caught the warm, smoky scent of his skin. He saw my reaction and laughed, which infuriated and excited me. "You really want to stop this. You want me to leave and never come back. Right?"

"Right."

We stared each other down. From above, I could hear the faint applause of a live studio audience.

"Right," Tyler said, lowering his face to mine. He kissed me and I let him, even though once had been enough and he was the one in control and my mother was upstairs and awake.

I knew I was supposed to refuse him, to squash this problem once and for all and become the girl most people saw each day—the smiling, confident girl who'd secured a place at the top of the high school food chain. But I could never truly be her, at least not permanently. So I turned off the lamp, wrapped my arms around Tyler's neck, and pulled him closer. I shut my mind to everything else, including the intrusive thoughts of Ben. Ben, who I possibly could have loved if only I was brave enough to love someone like him.

I didn't love Tyler Flynn. I didn't even like him.

Chapter Two

In the morning I took an extra-long shower, ridding my skin and hair of cigarette smoke and Tyler's scent. Then I got to work on my daily transformation routine.

My hair, otherwise known as the bane of my existence, took the longest to perfect. When I was little it was yellowish-blond and curly, but over the years it had evolved into a pale copper shade and the curl had loosened somewhat. Still, it needed vast amounts of product to tame, especially on damp days.

Next, a layer of foundation to hide the spattering of freckles across the bridge of my nose, and then a few dramatic swipes of black liquid eyeliner that always felt like too much. But heavy eye makeup was the trend and fitting in was imperative.

Lastly, the outfit—jeans and shirt and coat and boots, all the right fit and the right colors and the right labels. Dangly earrings, a few bracelets, a knotted scarf around my neck . . . check, check, and check. Costume complete, I was now fit for school.

Mom and I owned one car, a five-year-old Ford Focus that we shared. Maybe *shared* is the wrong word, since sharing generally means a fairly equal division. Mom took the car to work each day from Monday to Saturday, which meant I couldn't use it to drive to school. She was a massage therapist at a day spa and she usually worked well into the evening. By the time she got home, I was either too tired to go out or already gone. Maybe, if I was lucky and she happened to be too hungover from the night before to get out of bed, I got to use the car on Sunday, her day off.

No car on school days meant either walking in unpredictable weather or the bus. Or in my case, a friend with his own wheels.

Right on schedule, Ben's silver Acura TL pulled up in front of my house. The TL was his newest acquisition, a step up from his last car and utterly impractical for an eighteen-year-old boy, but you could get away with driving lavish cars when your father owned the dealership.

"Hey," Emily said when I slid into the backseat. She handed me a paper to-go cup and I breathed in the familiar scent of nutmeg. A large chai tea latte, my favorite.

"Hi." I leaned over to say good morning to Ben and Kyla, the girl he'd been seeing for the past month and a half. I'd made little headway bonding with her. She was much friendlier to Emily, but only because Emily was Ben's cousin and in no way a threat to her. I wasn't a threat to her, either. Ben treated me the same way he treated Emily—like a blood relative. When he was dating someone, which he almost always was, he didn't even look at other girls, let alone hook up with them. Kyla had nothing to worry about.

"Lexi," Emily said in a scolding tone as I settled back into my seat.

"What?" I knew exactly why she was frowning, but I was majorly talented at playing innocent and it never hurt to try. Suddenly, I was glad the thick stripes of eyeliner made my eyes seem wider and more naive. I blinked at her.

"You promised us you'd stop."

"I did!" For about a week . . .

She leaned over to sniff my hair and then drew back, her narrowed eyes steady on my face. "You didn't. You smoked."

I looked away and took a sip of latte. Okay, so I'd smoked a cigarette this morning while reviewing my math. My first one in nine days. I knew how much my friends hated it, and I *had* promised to stop, but I'd woken up feeling so rattled over last night's first-ever double feature with Tyler that I'd just needed something to calm my nerves. I was sure I'd stood outside long enough to air myself out, but apparently not. I felt doubly guilty. "I'm sorry."

Ben sighed and ran a hand through his short, golden-blond hair. *Everything* about him was golden, from his hair to his status at school right down to the flecks in his warm hazel eyes. Even after knowing him for two years, his greatness still intimidated me at times. Emily was the same, wholesome and admired and untouchable. Maybe it ran in their family. It was hard work, being worthy of these two.

"Where's the pack?" Ben asked, turning around and giving me a deliberate look, like he already knew I had it on me—which I did.

I'd thought I might be able to sneak another one by the soccer field later.

I extracted the half-full pack of smokes from my bag and passed it up to him. Wordlessly, he stuffed it into his jacket pocket, keeping it safe until he could get to a garbage can. Ben and Emily liked the idea of saving me . . . from cancer, from other people, from myself. And I let them, because frankly, I could use some saving.

"I'll quit for good this time," I told my friends, who were both wearing *I'm-very-disappointed-in-you* looks. Kyla stared straight ahead, sipping her coffee.

Emily opened her mouth to say something but was interrupted by a loud tapping noise. We all jumped and looked toward the driver's side window. My neighbor, Nolan Bruce, stood shivering beside the car, half-frozen water dripping off his jacket sleeves. He must have overslept and missed the bus again. Ben pressed the button to open the window.

"Can I get a ride?" Nolan asked, leaning over to see our faces. "I slept in and missed the bus again."

"Sure," Ben said, barely managing to sound civil. He wasn't done being miffed at me for my relapse. The annoyed set of his mouth grew even more pronounced when Nolan climbed in and tossed his soaking wet backpack against the back of Ben's seat.

I shot Nolan a look. He knew Ben was particular about his car, but that never stopped him from testing boundaries.

"Oops." Nolan made a big show of stowing his backpack on the floor and wiping at the wet leather with his equally wet sleeve. "There, good as new."

Ben grunted and hit the gas. We drove to school in total silence, which wasn't an unusual phenomenon whenever Nolan hitched a ride with us. Because he was my friend, Ben and Emily and my other friends tolerated him, but just barely. They didn't get our relationship, couldn't understand why I spent so much time with "that weirdo across the street." They assumed we were involved in some sort of clandestine romance, which was ridiculous. For one, Nolan and I had grown up together and interacted like siblings, and for another, Nolan wasn't hot, at least not by their standards. He was slightly overweight and a little geeky in an intellectual, artistic, oddball sort of way.

Basically, Ben and Nolan's personalities just didn't mesh. Nolan called Ben "Pretty Boy" behind his back and often commented that he looked like he belonged on a ski hill in Vermont (true) and Ben was convinced that Nolan deliberately antagonized him just for fun (also true). Being stuck in a car with the two of them at the same time made me want another cigarette.

By the time we got to school, it had stopped snowing and Ben seemed more relaxed. He held Kyla's hand as we all crossed the parking lot, Nolan trailing a few feet behind us. Ben paused for a moment at the trash can near the main doors and chucked in my pack of cigarettes. I glanced over my shoulder to say a mental farewell to my cancer sticks and saw Nolan cautiously dip a hand into the trash can. A second later, his hand reappeared, clutching my undamaged pack. He grinned at me and slid it into his pocket. I pressed my lips together to avoid laughing, but a snort slipped out.

Ben turned to me and smiled, oblivious to the cigarette rescue. "What's so funny?"

"Nothing," I said as I walked through the door he held open for us. Always the gentleman. "Nothing at all."

Inside, the five of us split up into groups and went our separate ways. Emily and me to math, Ben and Kyla to whatever classes they had, and Nolan to the stairs that led to the bottom floor, where he'd undoubtedly sneak out and have a smoke before—or during—first class.

"Are you ready?" Emily asked once we'd settled at our table in math class. The teacher hadn't arrived yet.

"For what?" I said, still obsessing about last night with Tyler, the feel of his hands on my hips, guiding me toward him, the triumphant look in his eyes when I finally surrendered. What had come over me?

"For the zombie apocalypse. What do you think?" She snapped her fingers in front of my face. "The test. Are you ready for the test?"

"Oh. Sure." Emily was always extra cranky in math class because it was her least favorite subject. "Are you?"

"I hope so," she said, biting her lip as she glanced over the notes in front of her. "If I don't get at least a ninety-five, my final grade will drop."

"Em, we've already applied to colleges. They probably won't even look at our final grades."

"Yeah, but my parents will," she muttered as if a slight dip in her average was grounds for hysteria.

I didn't get that about Emily and Ben's family, the focus on excellence. I may have hung around with the school brains, but I wasn't one myself. The only subject I really excelled in was math which, coincidentally, was the one and only class I shared with Emily. In fact, math was the reason we'd first become friends back in sophomore year.

Emily, like Ben, took mostly honors classes, churned out an impressive grade-point average, and cleaned up at the academic awards ceremony at the end of each year. But unlike Ben, one thing kept her from intellectual perfection: math. She was simply *good* at it, not great at it (which in her world translated to "I suck at it"). After trying honors math for a semester in tenth grade, she grudgingly accepted that she wasn't a well-rounded genius and transferred to the regular, less daunting math class, where she chose the seat next to me and stayed for the next two years.

I'd seen her around school before that, walking through the halls with the same dark-haired girl and sometimes a blond boy who I'd assumed was her brother because they were so similar in looks. I knew her name; everyone in school did. She was everywhere—on the girls' basketball and volleyball teams, yearbook committee, school newspaper. Almost every day her name blared over morning announcements as the go-to coordinator for such-and-such club or event. And with her long, sleek blond hair, sprightly walk, and funky black-framed glasses, she was hard to miss.

In sophomore math, the two of us bonded over trigonometry and the distracting sight of our young male teacher's cute ass. Within weeks I'd been introduced to her best friend, Shelby Meyer, and the blond boy who turned out to be her first cousin, Ben. Right from the start they all took me under their collective wing, like I was a poor, underprivileged child they felt the urge to protect. And at that point in my life, I needed it. I needed them. They were the right kind of friends, respectable people I could reinvent myself with and hide behind.

Yes, I thought the first time I'd walked down the hall with the acclaimed Emily Manning and her friends. *I have arrived. This is where I belong.*

And through a lot of hard work on my part, it was where I still stood today. Somehow, despite several pitfalls and many secrets, I held my position at the top of the Oakfield High food chain. But there was no getting comfortable, not when I knew that at any moment I could either lose my grip or be shoved off completely.

"Okay, folks, everything off the tables," Mrs. Cranston—our middle-aged, female, non-distracting, senior year math teacher—ordered as she sailed into the room. Right on her heels was Tyler, hair still damp from his morning shower. He sauntered toward the back of the room, avoiding not just my eyes but everyone else's, too. He looked tired. When I thought about why, I felt my face go warm.

"Still asleep this morning, folks? I said everything off the tables." Mrs. Cranston plunked her extra-large coffee on her desk and began to pass out the test papers. "All I want to see is a pencil, a calculator, and a great big smile."

As I passed the stack of tests to the table behind us, I caught another glimpse of Tyler, slouched in his chair and yawning. He ran his hands through his hair and glanced around the room. His eyes skipped over mine and landed squarely on Skyler Thomas, who was watching him, smiling, the end of her pencil resting on her plump bottom lip.

"Begin," said Mrs. Cranston, collapsing into her chair with her jumbo coffee.

I faced forward and got to work.

Chapter Three

"Lexi?" My mother poked her head into my room and then, when she saw what I was doing, immediately retreated. "Are you almost done?"

"Yes," I said, rolling my eyes. She acted like Trevor was going to leap out of my hands and close his mouth around her jugular. As if. I'd told her numerous times that corn snakes were not aggressive, but her fear was so bone-deep that it made her irrational. "You can come in, you know. He's back in his tank." I'd just finished giving him fresh water, exchanging the piece of Astroturf at the bottom of his tank for a clean one, and now I was dangling a dead, defrosted mouse in front of his face.

Mom peered around the door frame again and let out a strangled yelp. "I can't watch it *eat*."

I dropped the mouse and secured the lid on the tank. Trevor lay still, head up, as if checking his dinner for signs of life. I watched him fondly for a moment, enjoying the sinuous beauty in his movements, the vibrant oranges and reds in his skin. For as long as I could remember, I'd loved snakes. Emily, whose mother taught psychology at a high school in the city, often joked that I liked them because they were phallic-looking and I had penis envy. But that was hardly the reason. They just appealed to me. Who needed puppies and kittens when you could own something unusual, something exotic, something that stayed with you for decades.

"When are you going to get rid of that slimy thing?" Mom asked as I emerged from my room and shut the door behind me.

"I could ask you the same," I said lightly.

A tinge of pink leaked through her fake-and-bake tan. "And what is *that* supposed to mean?"

I walked past her to the stairs. She knew exactly what it meant. Her latest boyfriend, Pete something, was a forty-five-year-old unemployed construction worker with an ex-wife and four kids he didn't support. He also stole all our food, spent Mom's money, and called her names whenever she forgot to buy beer. He was the definition of *slimy*.

Then again . . . considering who I entertained in my bedroom on a regular basis, it wasn't like I had much room to judge.

"Anyway"—she followed me to the kitchen, where I washed my hands at the sink—"I went downstairs to tell you . . . shit, I forgot what I was gonna tell you." She kneaded her forehead for a second. "Oh yeah. You can use the car tonight. I don't need it after all."

"I thought you and . . ." I refused to say the jerk's name. "I thought you were going to the casino tonight."

"Nah." She caught her reflection in the microwave door and started picking at her hair, smoothing it down. Mom and I shared the same kind of hair, but hers had been chemically straightened into submission and bleached light blond. Like Barbie. "I have a date, actually," she said, a sly smile curling her lips.

I dried my hands on a dish towel and raised my brows at her. "What happened to . . . ?"

"Pete?" She stopped playing with her hair and sighed. "He's history."

Whew, I thought. We'd have food in the house again.

"This guy," she said, fanning herself with her hand, "is freaking gorgeous."

That was how my mom talked, like a teenager sharing secret crushes with her besties. She even looked the part, with her diminutive figure and heavy makeup and short skirts. At thirty-nine, she was edging very close to the "too old to pull off that look" category. My friends thought she was fun and cool, but they didn't see her makeup-free and sullen in front of the TV late at night, or smudged and wrinkled and smelling like a stale tavern on Sunday afternoons.

"He's not a client, is he?" I asked, suspicious. Because she worked at a day spa, most of her massage therapy clients were women, but the occasional straight man showed up. She'd dated a client once, years ago, even though it was unprofessional and possibly even against the rules. He must have really enjoyed her massages.

"No. I met him at Starbucks a couple days ago when I was out on my lunch break. There was this big mix-up and he accidentally grabbed my hazelnut latte." She giggled. "Anyway, everything got straightened out and we just started talking."

Moving over to the table, I idly started thumbing through yesterday's mail. Flyers, coupons, bank statements, and an innocent-looking letter from the cable company. I ripped it open.

"His name is Jesse," my mother babbled on, her voice honey-sweet and lilting like it did when she was in a good mood. Her *I-met-a-new-man* voice, full of promise. "He works in one of those huge office buildings on the waterfront. He's really smart and he must make good money because—"

"Mom," I said, not taking my eyes off the paper I was reading, the one from the cable company that claimed our bill was well overdue. Usually she hid this kind of mail from me, knowing I'd nag her about it. I didn't even have a key to our mailbox. "This payment was due *weeks* ago. They're cutting off our cable on Monday."

She finally shut up about the latte guy and stared at me, open-mouthed. "The cable?" Panic seeped in as it dawned on her that she'd soon be without The Game Show Network.

"Yes, the cable." The paper crackled as my fingers tightened around it. "What else didn't you pay?"

She closed her mouth and started gnawing on her bottom lip. "I'm *sure* I paid the electric bill this month."

I took one look at the uncertainty on her face and rushed down the hall to the spare bedroom where we kept the computer. She followed close behind. I brought up online banking and gestured for her to enter her username and password, information she refused to divulge to me no matter how much I begged. "I'm the mother and you're the child. *I* pay the bills around here," she'd say, even though it was only half true. Sometimes she paid them, sometimes she didn't, and we never knew which one it was until an overdue notice appeared in the mail or, in extreme cases, we lost the cable, phone, lights. We'd lived a few days in complete darkness more than once.

"Okay," she said slowly as she looked over her account. "So I didn't pay it. I will right now, don't worry." She sat down in the computer chair and started typing.

"My *God*, Mom," I growled. She was a child. I lived with a bleached, tanned, almost-forty-year-old child. "I set reminders for you on your phone and everything."

"Yeah, well . . . " She shut down the browser and spun around in the chair, her expression a mix of apology and belligerence. "They always get paid eventually, don't they?"

"No! That's the problem."

Her face turned pink again. "Get off my back, Lexi," she shouted. "So a bill gets paid a little late sometimes. Who cares? I'm sick of you constantly nagging at me. Nag, nag, nag. *I'm* the mother and you're the—"

"Right," I said, cutting her off. "*I'm* the child. And that dynamic has always worked so well around here, hasn't it?"

She stood up to her full five-foot-one height and glared at me. "And what is *that* supposed to mean, Lexi Claire?"

Oh, I knew she was angry when she brought out my full name, the name I used to go by when I was little but shortened to just Lexi when I was twelve. *Claire* came from my paternal grandmother, a woman I didn't even remember. I thought of her in the same way I thought of my father—a stranger who was probably dead by now.

"Nothing, Mother," I replied with false sweetness. She opened her mouth to yell at me some more but I didn't give her the chance. I turned and walked out, not stopping until I reached the front door. I yanked it open and stepped out into the cold, forgetting about my jacket. Too pissed to even notice the biting March wind, I tramped across the street to Nolan's house.

"I'd offer you a shot of vodka," Nolan said, smoothing his finger over a line in his pencil sketch, "but my parents put a lock on the liquor cabinet last weekend after they figured out that Landon had been into it. He and his friends were sneaking rum and then filling the bottle back up with water."

I laughed. We'd done the exact same thing at that age. Nolan's little brother was fourteen and apparently following in our devious footsteps. "It's okay," I said, shivering. I'd been sitting on the couch in the Bruces' basement family room, cocooned in a fuzzy blanket, for the past twenty minutes. The walk over here had taken forty-five seconds, just enough time to give me a lingering chill.

"No plans this evening?" Nolan asked, his eyes glued to his sketch pad. "Don't tell me the Preppy Posse is staying in on a Saturday night."

I shoved his leg with my foot, but even that didn't break his concentration. He was in the zone. I'd realized Nolan was going to be an artist the day he got mad at me for going outside the lines as we colored a picture of the Teletubbies together. We were four.

"We're going to the movies. The late show." With any luck, my mother would be long gone on her date before I ventured back over to get ready. "How about you? Any plans tonight? Amber?"

He shook his head as he shaded a section of eyebrow in his drawing. People were his specialty. He drew family, friends, celebrities, total strangers. Under Nolan's hand, faces came to life on paper. "Her grandmother died yesterday."

"Oh," I said, frowning. Amber was Nolan's girlfriend. They'd started dating this past summer. I liked her for several reasons—she was nice, she treated Nolan really well, and she didn't bat an eye when she came over to find me hanging out with him. Most girls would have been wary, but Amber was open-minded and trusting—necessary qualities for a girl who dated a guy whose best friend was me. "That sucks."

"Yeah."

"You can come out with us tonight, if you want."

He laughed. "I think I'll stay here."

I snuggled down into my blanket and contemplated doing the same. I loved being in Nolan's family room. His house was almost identical to the one I lived in with Mom—split-level, four bedrooms (our house had three), two bathrooms, and a family room on the lower level. But while my family room at home was a graveyard of boxes and dusty exercise equipment, the Bruce family room lived up to its name with its comfortable furniture, wood stove, big-screen TV, and every video game system known to man. It was our favorite place to hang out, except when Landon was down here with his friends, polluting the room with potato chip crumbs and odors that made me glad I didn't have a brother of my own.

Teresa, Nolan's mother, came down the stairs, a stack of folded towels in her arms. "Check the bottom drawer!" she hollered over her shoulder as she entered the room. Those words, I assumed, were directed upstairs toward her husband or younger son. She turned back around and spotted me curled up on the couch with just my face and a few strands of hair showing. "Oh, hi, sweetie," she greeted me, continuing on to the bathroom. When she returned empty-handed, she started gathering up game controllers and empty soda cans. "You haven't been over in a while," she said, peering at me closely. It didn't matter that the blanket hid ninety-nine percent of my body; she always knew when something was amiss with me.

"I've been busy," I told her. "Studying hard. You know me." That's the problem, I thought. She did know me, all too well. The entire family did. They knew when I arrived at their door, shivering and out of breath, my cheeks flushed with anger, I'd had enough of being in my own house and craved the normalcy and warmth of theirs.

Teresa narrowed her eyes, which were light brown like Nolan's. "Is she drinking?"

"No. The bills again."

Teresa sighed and went back to hunting for discarded wrappers and cans. Nolan kept drawing, barely paying attention. He'd heard conversations like this between me and his parents more times than either of us could count.

It started when I was six, the first time Mom passed out from drinking too much wine and didn't hear me when I called out in the middle of the night with one of my nightmares. When I went to her room and found her sprawled on her bed, fully dressed and unresponsive, I panicked and ran—in my bare feet at two in the morning—across the street to the Bruces' house. That was back when Nolan's mother and mine were still best friends.

"Let me know if you need anything, okay?" Teresa told me before going back upstairs. I assured her I would. "And Nolan, sweetie . . . could you please not get pencil smudges all over the couch?"

Nolan smoothed another line, blurring it, before nodding in his absent, preoccupied way.

I peeked over at his drawing and came face-to-face with Mr. Teng, our physics teacher. "That's incredible, Nolan." It blew me away that he could recreate facial features just from memory. I was barely able to draw a straight line.

"Eh," he said, shrugging and closing his sketch pad. "It's not done yet." He threw the pad and pencil on the coffee table and stretched out his hand. His fingertips, as usual, were stained black with graphite. "Let's play *Call of Duty.*"

I glanced at my watch. Seven-fifteen. I still had plenty of time. "Okay."

He set up the game and handed me a controller. "Want some pretzels?"

"Sure." Just as I uttered the word, my stomach let out a thunderous growl. My body felt empty. Concave. When Nolan was halfway up the stairs, I called, "Bring down some cookies too, would you?"

"Oreos or chocolate chip?" he called back from the top of the stairs.

"Oreos!" I replied at the same volume. One of my favorite things about this house was the constant, good-natured yelling back and forth, disembodied voices communicating from different rooms of the house. Always loud and chaotic, but rarely angry. At home, I'd never even think to bellow a question to my mother in the kitchen while I was using the toilet or something. But here, I did it just as easily as Teresa called me "sweetie," the same term of endearment she used for her husband and her sons. And the dog and cat, too.

While Nolan was up in the kitchen, I sent a text to Emily, letting her know I had the car and could pick everyone up for the movie later. Then, as quick as I dared, I pulled up the message Tyler had sent me an hour ago—can I c u tonite—and tapped out a response.

Yes. 1:00.

"Sorry, all we have left is stale gingersnaps."

I startled at Nolan's voice and shoved my phone back into the pocket of my sweater. "Yum," I said as he dumped the box in my lap and settled in next to me with a giant mixing bowl of pretzels. I dug into the box and grabbed a handful of cookies, even though I knew no matter how much I tried to relieve the hollow ache in my stomach, I'd never truly feel full.

Chapter Four

My mother's date with Latte Guy must have gone well because she was up bright and early on Sunday, hangover-free and blasting Green Day on the stereo as she vacuumed the living room. For the rest of the day, she cleaned the bathrooms and organized our finances and made a chicken pot pie for dinner. I liked my mother's New Man phase the best. It was when she most resembled a normal parent. Too bad it never lasted.

She stayed in maternal mode all day and then went to bed at the reasonable hour of eleven o'clock, where she watched the news instead of *Wheel of Fortune*. Man, I thought, this new guy must be something special.

Her good mood still hadn't waned by Monday morning. When I strode into the kitchen, dressed and ready for school, I discovered half a bagel sitting on a plate in the middle of the counter, a small piece of paper beside it. A note. *Have a good day!* it said in my mother's girly script. Two days ago she was screaming at me, and now she was wishing me a good day. I munched on the bagel and shook my head. She was certifiable.

Like clockwork, Ben's Acura appeared at my curb at eight-fifteen on the dot. I was standing in the driveway, waiting. As I walked toward the car, I realized something was off. Emily was sitting next to Ben in the front, and

Kyla was nowhere to be seen. She could be sick today, I reasoned. But no. When I climbed into the backseat, the crackle of tension in the air told me otherwise.

"Hey," I said, storing my backpack next to my feet and buckling my seat belt.

"Hey," Emily said, tossing a smile over her shoulder.

Ben said nothing. Just put the car into drive and hit the gas.

"Uh," I said after a minute of silence. "Where's Kyla?"

"Couldn't tell you," he replied with an apathetic shrug.

Emily glanced back at me, her glasses glinting in the sun, and quickly rolled her eyes. She never had much patience with Ben when he was acting quiet and sulky, which happened every time one of his girlfriends did something to piss him off. Okay, so he and Kyla were definitely done. I could barely wait to get to school.

As it turned out, I didn't get the chance to talk to Emily until after math class. My stomach fluttered in anticipation as we gathered our books. As much as I wanted to demand details, it was important that I wait for her to bring it up. She had no idea I had a crush on Ben.

Ben didn't even know I had a crush on Ben. I hid it well. He liked peppy, cheerleader-type girls who laughed easily, drew hearts on everything, and wore their hair in smooth ponytails. And no matter how hard I tried to tailor myself into what he wanted, he seemed to sense it was all an act. That he was too good for me. I'd never be anything more than his friend, and any romantic feelings I felt for him had to stay locked up inside, along with so many other things.

It was a shame. He had more in common with me than he did with those cheerleader girls. We'd both been raised by single parents. Only with him, it was his father. His mother died in a car accident when Ben was four, a tragedy that made him even more endearing to the girls around school ("Poor baby, he needs mothering!"). As for me, I only pretended my other parent was dead. It sounded better than "he was an addict who abandoned me when I was four." All I'd told my friends was that my father was gone, which was the truth. He hadn't been in my life for over thirteen years and I barely even remembered him. My mother said he was most likely dead of a drug overdose by now, but that was just speculation. I often wondered what it felt like to *know* your parent was dead, to never have to wonder if he was out there somewhere, ignoring your existence.

"Stupid geometry," Emily grumbled as we left the classroom together. We'd gotten our math tests back and she hadn't done as well as she'd hoped. "Why do I even have to take this class? When does a journalist ever need to do math? It's not like I dream of being an accountant or something." She cut her eyes toward me.

I'd mentioned to her months ago that I might want to study accounting in college. I liked numbers. They were steady and reliable. Not like letters and words, which could be misread and twisted and designed to hurt.

"Three more months until graduation and then you'll never have to think about it again," I said, wishing she'd spill about Ben and Kyla already. "You eating lunch with us today?" I asked her. Emily pretty much ran the school newspaper, which meant she spent a lot of her lunch hours editing instead of eating.

"Yeah. Shelby's coming, too. She said to wait for her."

We rounded the corner to the hallway that contained our lockers. I dumped my books, extracted my lunch, and waited with Emily for Shelby to arrive. The three of us preferred to steer clear of the cafeteria—and its soggy cuisine—and eat our brown-bag lunches downstairs in Ms. Hollis's history classroom, which we'd gotten permission to use at lunchtime. Ms. Hollis liked us and had no problem leaving us unattended while she went off to eat her salad and gossip in the teacher's lounge.

"She must be in the bathroom again," Emily commented when Shelby failed to show up after five minutes.

"Uh-huh," I said vaguely. I was distracted by the sight of tousled dark hair and broad shoulders. Tyler was heading down the hallway with a few of his stoner friends, all of them looking like they'd just rolled out of bed. As they passed us, a couple guys turned to check us out, but Tyler kept moving like I wasn't even there. Just like I'd instructed him to do.

I looked over at Emily to find her inspecting my face as if it was one of those giant frogs we'd dissected last semester in biology. *Damn it.* She'd noticed me noticing Tyler. Time to backpedal.

"They smell like weed," I said, wrinkling my nose.

She continued to study me, her pale eyebrows lifting toward her hairline. It was true; they did give off the sweet, pungent scent of weed when they walked by. The same scent that clung to Tyler's skin some nights, and my hair when we smoked it together.

Emily nodded and backed off, even though she was obviously still suspicious. Shelby was unobservant and constantly distracted, but this girl missed nothing.

I took a deep breath and let it out through my nose, wondering as always what my friends would do if they knew the real me, the me who sneaked the school bad boy in through her bedroom window at night. The me who reverted to her old bad girl ways, on occasion. They'd be shocked, of course, and disappointed, and probably mad enough to ostracize me forever. Like most of the school—staff included—they thought Tyler was a loser. A troublemaker. I'd learned this in the spring of sophomore year, when I laid eyes on him for the first time. I'd been walking with Emily and she'd noticed me doing a double take as we passed him in the halls. He was hot even then, tall and lean with deep brown eyes and dark brown hair that always looked like he'd just run his fingers through it.

"Don't even think about it," Emily had told me. "That's Tyler Flynn. He might be nice to look at but he's a total douchebag. He got suspended once for shoving Mr. Quinn, the shop teacher, into a filing cabinet. And he's been arrested for breaking and entering and apparently he's gotten, like, three girls pregnant. I hear he deals drugs, too. Believe me, you are way too good for him."

It wasn't until almost two years later, after he'd been in my bed a few times, that I got the real story from Tyler himself. He'd pushed Mr. Quinn, yes, but not into a filing cabinet and only because Quinn grabbed the front of Tyler's shirt during a disagreement. It was true he'd been arrested for B and E, but the pregnancy rumors were false. ("I cover my junk," he'd said—a claim I could attest to.)

As for the drugs, well, it was only marijuana, and he sold only to his friends.

"Finally," Emily said when Shelby joined us a few minutes later. Actually, Shelby's stomach arrived first and then Shelby herself.

"Sorry," she said, her cheeks pink with the exertion of walking. "I had to pee. Piper spent all of French class stomping on my bladder."

I glanced down at her stomach, which seemed to expand by the second like one of those time lapse movies with the flower growing from seed to bloom. Shelby wasn't the only pregnant girl this school had ever seen, but she was certainly the most memorable. For one, she was a straight-A honors student and (formerly) one of the most popular girls in school. And two, she wasn't one of those women who barely looked pregnant at six months along. No, Shelby looked thirty months pregnant at six months along. My mother said she was "all baby," meaning she was thin everywhere else, making her torpedo belly stick out even more. Every time I looked at that bulge, I wanted to run home and swallow my entire birth control pill prescription.

The three of us headed downstairs to Ms. Hollis's classroom, dodging several freshman girls on the stairs who stopped to gape at Shelby's middle. Shelby didn't even bother giving them dirty looks; she was already used to stares and snickering and rude remarks.

"I feel like a zoo exhibit," she said as we settled in the classroom with our lunches. Emily and I sat in desks in the front row while Shelby lowered her body into the teacher's chair. She couldn't sit comfortably anywhere else. "And here we have a pregnant teenager of the human species," she added in a dead-on Australian accent. "See how she moves, arching her back so she won't lose her balance and fall on her face. She is an exotic creature, and very, very dangerous when provoked."

Emily and I cracked up. "Just ask Evan," Emily added, and we all cracked up again.

Shelby and Evan—her on-again-off-again boyfriend and the baby's father—had been in one long, ongoing fight since she'd announced she was pregnant back in October. One minute he was there and they were planning a happily ever after with their little family. The next minute, he was gone and Shelby was crying, overwhelmed at the prospect of single motherhood. The tension between them had only increased when Evan skipped out on the eighteen-week ultrasound in January. It was Emily and I who stood by her side, holding her hand as she found out the baby's gender. A little girl. Piper Olivia.

"So," I said a few minutes later, keeping my voice casual and just vaguely curious. *Screw it*, I thought. I couldn't wait any longer. I had to know. "What happened between Ben and Kyla?"

"They broke up," Emily said, watching me as she picked up an orange and started to peel it.

I kept my face smooth. I swear, the girl could see right into my thoughts sometimes. She was going to make an excellent investigative journalist someday.

Shelby slurped up the last of her milk. "Why? Oh wait, let me guess. She got drunk at a party. Or . . . oh! I know! She forgot to use proper grammar in a text."

Emily stuffed a section of orange into her mouth. "She went back with her ex-boyfriend."

"Oh." Shelby seemed disappointed that she couldn't make fun of Ben's high standards some more. "Is Ben all broken up about it or has he moved on to the next girl in line already?"

I didn't get why Kyla would choose someone else over him. "He seemed pretty upset this morning in the car." *I'll console him. . . .*

Shelby made a *psshht* sound. "Yeah, he always gets upset when he finds out the girl he's dating is an actual human being with flaws like everyone else. Making mistakes is an inexcusable offense, you know. Believe me, I've been there."

To hide my expression from Emily's all-seeing eyes, I feigned a sudden interest in my sandwich. It still bothered me to be reminded that Ben and Shelby had dated once, back in junior year. For three agonizing months, I'd had to pretend not to care when I saw them together, holding hands in the hallways or kissing at parties. It didn't help that they looked great together, too. Due to Shelby's long dark hair and full lips and Ben's blondness and commanding presence, people at school had nicknamed them "Brangelina," as in Brad Pitt and Angelina Jolie—only without all the kids.

Oakfield High's version of Brangelina broke up when Shelby downed a few too many vodka shots at a party and ended up grinding on the makeshift dance floor with Evan Sharp, a friend of Ben's from the track team. Seeing his girlfriend pressing her ass into another guy's groin—and in front of everyone—proved to be too much for Ben. He dumped her later that night and Shelby started dating Evan soon after. Four months and one condom mishap later, she was pregnant.

Emily eventually forgave her friend for humiliating her cousin, but Ben had barely glanced at her since.

"Kyla was too ditzy anyway," Emily said through a bite of orange wedge. "Ben needs someone who's like him."

"Inflexible?" Shelby said. "Unforgiving?"

"Perfect," I blurted without thinking. They looked at me. My face started burning and I turned away to pack up the remnants of my lunch.

"If that's perfect," Shelby said wryly, "then I'll gladly take damaged."

I could feel Emily's gaze on me again, sharp and speculating.

No way could I ever let it show, this bone-deep longing I felt to be with Ben, to touch him and sit next to him and feel protected by the warmth of his shine. Showing it would lead to admitting it, and admitting it would only end in humiliation. Pining for a boy who was completely out of my league—not to mention totally uninterested— was just plain sad and pitiful. I'd worked too hard and come too far to be seen in that light again. I was a different person now. Better. Before I met Emily, I'd spent most of my time playing video games with Nolan or hanging around with kids like me, kids with no boundaries whose parents didn't give a shit about them. Nolan had his art and his caring, nuclear family to keep him grounded, but what did I have? An immature mother, an absentee father, and no special talents or skills to distract me or set me apart. I had Nolan's family, sure, but they weren't really mine. I didn't technically belong there.

So I'd found somewhere else to belong. Integrated myself with the smartest and most admired clique in school, changed my image to align with theirs, tricked them into thinking I was confident and stable, and secured a spot within their privileged circle. With them, I felt like I'd finally overcome my past. I wasn't some pathetic, fatherless girl who felt like trash inside; I was normal, at least on the outside, and I used this illusion to distance myself from who I really was.

Nolan was the only one who knew the real Lexi Shaw, and that was exactly how I intended to keep it.

Ben and Emily had various commitments to attend to after school, so I usually took the bus home with Nolan in the afternoons. Sometimes I'd go to his house and help him raid the cupboards until his parents got home, and other times, like today, I just wanted to be alone.

In my room, I lifted Trevor out of his tank and let him coil around my fingers as I straightened the quilt on my bed with my free hand. When it was perfectly neat, I sat down, opened the drawer of my nightstand, and brought out my snake book. The title, *Corn Snakes: An Owner's Guide*, hovered over a picture of a snake that looked a lot like Trevor.

My mother, even if she'd been brave enough to come into my room to snoop through my drawers, would never open a book with a full-color picture of a snake on it. This made it a perfect place to store things like pictures, especially pictures I'd stolen from the shoebox I'd found in her closet when *I* was snooping through *her* room.

At age nine, when I'd first seen these pictures, I'd known immediately that the guy looking back at me was my father. Five years had gone by since I'd last seen him, and my memories of him were fuzzy, but one glimpse of his eyes erased any lingering doubt. They were just like mine.

Instinctively, I'd hidden the pictures and never told my mother I'd seen them. I knew she wouldn't like it. She didn't even like to talk about my father unless it was to remind me that she'd saved us from him and that he was a horrible dad, the kind who didn't think twice about driving drunk with his baby in the car and spending the rent money on crack. He was so awful, Mom told me, so destroyed by drugs, she'd had no choice but to rip me from my home and move us several thousand miles away to a town where she knew no one except for her old friend Teresa. Once here, my mother made sure the dangerous man who was my father could never follow us or contact us. Restraining order issued, sole custody granted, ties severed. All for our own protection.

Pictures were destroyed too, except for these two that had somehow survived. In one, my parents sat together on a ratty brown couch, fingers curled around bottles of beer. My mother's hair was reddish blond, like mine, only she had bangs that defied the laws of gravity. She wore a loose neon-blue shirt that revealed one creamy shoulder and she was smiling, face flushed with happiness. She looked thrilled to be beside him, this guy with the shaggy brown hair and tattoos on his arms and eyes the exact color and shape of my own.

In the second picture, the same shaggy-haired, tattooed, blue-eyed man was holding me in his arms, helping me blow out the candles on my second birthday cake. I was a chubby-cheeked toddler with a mop of yellow ringlets for hair and a smile that mirrored the one on my father's face. We looked happy and relaxed, and completely unaware that in just two years, we'd be torn apart.

He looks so normal, I thought whenever I looked at these pictures. *This* was the man we'd escaped in such a hurry? The man who'd helped create me only to choose drugs and alcohol over his own daughter? The man who gave me up when I was just four years old, barely old enough to form any clear memories of my time with him?

I did have one memory, one that came back to me often, the image so vivid I knew it had to be real and not just something I'd fabricated from the various things I'd heard about him. No one had ever told me about walking in the woods with my father, holding his hand as he pointed out birds and squirrels and bugs. But I was positive it was something we used to do together. Even now, I remembered the warmth of his hand, wrapped snugly around my small one, and the smell of those woods, fresh and damp. More than anything, I remembered what I'd felt, being there with him. Not fear, not anxiety, but security and contentment, the way a little girl should feel with her father. This happy memory conflicted with everything my mother had ever told me about him, but I refused to let her words twist it or tamp it down. It was the only connection to him I had left. That, and the pictures.

Whenever I felt that familiar ache in my gut, I'd open my snake book and study those two pictures until my eyes watered. Rarely did it help, but I liked the feel of them in my hands, solid proof that at least one time in my life, I had a parent who held me close and seemed glad that I'd been born.

Chapter Five

"Wexi, can you wead this My Wittle Pony book to me?"

I jumped and looked over toward the side of the couch, where Grace stood with her blanket and a glossy pink book. I smiled at her, even though this was the fifth time she'd gotten up since I'd put her to bed less than an hour ago. Her big brown eyes and the way she pronounced my name melted me every time.

"Sure," I said, and she cuddled in next to me on the couch. I breathed in the smell of her blueberry-scented kid shampoo and began to read.

Somehow, despite growing up with a woman whose idea of mothering was storing easy-to-open, pre-made food within my reach so I wouldn't starve to death on weekends when she slept through breakfast and lunch, I loved taking care of little kids. Maybe maternal instincts skipped a generation, or maybe being around Nolan's nurturing mother had impacted my psyche. In any case, I'd graduated from the Babysitter Training Program at age eleven and had been taking care of children ever since. And I was good at it.

I'd been babysitting Grace ever since she and her parents moved onto my street about three years ago. She was only eight months old then. Her parents, Todd and Rachel, paid me well and trusted me implicitly. And Grace . . . she literally couldn't remember life before me. I watched her at least once a week, whenever her parents went out for a date night or had a scheduling conflict with work. She was always excited to see me.

"One more book? Pwease?" Grace begged after the Little Ponies had solved all their pony problems and lived happily ever after.

"It's nine-thirty, Gracie. Time to go to sleep."

She sighed and shook her head, making her chin-length brown hair flick against her face. She could be quite the diva. "I'm not tired."

"I am," I said, tossing the book on the expensive-looking coffee table in front of me. Todd and Rachel's house was a lot nicer than ours. Rachel was a registered nurse and Todd managed a car rental company. "Maybe *you* could put *me* to bed."

She giggled. "Okay." She went to use the bathroom and then tucked me into her twin-size bed. Only then did she climb in herself, clutching her yellow blanket in one hand and my fingers in the other.

We stayed that way, both of us passed out after a hard evening of coloring and dollhouse decorating, until her parents arrived home at midnight.

Todd offered to drive me home, but as usual, I declined. My house was a two-minute walk up the street and we lived in a very safe, quiet neighborhood. The only creatures I ever stumbled across between their house and mine were outdoor cats and the occasional raccoon.

The air felt mild and damp on my face as I trudged up the road. When my house came into view, my stomach dropped. An unfamiliar car sat in the driveway next to our Ford. *Great*, I thought as I passed it. Upon closer inspection, it was a Lexus SUV. Pricey. Usually, my mother's boyfriends drove pick-up trucks or dented cars with rust stains the size of my head.

Please, I thought, closing the front door with more force than usual. *Please don't let them be in bed together.*

They weren't. To my surprise, they were sitting at the kitchen table, mugs of some kind of dark liquid in front of them. My mother, showing all thirty-two of her bleached white teeth, and a man I assumed to be Latte Guy, smiling back at her.

"Oh," my mother said when she saw me, as if she'd forgotten I lived there. Or she was disappointed to see me. Probably both. "This is my daughter Lexi."

When the guy stood up to greet me, the first thought to enter my mind was *He's young.* Younger than my mother, for sure. Maybe early thirties.

"Jesse Holt," he said, his grip firm around my hand.

The second thought to enter my mind was that he was as good-looking as my mother had claimed. Tall, well-built, with close-cropped black hair and gray, almost colorless eyes. Eyes that stayed locked on mine as we shook hands. He oozed confidence.

"Hi," I said, nodding politely and then backing away. I knew from the strained smile on my mother's face that I was interrupting this . . . whatever it was. "Nice to meet you."

He smiled and maintained eye contact with me for a few more seconds, then sat back down across from my mother. Flustered, I excused myself and headed for my room. There was something about him, something not altogether pleasant. *Slick* was an apt description. He seemed like the type of guy who would sleep with someone and then steal her purse. Hopefully, Mom hadn't left any valuables lying around.

Once in my room, I closed and locked my door and then checked on Trevor. He was all curled up in his hide, digesting his weekly mouse meal. From where I was standing, I could just make out the muffled conversation going on above me in the kitchen—a high, giggly voice mingling with a deep, smooth one. Even though my room was toasty warm, a shiver ran through me. I unlocked my door and slipped next door to the bathroom, where I scrubbed my hands in the hottest water I could stand.

A loud thump woke me out of a dead sleep sometime later. I jolted upright in bed and looked around my dark room, trying to identify the source. My pounding heart almost stopped altogether when I saw a dark shadow pass by my window. Seconds later, there was a bang against the glass and then a face appeared. Relief filled me, quickly followed by anger. Tyler. He knew he wasn't supposed to just show up unannounced.

I scrambled out of bed, still half-asleep, and opened the window a few inches. "What are you *doing*?" I whisper-yelled.

He poked his head into the opening. "Can I come in?" he asked, giving me a blast of his alcohol breath.

"Are you insane? You're supposed to text me before coming over here."

He grinned and lowered his body so that his chest and legs were flush with the wet ground. "Insane? No. Drunk? Maybe. And I did text. Five times."

Just then I remembered that my phone was upstairs in my coat, stone cold dead.

"Let me in, Sexy Lexi." He laughed at this unoriginal nickname and then repeated it three more times. He was toasted. "Please? It's fuckin' cold out here."

Normally I would have slammed the window on his

neck in response, but for some reason I opened it wider and stepped aside. Tyler rolled over and then stuck his legs in, the rest of his body clumsily following.

I reached behind him to shut the window and then spun around to face him. "You have to be quiet. My mother has . . . " I cocked my head and listened for signs of life upstairs. Nothing. "Is there an SUV in the driveway?"

"No." His hands found my hips in the dark and he pulled me closer. "Why?"

"No reason."

He leaned in for a kiss. I wasn't exactly in the mood, but I kissed him back anyway.

He smelled like fresh air and smoke and whatever he'd been drinking earlier. As I slid my arms around his waist, my hand knocked against something solid near the inside pocket of his jacket. Shifting my face from his, I reached into the pocket and freed its contents: a small, half-empty bottle of spiced rum.

"Trying to get busted for underage drinking again?" I asked, dangling the bottle in front of his face. "Walking the streets, drunk, with this in your pocket? Not very bright of you."

He made an uncoordinated grab for the rum, but I snapped it away before he could make contact.

"Uh-uh-uh," I said as if scolding a naughty toddler and then watched his dark eyes flash as I opened the bottle and took a slow drink. The rum burned going down, making me gasp.

"Got any mix?" he asked. Smiling, he tugged on the bottle until I finally let go.

A few minutes later, we were sitting side by side against my headboard, chasing mouthfuls of spiced rum with sips of the warm Coke I'd swiped from the stockpile of cases in the laundry room. When our cans reached the half-empty mark, we filled them back up with the rest of the rum. The icky feeling I'd had going to bed had become a distant, fuzzy memory.

"So what have you been up to tonight?" I asked, wincing through another swallow. "I mean, before you decided to slam my window and scare the shit out of me." I was just buzzed enough not to care about the interested tone in my voice. Usually, I felt it best not to question Tyler about where he'd been and what he'd been doing before he showed up at my house. I didn't want to think about whose sloppy seconds I was getting whenever he kissed me.

"Party at Skyler's," he replied.

"Oh." Skyler was the one who always stared at him in math class. I was pretty sure he'd either already slept with her or was planning to. "How did you get here?"

"Walked, of course." He drained his Coke can and burped quietly. "You think I'd drive like this?"

"Maybe, if you still had a car."

He shot me a dirty look, and not because I'd accused him of being capable of impaired driving. He was still annoyed that his parents had taken away his car after one too many speeding tickets. He wouldn't get it back until—or *if*—he graduated. "And what have you been up to tonight, Sexy Lexi?" he asked, tugging on one of my curls.

I slapped his hand away. "I babysat. You know, one of those *honest* ways to make money?"

He reached for his discarded jacket and rooted in the pocket for his pack of cigarettes. "Are you saying"—he slid one out and stuck it between his lips—"I don't make an honest living?" He flicked his lighter and held the flame against the end of the cigarette, but his hand was swaying too much to ignite it. "I'm an entrepreneur," he added, stumbling over the word.

I let out an ungainly snort and started to laugh. "Give me that," I said, taking the lighter from him and holding it steady against the cigarette. When it was lit, I snatched it out of his mouth and put it in mine.

"First you steal my rum and now my cigs," Tyler said, indignant. "What's next? You want my wallet? My heart? No, wait . . . you already stole that."

The lighthearted atmosphere drained from the room and all of a sudden I felt completely sober. There it was again, that impending-storm feeling. That shift in the air between us. He'd never said anything like that before, and even though I knew the alcohol had surely loosened his tongue, the implication in his words was pretty clear. To him, I wasn't just an outlet or a booty call or someone to share rum and a smoke with. Somehow, without any encouragement on my part, I'd become more.

I passed the cigarette back to him. "Tyler—"

"I was just kidding." He chuckled a little, but it sounded hollow. Forced. He looked away and took a drag off the cigarette, holding the smoke in his lungs for several seconds. It must have burned.

I felt the stirrings of nausea. "You should probably go. It's really late."

He exhaled, finally. "I don't even have a heart."

I'd thought so too, until that moment. His apparent lack of a heart was why I'd chosen him in the first place, back in September. For months, I'd studied him at school, watched him in action, witnessed him walking, making out, arguing with a different girl each week. I'd heard all the stories about him. *This guy is exactly what I need,* I'd thought. *Someone who obviously can't handle a real, long-term relationship. Someone who never gets attached.* And I knew, even before I approached him that day in the vacant stairwell, that he'd be on board with my request to "help him study" before our first big math quiz. Knew he'd come over to my place that Wednesday afternoon, when my mother was at work. Knew he'd be okay with using my bedroom window so no one would see him enter my house. He was cool like that. Agreeable.

We didn't even sleep together that day. It was enough just to have him in my room, this boy whose mere presence set off mini fireworks inside my stomach. He made me feel uneasy, unbalanced, alive. He made me feel wanted.

He'd wandered around my room like he owned it, poking at Trevor and eyeing the series of sketches I'd taped across the length of one wall. "In love with yourself?" he'd asked, tilting his head at the row of drawings . . . all of my face at different angles and stages of my life.

I'd put them in order because I liked to see the subsequent progression of my looks and of Nolan's artistic skill. The older drawings were rough, childlike, the penciled features just barely recognizable as mine. The last one, done most recently, had showed an exact likeness of my face, right down to the precise spattering of freckles across my nose, unhidden by foundation.

"My friend Nolan drew them," I'd explained.

"Is he in love with you?"

I rolled my eyes. "No. He draws all kinds of faces. Even male ones."

"Is he gay?"

"Not that it's any of your business, but no."

"Are *you* gay?"

I let my eyes roam over his body, from his smirking lips right down to the zipper on his well-worn jeans. Then I looked directly into his teasing brown eyes. "What do *you* think?"

He laughed, surprised but clearly intrigued. We did study math that day, but we also made out for a while. Just testing the waters. After that, it was settled. I'd use him and he'd let me, and no one would ever know our secret. We'd have sex, but it wouldn't mean anything because he was a total man-whore anyway. It wasn't like he was *my* first either. No, that title went to Blake Woodward, who I'd dated the summer before tenth grade. I gave him my virginity and he dumped me a week later. Blake was one of the many reasons I'd decided to cultivate my good girl image and move on from troublemakers like him. Bad boys, exciting as they may be, would only break my heart.

But not Tyler. With him, I'd keep emotion out of it altogether. It wasn't exactly a difficult task. He was cocky and rude and insensitive and exasperating. He'd screwed a good percentage of the female population of Oakfield High. He did drugs and smoked and drank too much and drove like a maniac. He was a total douchebag, just like Emily had warned me, and whenever I was with him I wondered how it was possible that he could disgust me and turn me on, all at the same time.

Like right now, for instance.

"It's time to go, Tyler," I told him again. The words scraped past my throat, slow and raspy.

"Not yet." He took my almost-empty can from me, dropped his cigarette in it, and placed it on the nightstand. Then he held both my hands, urging me over onto his lap.

I went. Even after all these months, he still made me feel uneasy, unbalanced, and alive.

"We can't keep doing this," I said, settling my legs on either side of his hips and pressing into him.

He didn't answer. His fingers tangled in my hair as he lowered his mouth to my neck, seeking out the sensitive spot under my ear. I clutched the back of his shirt, bunching it up in my fists and pulling until my palms met warm skin. He did the same to me, yanking my T-shirt up and over my head like it was on fire and I'd burn if he didn't get it off me right this second. Then his hands were on my waist, lifting and twisting me until I was splayed out on my back on the bed. He hovered over me and I closed my eyes, skin tingling, impatient to find out where his lips would land next. I felt them brush against my stomach, feather-light and familiar.

"I'm sorry," he mumbled against my hipbone.

Was he was sorry because he'd said those words or sorry because he'd meant them? Right then, I didn't really care.

Chapter Six

A few days later, Nolan appeared at my locker as I loaded up my backpack after school. He pressed his shoulder against the locker next to mine. "Hey, Lex. Mom wanted me to invite you over for Sunday dinner."

I smiled up at him. "Oh? Since when do I need an invitation?"

He shrugged and scratched at his chest. He was wearing a black T-shirt with the words *I never finish anyth* across the front in white letters. "Beats me. She told me before I left this morning to invite you. I just remembered five minutes ago."

"Well, tell her thanks and I accept." I turned back to my open locker. I'd eaten more meals at the Bruces' table than at my own, but formal invitations were typically reserved for holidays and birthdays. As far as I knew, there were no special occasions happening at the end of March.

"She said to come over at around four and—what are you doing with *that*?"

I glanced down at the bottle of red poster paint in my hand. Quickly, I stuffed it into my backpack. "Nothing."

Nolan crossed his arms and leaned over to peer into my locker where a box of markers and several more bottles of paint sat in plain sight on the top shelf. "Since when do you paint?" he asked with a snicker. He knew as well as I did that I could barely paint my nails without making a mess, let alone a decipherable picture. When we were little, my drawings and crayoned masterpieces looked like chicken scratch next to his. Even now, when I colored with Grace, I went outside the lines.

I moved my locker door until it blocked his view inside. "I, um . . . I'm helping one of my friends with some posters."

"What kind of posters?"

I spotted Amber at the other end of the hallway, heading toward us. Relieved, I waved at her. Nolan looked in the direction of my gaze and I used the distraction to sweep the rest of the art supplies into my backpack.

"What'd I miss?" Amber said when she reached us. Her purple-streaked brown hair was twisted into tight knots on either side of her head.

"Lexi is making posters," Nolan said in the same tone he might use for *Lexi is murdering kittens*.

"What kind of posters?" Amber asked.

"Hey, I'm sorry about your grandmother," I told her. I hadn't seen her since Nolan told me about her grandmother's death. She'd been out of school for a few days.

"Thanks." Her mouth quivered and I instantly regretted bringing it up. Grandparent-grandchild relationships were totally foreign to me. My mother's parents had been dead for years and I didn't remember my paternal grandparents. All I had of them was the quilt on my bed, made for me by my father's mother and one of the only items from his side of the family that made the move with us across the country. That and my middle name.

Nolan reached over to squeeze Amber's hand and she glanced up at him, her lips curling into a tiny smile. In spite of being total opposites—or maybe *because* of—they looked really cute together. While Nolan was over six feet tall and wore mostly black, Amber barely skimmed the five foot mark and everything about her was colorful. Her hair, her makeup, her clothes, the dozens of patterned bracelets she wore up each arm. She was a walking rainbow. Even the bands on her braces changed color every few weeks.

"So what kind of posters?" she asked again, smile back in place. "I didn't know you painted."

Nolan snorted and I gave him a quick jab to the shoulder. "I don't. It's just posters about food donations. Student council is collecting non-perishables for the food bank."

"You're not on student council," Nolan pointed out.

I shut my locker and slung my backpack over my shoulder. "I know. Someone I know who *is* on the student council asked me if I wanted to help with the posters. That's all."

"Lex, you can't even form intelligible letters with a ballpoint pen. Why would you agree to make an entire—"

"Ready, Lexi?"

All three of us spun around to see Ben standing a few feet away, his arms loaded with poster paper. My face started to burn and I hoped with everything in me that he hadn't heard the last exchange.

"Ah," Nolan said, all caught up to speed. He cleared his throat and I could tell he was trying not to laugh. My interest in poster-making suddenly made sense. That's the problem with lifelong friends—they know you far too well.

I turned back to Ben. His eyes skimmed over Nolan like he blended into the lockers before coming to rest on me.

"Yeah, I'm ready," I said, walking toward him. As I passed by Nolan, I shot him a withering glare.

Ignoring me, he lifted his chin at Ben in that '*sup* ges-

ture guys do and then he and Amber headed in the opposite direction, hand in hand.

"I got the supplies from the art room," I said as Ben and
I made our way to room 216, the ad hoc spot for the student council meeting.

"Great." Ben sounded distracted and harried. He transferred the paper to his other arm and sighed. Practically
running the school really stressed him out sometimes, no
matter how capable he tried to appear. "I never would
have asked you to do this if half the reps weren't out sick
with that flu."

"It's no problem." However, it might become a problem when he saw my shoddy posters. I knew Ben liked
things done a certain way, meaning *adequately*. "Um, why
can't you use the computer to make these posters?"

We reached room 216 and Ben held the door open for
me. "Poster paint and markers are way cheaper than
printer ink."

I should have guessed. Our school board was notori-
ously stingy. I went into the room ahead of Ben, inhaling
his soapy-clean scent as I passed. He always smelled like a
cross between clothesline-dried bed sheets and fresh-cut
grass. Like summer.

"So," Ben said, plunking the paper onto a table with a
swift bang. "We want the posters to say something like
Oakfield Food Bank needs donations. Drop off your non-
perishable items in the main office by April fifth. You can
get creative too, if you want. Paint some soup cans or
whatever."

Seeing as how any soup can I painted would resemble a
giant blob of nothing, it was best not to get too inventive.
Stick with the words, I told myself. I could spell, most of the
time. Nolan was right, though . . . my handwriting was
barely legible.

Ben left me to my posters and went to join a large

group of students gathered together in one corner of the room. From where I was, it sounded like they were deep in discussion about the upcoming talent show. The only other people making posters besides me were two freshman girls who were doing more giggling than working and one pimply sophomore guy whose poster already looked like cool graffiti art. Nolan would have loved it.

Speaking of Nolan, I could have used his artistic talents right then. My poster was starting to resemble a kindergartener's art project. My letters didn't seem to want to go straight. Still, every time I asked myself why I was sitting there, breathing in stuffy school air and cheap paint, I'd peek over at Ben. Because he was student council president, he spent most of the afternoon presiding over the group's discussions. When he wasn't presiding, he was working the room, speaking to individual people and conferring with Mr. Isaacs, the teacher advisor. I could totally picture Ben in politics someday, but he had even bigger dreams. He planned to major in economics in college so he could someday make a living helping people in impoverished countries. Like I'd said—perfect.

At one point, he came over to check on us. He put his hand on the back of my chair, leaning over my shoulder to inspect my progress. His summer scent surrounded me and I felt a fluttering in my chest. Being around Tyler did things to my stomach, but Ben affected my heart.

"Not bad," Ben told me, and he sounded like he actually meant it. He was nothing if not diplomatic.

"Thanks," I replied, frowning at my poster. *Bad* was the only part of his comment that applied.

He moved on to the pimply guy and I noticed the two freshman girls watching his every move, their hands fidgeting anxiously with their markers. I remembered being their age, ogling senior guys and thinking they looked *so old*, like men. When it came to Ben, I understood their nervousness. Not only was he good-looking in a wholesome, slightly nerdy kind of way, he also gave off an air of authority that made people want to please him. Even me. *Especially* me, as evidenced by the splotches of red marker on my hands.

An hour and several lopsided lines later, it was time to go home. Ben came over to thank me for my help and to ask me if I'd be available to finish the posters tomorrow at lunch.

"Sure," I said . . . because he was Ben and I was a sucker for punishment.

"You're a lifesaver, Lexi."

I shrugged modestly. That was me, Lifesaver Lexi to the rescue.

A cute blond girl who I recognized as one of the eleventh grade council representatives walked up to us then and bumped her hip against Ben's. He turned to her, smiling for possibly the first time all afternoon, and wrapped an arm around her waist. I struggled to keep my reaction from showing on my face. *Of course*, I thought. *Of course he has someone else already.* Kyla had been history for over a week, after all.

"Have you guys met?" Ben asked, glancing at me for a second and then returning his gaze to the beaming girl beside him. She was exactly his type.

"You're Ben's friend Lexi," the girl said, nodding at me. "I'm Tori."

"Hi," I said, stretching my lips into a credible version of a smile.

Tori smiled back at me the way most of Ben's girlfriends did—with a hint of a warning simmering underneath. *Watch your step.*

Don't worry, I wanted to assure her. "Ben's friend Lexi" was a permanent position.

★ ★ ★

Ben offered to drive me home, of course, but I wasn't in the mood to sit in the backseat of his car and watch him and Tori make googly eyes at each other in the front. So I lied and told him a friend was picking me up. Then, first making sure the happy couple was long gone, I walked home in the early spring drizzle.

By the time I reached my house, it was starting to get dark and my stomach gurgled with hunger. I found my mother in the kitchen, dumping spaghetti noodles into a colander. Steam rose up, half-obscuring the expression of annoyance on her face.

"Is it too much to ask that you be here on time to start dinner?" she asked, shaking the colander in short, jerky movements. "The last thing I want to do after nine hours on my feet is come home and cook."

Like boiling pasta and opening a jar of sauce is difficult and time-consuming, I thought, opening the fridge to get the parmesan. Barer-than-usual shelves greeted me, and I tried to figure out what was missing. It hit me as I sifted through the jars of condiments in the door. Mom's ever-present box of wine was gone, along with the several bottles of beer we always kept on hand. *Interesting.* I found the cheese and shut the fridge door, studying my mother as I did so. She didn't *seem* drunk.

"I had something to do after school." I turned to place the bottle of parmesan on the table and noticed a pink vase filled with a dozen red roses sitting by the salt and pepper shakers. I ran my index finger over a silky petal. "Where did these come from?"

The irritation on her face melted into a sort of dreamy glow. "Jesse sent them to the spa today. For no reason at all. Isn't that sweet?"

An image of those eerie colorless eyes flashed through

my mind and I held back a shudder. "So you like this guy?" I extracted a couple of plates from the cupboard. "Don't you think he's a little, uh . . . young?"

The spoon she'd been using to stir the sauce slammed down on the counter, sending red drips flying. "Spare me the judgmental attitude, Lexi, okay? He's thirty-two. I'm not one of those . . . what do you call them . . . *cougars.* God, you just have to find something wrong with everyone I date, don't you?"

"But it's so easy," I shot back.

Her eyes narrowed into slits and she yanked one of the plates out of my hand. Turning away from me, she grabbed the pasta spoon, scooped a clump of noodles onto the plate, and ladled on some sauce. She carried it to the table, where she sat and began to eat, ignoring me. Calmly, I fixed my own plate and sat down across from her. The cloying scent of the roses tickled my nose.

"Where's all the booze?" I asked, cocking my head toward the fridge.

Mom twirled some spaghetti onto her fork and shoved it into her mouth. She chewed slowly, making me wait for her answer. "Got rid of it," she said after a minute. "Jesse doesn't drink. He's . . . he's a recovering alcoholic."

I covered my dinner with parmesan and dug in. "Better than a practicing one, I guess."

She opened her mouth as if to chastise me some more, but realizing what I'd said wasn't a dig, she shut it again. We ate in silence for the remainder of the meal.

"I could stand to cut back a bit on the wine, anyway," Mom said as we cleared the table together.

I just shrugged noncommittally. It was far from the first time she'd vowed to stop or cut down on drinking. Nor was it the first time she'd tried to change for a man. She always went back to her old self, eventually.

"Jesse's great. Really. He has a stable job, he doesn't drink, no kids. I'm telling you, he's not like the men I usually date. He's different."

"Okay," I said flatly. I was still unable to shake my first impression of him. That icky vibe.

Mom's mood seemed to improve as she loaded the dishwasher. "I'll have to invite him over for dinner one night. So you can get to know him better. It'll be fun."

I scrubbed hard at a patch of burnt tomato sauce on the stovetop and thought about how getting to know Creepy Latte Guy wasn't high on my list of fun things to do. "I guess so. Just don't make it for Sunday. I'm going to the Bruces' house for dinner."

"Oh." Her face contorted the way it always did when I mentioned them. Nothing dampened her mood faster than the thought of me across the street, bonding with her ex-best friend, the woman who almost succeeded in taking me away from her. I'd never blamed Teresa for that— she did what she felt she had to do—but Mom was a different story altogether. Five years later, she still blamed her.

My mother and Nolan's mother had grown up together, just like he and I did. The only time they were ever apart was when Teresa decided to go east for college. Mom stayed out west in Alton, the same town in which they'd both been born and raised, and skipped college for a series of minimum wage jobs. Two years later, she met a tattooed bass player named Eric Davis and got caught up in his wild cyclone of bar gigs, liquor, drugs, and partying . . . until she got pregnant a couple years later, that is, and put a stop to it all. My father stopped too, for a while, until the music scene—and everything that went along with it—beckoned to him again.

Through all this, my mother kept in close contact with

Teresa, who'd married Malcolm Bruce, a local guy, and settled down with him in his hometown of Oakfield. Despite their distance and contrasting lifestyles, my mother and Teresa's friendship was as solid as ever. So when Mom called her up one day, crying, saying she needed to get as far away as she could from Alton and the horrible man who'd fathered me, it made perfect sense for us to go and stay with Teresa and Malcolm for a while. Until we got back on our feet, they said. They'd even pay for the plane tickets.

We lived with the Bruces for two years. During that time, Mom took a massage therapy course while I stayed home with Teresa and quickly became attached to her and to Nolan, who was only a few months older than me. He and I did everything together, even though he was bossy and pushy at times (qualities he still possessed). I didn't remember much of those years, but what few memories I had were all happy ones. We were a family.

One of my sharpest childhood memories was the day my mother found a stable job and told me we were moving out of the Bruces' house. I remember throwing myself on the floor in an epic tantrum, and I didn't shut up until I heard where we were moving. Not back to "that place I was born" like I'd feared, but to the house right across the street with the pretty lilac bush in the front yard. Teresa, who was a realtor by then, had received some inside info on when it would go up for sale. When it did, we grabbed it.

Having our own place was fun at first, but I hated not having my best friend beside me full-time. And my mom wasn't sweet and fun like Teresa. She didn't cook chicken nuggets for me or remind me to brush my teeth. She didn't give me hugs at bedtime or praise me when I cleaned up my toys. I wanted to live with the Bruces again, but I knew I couldn't because my mother needed me way more than they did.

Even though Teresa didn't agree with many of Mom's life choices or her parenting style, she tried not to interfere. But when I turned twelve and Keith Langley exploded into our lives, all bets were off. Keith was a nightclub bouncer with a fondness for Jack Daniels and a hair-trigger temper. The first time he beat the crap out of Mom, I cowered in my room with the lights on, too scared to react. The second time, I threw a can of mixed vegetables at his head and ran across the street for help. Teresa called the police while Malcolm stomped over to break it up and I huddled in the family room with Nolan, shaking under the blanket he'd gently wrapped around me.

Teresa and my mom had a screaming fight in my house that night, one I did not witness. I stayed at the Bruces' house overnight, and in the morning, Teresa told me what had happened. When she'd arrived across the street, Keith was being led to a police car while my mother sat in the living room, a dishcloth packed with ice pressed up against her swollen lip. The cops came back inside and Mom declined to press charges, which sent Teresa into an uncharacteristic rage. "If he ever comes back," she'd warned Mom, "if he ever so much as shows his face around here again, I'll call Child Protective Services and have that beautiful little girl taken away from you for good. She deserves better than this, Stacey, and so do you."

Teresa never had to follow through on her threat because Keith never came back, but it didn't matter. My mother was so insulted by her best friend's words, she stopped speaking to her altogether. They hadn't exchanged a civil word since. In the years following that night, Mom had worked her way through a parade of skuzzy boyfriends, but there was never another one as volatile as Keith Langley.

Maybe this Jesse guy will be different, I thought as I wiped the kitchen table and inhaled the scent of those perfect, fragrant roses. Maybe he'll be good for my mother. After years of kissing frogs, she was long overdue for a prince.

Chapter Seven

I showed up early at the Bruces' house on Sunday afternoon and was greeted by Gus, their hyper rat terrier. After sniffing me for a minute, he took off in the direction of the living room, where he curled up on his bed and started gnawing on a rawhide bone. Their cat Hugo, a plump black and gray tabby, dozed on the back of the couch. The house smelled amazing, like roast turkey and onions frying in butter. I wandered into the kitchen, salivating.

"Hey there, Lexi." Nolan's dad stood at the counter, pouring beer into a tall glass. "How goes it?"

"It goes good," I said. We had this exchange every single time we saw each other, which wasn't too often. He was a field service technician for a heavy equipment company and traveled a lot. "How goes it with you?"

"Oh, can't complain," he said, curling his thick fingers around the beer glass. Nolan and his father were nothing alike, aside from their height. Malcolm was big and burly, his forearms thick with muscles after years of working on heavy machinery. He'd played football in college and dreamed of doing it professionally. Instead, he married Teresa, took a steady job, and transferred the dream to his sons. Nolan had zero interest in sports, but Landon fortunately inherited enough of the jock gene to keep their father satisfied.

Teresa breezed into the kitchen, tossing me a "Hi, sweetie" as she made a beeline for the oven. She opened it a few inches, peeking inside at the delicious-looking bird. Pleased with its progress, she shut the oven door and adjusted the timer on the stove.

"Can I help?" I asked, watching her dart around the room like a flea on crack. Strands of light brown hair stuck to her forehead and she had what looked like grease stains all down the front of her jeans.

"Sure." She nodded toward the pile of produce by the sink. "Peel carrots."

I went to work on the carrots while Malcolm took his beer and fled the scene. I felt like dragging him back and sticking an apron on him. He was one of those gruff, old-fashioned types, the kind of guy whose only contribution to a dinner like this was to sit at the head of the table and carve the meat. Nolan didn't get along with him all that well, mostly because they had no common ground. Artistic talent, according to his dad, wasn't nearly as impressive as a good defensive tackle.

"Where's Nolan?" I asked as I dug around in the bottom cupboard for the cutting board.

"I sent him to the store for milk." She dried her hands on a dish towel and looked at me sideways. "He mentioned something the other day about your mom having a new boyfriend."

I heard that familiar undercurrent of concern in her voice, the one she'd adopted way back in the Keith Langley days. *Do I need to worry about you?* it said. I told her everything I knew about Latte Guy so far, leaving out the whole creepy vibe thing. For all I knew, I was just imagining that. She visibly relaxed when I mentioned that he didn't drink.

"Well," she said, hauling the turkey out of the oven. "Let's hope this one's a winner."

Nolan returned with the milk, looking like he'd just rolled out of bed. His hair was sticking up and he wore torn sweatpants and a black T-shirt that claimed I SEE DUMB PEOPLE. He attempted to shove the carton of milk in the fridge and leave, Malcolm-style, but I ordered him to stay and help me with the veggies. I was slowly training him to be well-rounded husband material for the future Mrs. Nolan Bruce.

An hour later, the five us were seated around the kitchen table, plates loaded with turkey and all the trimmings. Hugo wove his fat body around our chair legs, hoping for scraps, while Malcolm and his youngest son discussed the upcoming NHL playoffs, Nolan yawned into his mashed potatoes, and I enjoyed the first peaceful moments I'd had all week. Usually, during Sunday sit-down dinners, Teresa would spend the entire time asking me questions about school and my life in general, but she seemed distracted. In fact, she barely even looked at me, focusing instead on her food and glass of chardonnay. I had the distinct feeling I was missing something.

After dinner, Malcolm and Landon took their dishes to the sink and retreated to the family room to watch a game. Nolan looked like he wanted to escape, too, but fearing my wrath, he helped load the dishwasher.

When it was full, Teresa shooed him out of the kitchen. "Lexi and I will finish up."

Nolan shrugged and went off to draw something.

Teresa filled the sink with soapy water and submerged one of the pots that hadn't made it into the dishwasher. Feeling so stuffed I could barely move, I stood next to her with a dry dish towel. We worked in silence for a few minutes, her washing and me drying, the lemony scent of the dish detergent rising up between us.

"Lexi," Teresa said as she rinsed the turkey roaster under cold water and then passed it to me. "There's something I need to tell you."

Going by the weightiness of her expression, it wasn't going to be good. A nervous jolt shot through my stomach. "Okay."

She dunked another pot and attacked it with the scrubber like she was trying to scour the stainless steel coating right off. When she looked at me, I saw something similar to fear in her eyes. "I have this friend named Josie," she said, focusing again on the pot. "We went to high school together and she still lives in Alton, where your mom and I grew up." She paused for a moment and glanced at me.

I nodded to show I was listening, even though I had no clue what her friend Josie had to do with me.

"Anyway, Josie and I have kept in touch all these years. We talk on the phone once a month or so and she keeps me updated about the goings on in Alton. Not that anything exciting ever happens in that boring little town, mind you. Still, I like to hear about what my old friends are up to and who died and who—"

"Um." I gently cut her off. "Is that what you needed to tell me?"

She studied me for a moment, her mouth slightly open as if she hoped the right words might tumble out on their own. "Sweetie, it's about your father."

Ice water surged through my veins. "Is he dead?" The question came out on a whoosh of breath.

"Dead?" Teresa asked, surprised.

"Well, Mom said . . . " My voice cracked like an adolescent boy's. I cleared my throat and tried again. "Mom said he probably was by now. Dead. From the drugs and stuff."

Surprise flickered in Teresa's eyes. "No, sweetie. After you and your mom . . . after you came here, he stayed in

Alton for a couple months and then moved away. No one seemed to know where he went, but rumors were going around that he was staying in a rehab center in Vancouver."

I nodded; she'd mentioned that before, years ago, back when I'd been curious enough to pester her for information. My father had made it to rehab, apparently, but the rumors stopped there. It was as if he'd disappeared off the face of the earth. I'd always assumed the stories were either false or he'd relapsed after rehab.

"Your father isn't dead, Lexi." Teresa dropped the scrub brush into the water and turned toward me. "He's back."

"Back?"

"In Alton." She placed her dripping hand on my forearm. "Josie said he moved back in January after his father—your grandfather—passed away and left him his backhoe company. Your father took over. He owns the business now."

All I could do was gape at her. My father . . . alive . . . living in Alton and running a backhoe company? This Josie woman had to be mistaken. "But"—I shifted away from the moist heat of her hand—"but the drugs. He's a drug addict. How can he . . . ?" I couldn't say what I wanted to say. How can he be back in Alton? How can he run a business? How can he be alive and thriving and still forget he has a daughter?

"Josie says he's sober as a judge now. And . . . " She let out a sigh and my entire body tensed, bracing for more. "He didn't come back alone. He's got a wife and two kids. Josie said—"

A roaring sound filled my ears, blocking out the rest of her words. I threw the dish towel down on the counter and brushed past her to the door. Her fingers skimmed my arm as I passed, trying to hold me there, but I dodged them and kept going. When I reached the doorway, I turned around to face her. "When did you find out about this?"

Her hand, still dripping with dish water, returned to her side. "Josie called me shortly after he came back."

"You said he moved back in January. So you've known for *two months*?" Acid stung the back of my throat as my dinner fought its way back up my esophagus. I swallowed it down again. "Why would you keep this from me?"

Teresa blinked a few times and then dropped her gaze to the floor. "Because I knew it would hurt you. It wasn't my place to tell you, Lexi. Your mother would be furious if she ever found out I spoke to you about this. As if she needed another reason to hate me."

"But it's not *about* her. It's about *me*. He's *my* father, and I had a right to know." My stomach gurgled and I inhaled deeply, willing its contents to stay put. "Why tell me now if it's not your place?"

"It's been eating me up for weeks. I had to tell you." Her eyes found mine again. "You'll be eighteen in June. An adult. Old enough to contact whomever you want, and your mother can't do a thing to stop you." She walked over to the big oak cabinet that sat along the far wall in the kitchen, opened one of the drawers, and removed a small piece of paper. The kind people wrote grocery lists on. After a moment of hesitation, she handed it to me. "His information," she said softly.

I looked down at the paper. My father's name was written there along with the words *Davis Excavating Ltd.* And a phone number. His phone number. As if I'd call him, this stranger who existed only in photographs stuck between the pages of *Corn Snakes: An Owner's Guide.* As if I'd give him another opportunity to reject me.

"Keep it." I tossed the paper across the kitchen. It floated in the air for a few seconds and then landed, writing side up, under the table.

"Lexi, sweetie, I'm sorry. I should have told you sooner. I just . . . " She put a hand over her face and started to cry. Under normal circumstances, her tears would have immobilized me, but right then her betrayal was like a sharp poke between my shoulder blades, spurring me forward. I bolted out of the kitchen and ran smack into Nolan's I SEE DUMB PEOPLE shirt.

"What's going on?" he asked.

I ignored him and continued on to the front entryway. Gus shot ahead of me, whimpering to go outside. I ignored him too, grabbed my jacket, and got the hell out of there.

Going home and facing my mother wasn't an option, so I just started walking.

"Lexi!"

I heard Nolan's voice behind me as I strode past Grace's house at the end of the street. Their driveway was empty, and I vaguely remembered Grace mentioning something about going to visit her grandmother this weekend.

"Lex! Wait up!" Nolan's voice was closer and wheezy in that *I-really-should-quit-smoking* kind of way.

I didn't want him to pass out in the street on top of everything else that had already happened, so I stopped walking and turned around. He was just a few feet away. Gus trotted along ahead of him, straining against his leash in his eagerness to reach me.

"Thanks," Nolan panted when they finally caught up. Gus circled around me, binding my legs with his leash like he was trying to prevent me from going any farther. "Holy shit, it's cold out here."

He was right; it was freezing outside, but I'd been walking along with my coat wide open, barely noticing the weather. The icy air felt good on my puffy eyes. I untangled myself from Gus's leash and started moving again. Nolan walked beside me, a foot or so of space between us.

"Did you know, too?" I asked after several minutes of silence.

"Know what? I have no idea what happened back there. Mom was crying and then you ran out the door and the next thing I knew, she was telling me to take Gus for a walk. I'm pretty sure that was her way of saying go find Lexi and make sure she's okay." He stepped over a slick patch on the sidewalk. "So are you? Okay?"

I shook my head. "My father's alive." I could feel Nolan staring at me, perplexed, so I told him the rest of it. My voice faltered when I got to the part about my father's new family and, oh my God, the fact that I had *half-siblings*. "You really didn't know anything about it?"

"No," he said.

I believed him because Nolan never lied to me.

"I would've told you, Lex. You know that. Mom shouldn't have kept it from you for so long. It was shitty, but you know her. She always means well."

I made a grunting sound and zipped up my jacket to my chin. The cold was starting to penetrate. "It's not that I even want to contact him, you know? I mean, he let my mother take me halfway across the country and then never tried to see me or talk to me again. So screw him for that. It's just . . . I guess I wanted the option."

Nolan nodded. "Makes sense."

We paused for a few moments to let Gus water the snow beside a telephone pole and then kept going. We practically had the neighborhood to ourselves at that time of the day. All the families and dog walkers and middle-aged joggers were relaxing in their warm, cozy houses, eating Sunday dinner and watching sports on TV. No one in their right mind would be out in the cold voluntarily.

"I wonder how much my mother knows," I said as we passed by the desolate playground, basketball court, and soccer field area. "Maybe she really did think he was dead."

Nolan contemplated that for a minute. "If I had to guess, I'd say she's been keeping tabs on him. I think she probably knows more than she lets on."

I thought of all the times I'd tried to ask her about my father, who he was, where he was, what kind of person he'd been. Each time I pressed her for info, she'd say something like, "He was a drug addict and a drunk, Lexi, and he didn't give a damn about either of us. Forget him. We're better off without him, trust me."

I did trust her, at least on that topic, and after a while I stopped asking about him altogether. My father was no good, a deadbeat, a loser. Good riddance.

But, unfortunately for me, I'd always had trouble staying away from no-good losers. Just like my mother.

"You must be at least a *teensy* bit curious about him, though," Nolan said, tucking his un-gloved hands into the sleeves of his jacket. "Don't tell me you've never Googled him."

"Of course I've Googled him," I admitted, cracking a tiny smile. "Willpower isn't exactly my strong suit. I searched his name a few times over the years, but it's so common, I got like a million results. I hardly had any info about him, so it was like finding a needle in a haystack."

"Well, now you know where he lives and works."

My still-full stomach tilted again and I slowed my pace. Nolan slowed with me, but Gus, oblivious, dashed ahead until he met resistance and almost strangled himself. He looked back at us, tail wagging impatiently.

"Right." I'd only looked at that paper for a second before hurling it back at Teresa, but the name of his company was burned into my brain. I could Google that and possibly find his email address and maybe even a current picture of him. If I ever wanted to—which I most definitely did not. He'd let me go once and probably wouldn't hesitate to do it again. Why give him the chance?

Nolan and I walked Gus until the streetlights flicked on and we were all too frozen to go any farther. We turned and retraced our steps along the snow-crusted sidewalks, passing Nolan's last cigarette back and forth in an attempt to restore circulation to our hands.

"I'm quitting after this one," I said, exhaling a lungful of smoke into the bitter air.

"Me too."

"I'm serious this time."

Nolan tossed the butt on the pavement and ground it out with his boot. "Me too. Amber said she's sick of my ashtray mouth."

"We'll quit together then. Deal?" I paused to hold out a partially numb hand.

He transferred the leash handle to his left hand and shook with his right. His skin felt even colder than mine. "Deal."

When we reached my house, Nolan dug in his pocket and brought out a small piece of paper, carefully folded in half. "Mom told me to give you this." He pushed it into my hands. Before I could react, he turned and jogged across the street to his house, Gus loping cheerfully behind him.

I didn't even glance at the information. I knew exactly what was written there. I just slid the paper into the back pocket of my jeans, intending to throw it away or perhaps even flush it down the toilet the first chance I got. But it stayed in my jeans for the rest of the evening, perfectly undamaged.

Sometime near dawn and still half-asleep, I got out of bed, fumbled around for my discarded jeans, and tucked the paper in between the pages of my snake book.

Chapter Eight

Pregnancy had granted Shelby the title of permanent designated driver. It also had granted her the right to erupt into hormonal rages over every little thing that annoyed her, like the way her seatbelt dug into her stomach and that she couldn't indulge her occasional vodka cooler craving.

"You guys suck," she yelled out the driver's side window when Emily and I emerged from her house, our hair and makeup party-perfect. As we approached the car, Shelby eyed our flat middles and non-maternity-wear jeans and sighed. "I can't wait to be skinny again."

I snorted as we climbed into her white Jetta, a gift she'd received from her parents about a year ago, before she got pregnant and broke their hearts. "Me too," I said to her *skinny* comment. Emily had the build of a prepubescent girl, but my body type hovered in the land between slender and voluptuous. I was always one or the other, depending on how much I ate and how stressed I happened to be. At the moment, I felt thin, but only because I'd skipped dinner.

"Remember, ladies," Shelby said once we were parked along the road near Dustin Sweeney's house in Rocky Lake, a rural-ish town about a ten minute drive from ours.

"Pregnant girls bore easily and tire easily, especially at parties. So when I tell you we have to leave, get your asses in the car and don't give me any 'tude. Okay?"

"Okay, cranky," Emily said as all three of us stepped out of the car and walked toward the house. She stumbled as her high-heeled boot hit a patch of slush in the driveway.

I grabbed her arm to steady her, and then grabbed Shelby's arm, too. Falling could be disastrous for her. Plus, it was dark and spooky with the mammoth trees and weird howling noises coming from the woods in back.

Dustin Sweeney answered our knock and ushered us into his warm house. The place was already packed with bodies, and I took a cursory glance around for Ben. Emily had mentioned earlier that he was going to be there, which made me even more anxious to get there myself. Ben rarely went to parties, and I didn't think I'd ever seen him drink more than one beer. He was too mature and responsible to cut loose on a Friday night, unlike his cousin. Emily may have been a little uptight at school, but she wasn't opposed to slamming a few drinks on the weekends.

As for me, I'd been looking forward to this party all week. One night—that was all I needed. One night of deafening music and mindless conversation and the obliterating sensation of a good buzz. Just for tonight, I wanted to forget about my not-dead father and Teresa's tears and the folded paper in my snake book, still untouched and un-Googled five days later. I'd be Smiling and Confident Lexi, the girl my friends saw, the girl who didn't have a father but was fine, fine, fine, regardless.

"Did you get our Corona?" Em asked Dustin as we shrugged off our coats and added them to the pile in the corner.

She and I had decided to go splits on a case of beer.

Whenever Dustin threw a party, he'd collect drink orders and money at school a few days beforehand and then get his older brother to buy it for us.

"Of course," he said, unveiling his cute, dimpled smile. He was one of those likable, friendly, well-known people who got along with everyone and had zero enemies. His house was well-known, too, mainly for its secluded location, outdoor hot tub, and lack of parental supervision. I'd participated in my fair share of drunken hook-ups in and around his house during my high school career, a few of them with Dustin himself.

Five minutes later, I was sipping on a frosty bottle of Corona and leaning against the kitchen counter, talking to Gisele Hargrove, a girl I barely knew from my English class. Shelby had disappeared to hunt for Evan, who was back to being a doting baby daddy this week, and Emily's whereabouts was anyone's guess. As Gisele made small talk with me, I kept one eye on the crowd.

After a while, I spotted Ben's other half, Tori, in the dining room. She was talking to one of her friends, gesticulating wildly as if to illustrate a crucial point. She was so into her conversation, she barely even reacted when Ben came up behind her, wrapped his arms around her waist, and laid his cheek against her hair. She just rested her hand on his and kept talking, taking his presence for granted in a way I could never imagine myself doing if I were in her shoes.

I shifted a few inches to my right to see them better—sometimes I couldn't help torturing myself—and Gisele stopped talking mid-sentence to stare at me. She probably thought I was hitting on her.

"Sorry," I told her, tearing my eyes from Ben and Tori and backing away. "I gotta . . . go to the washroom."

But instead of heading down the hallway to the bathroom, I grabbed a couple beers from the fridge, made my way down to the cooler, less crowded basement, and plopped onto the sectional couch. In one corner of the room, three guys and a girl threw darts at an electronic dart board. The plasma-screen TV was on, showing a car race that no one appeared to be watching. I folded my legs up on the couch and downed my second beer, which was followed closely by the third.

"*Here* you are," said a voice somewhere above me, and then all of a sudden, Dustin was beside me, his arm circling my shoulders. "I've been looking for you."

"Why?" I said sullenly, resting my bottle on the arm of the couch.

"Because." The word came out garbled so he tried again. "Because." He was totally hammered.

I inched away. "Have you seen Emily?"

"She's in the hot tub. You wanna go in the hot tub? You don't need a . . . one of those things."

"A swimsuit?"

His gaze landed on my cleavage. "Yeah, one of those."

"No, thanks. It's cold out."

"The air is cold but the water is boiling. 'S nice." He rested his head on my shoulder. "You're so pretty, Lexi. I want us to get back together."

I sighed. I wasn't drunk enough for this. "We were never together, Dustin. We just kissed a few times last year. Remember?" We'd done a little more than kiss, but I didn't feel like reminiscing at the moment.

"I remember," he said, tilting his head until his lips grazed my neck.

A shiver went through me and I closed my eyes. *Maybe I'll let him kiss me again,* I thought. *Maybe I'll let him . . .*

"Yo! Dustin! You got company, man."

Dustin stopped nibbling my neck and my eyes popped open. I blinked a few times, trying to focus on the faces in front of me. I saw Colin Hewitt, Dustin's friend and the owner of the voice we'd just heard, and then my eyes shifted over to the guy standing next to him. *Tyler.*

At first, I thought I must be drunker than I actually felt. Or maybe hallucinating. I couldn't think of any logical reason why Tyler Flynn might be standing in Dustin Sweeney's basement. Looking at me. Looking at Dustin's hand, high up on my thigh. But I wasn't that drunk, and he was real.

"Oh hey, dude!" Dustin said, taking his hand off my thigh to wave at Tyler. Like they knew each other.

How did they know each other? *Dustin knows everyone*, I reminded myself, *even the stoners.*

"Come on in and have a drink."

Tyler shook his head and lifted his chin ever so slightly, a gesture I recognized as *come here.* While Dustin lurched to his feet, Tyler's gaze shifted to me again.

I couldn't decipher the expression on his face. It was just . . . vacant. Closed off. I looked away and took a drink of my Corona. The guys disappeared upstairs together while I stayed there alone on the couch, reeling from my sudden buzz and the fact that Tyler had just witnessed another guy putting his lips and hands on me. Good thing he wasn't the jealous type. Guys like him didn't care enough to get jealous.

Dustin didn't return to the basement until my beer was almost gone. He dropped down next to me, practically on my lap, and slid his hand over my stomach. "Now where were we?" he said in my ear.

I pulled away. I didn't feel like letting him kiss me anymore. "Nowhere." I stood up, drained my bottle, and carried my empties with me back upstairs.

The upper level was still bursting with people. Music shook the house, the heavy bass thumping through me like a heartbeat. Familiar faces floated by, sweaty and laughing, but none of them belonged to my friends. I rounded the corner to the kitchen to dispose of my bottles and almost collided with Ben, who was leaning against the stove and talking to some guy I didn't know. Tori stood beside him, arms crossed, a pissed-off expression on her face. Before I had time to contemplate that, I grabbed another beer and slipped out the front door. I needed to be by myself for a few minutes, in case I decided to cry over the total clusterfuck that was my life.

I wandered around the front yard for a while, sucking in the pine-scented air and listening to the crunch of snow under my feet. In fact, I was so distracted by the sound, I somehow failed to notice the figure of a man lurking in the shadows near the side of the house.

"Hey."

I screamed and dropped my bottle, splattering beer all over my shoes. "What the *hell*?" I looked from my shoes in the direction of the voice, which my alcohol-soaked brain had finally registered as Tyler's. I stormed over to him, all set to give him hell for startling me and making me drop my beer. The next thing I knew, my back was pinned against the house and he was kissing me with a ferocity that turned my chilled body into liquid. I kissed him back, my anger dissolving as I melted into him.

But only for a moment. Then I pushed him away and delivered a swift kick to his right shin.

"Jesus!" he yelped as he staggered backward, almost falling into the barren flower garden beside us. "What was that for?"

I waited until he righted himself and then shoved him again. He was prepared and kept his balance.

"You can't just creep around in the dark and scare people, you asshole," I said, fuming.

He didn't respond with a smartass comment like I expected. He just stared down at me, breathing hard, that dark, intense gaze of his burning into my face. I broke eye contact and glanced around the yard, making sure we were alone. Luckily, all I saw were trees, bushes, and more trees.

"Don't worry," he said, his tone dripping sarcasm. "None of the popular kids are watching. You're safe."

I looked back at him. "What are you doing here, Tyler?"

"Having a smoke."

"No, what are you doing *here*? At Dustin's house?"

"What do you think?" he said, patting his jacket pocket.

Ah. His "honest living." Parties were good for business. He'd probably made a fortune tonight.

"Well," I said with a sigh. "You made me drop my beer."

He looked over at my empty Corona bottle, lying on its side a few feet away in the snow. "My apologies," he said, his eyes on me again. The fire in them made my heart pound even harder than it had when he'd scared me. "Why don't you go inside and ask Sweeney to find you another one? I'm sure he'd be more than willing to share with you."

The air suddenly felt very cold against my face. "What do you care?" I said, matching his scornful tone with one of my own. "You and me, we're not even . . . we're just . . ."

"Fucking?"

I folded my arms across my chest and leaned back against the house, putting some distance between us. "Right," I said quietly. "Aren't we?"

Again, he chose not to respond. He turned and walked away, moving toward the front yard and the dark road beyond. When he came upon the empty Corona bottle, he kicked it hard, sending it careening into a nearby shrub. Without turning around, he said, "Have fun with Sweeney."

Anger and confusion and the leftover sourness of beer bubbled up in my throat and, not caring who might be in hearing distance, I yelled, "I will!"

Back inside, I avoided Dustin and his roving hands and joined some people doing tequila shots until I could no longer hear my thoughts or feel my limbs. Then I curled up somewhere—I found out later it was the laundry room floor—and went to sleep.

The rest of the night seemed to happen in fragments. Emily's voice, repeating my name over and over. Small arms around me, pulling for what seemed like hours. Then bigger, stronger arms, lifting me easily. Cold air on my face and the scent of fresh-cut grass and summer strong in my nostrils. Smooth fabric under my cheek and Shelby's voice muttering a grudging, "thanks." A deeper voice, Ben's, answering her. "Watch her head." The hum of tires on the highway. And then a long stretch of nothingness that ended when I woke up the next morning on my bathroom floor, sick and humiliated and wishing I was dead.

Chapter Nine

The *wish-I-was-dead* feeling held on for the rest of the weekend, most of which I spent in bed, wrapped up in my grandmother's quilt and trying not to think. Sleep helped, so I let myself drift into it for as long and as often as I could. In fact, I was right in the middle of a lovely Sunday afternoon nap when my bedroom door opened and jolted me awake. I cracked open one eye and then shut it again as my death wish rushed back with a vengeance.

"Enough of this, Lexi. Get up."

I opened both eyes and looked at them. Nolan in a faded *Star Wars* T-shirt, a scowl darkening his usually pleasant face. Amber, standing a little behind him, the colors in her clothes and jewelry and hair so vibrant they made my eyes water. She seemed embarrassed, either for me or for her inexplicable presence in my room. I buried my face in my pillow and groaned. "Go away."

"Not happening."

I listened as he crossed the room and started yanking on the window lever, grunting when it wouldn't dislodge. Finally, it loosened and I caught a whiff of balmy spring air. "It's like summer out there today," Nolan said over the creak of the window hinges. "Time to get up, get a shower, brush your teeth, get dressed . . ."

The mere thought of doing all those things exhausted me even more. "I'm sick," I said, my voice coming out gravelly from disuse.

"Yeah, I bet. I can still smell whatever it was you drowned your sorrows in the other night." His hand closed around my ankle through the quilt. "Seriously, Lex. Get up or we'll dump a bucket of cold water on you."

I shook his hand off and glanced at Amber, who gave me an encouraging smile. What the hell was she doing here? What had Nolan told her? I didn't mind him seeing me like this—he'd seen me in worse condition—but why drag his girlfriend into the insanity along with him? What would she think of me now?

"Lexi, come on," Amber said, her voice light and much gentler than Nolan's. I felt the bed sink as she sat down next to me, a brave feat as I couldn't have smelled too pretty. "I'll run the shower for you while Nolan makes you something to eat. Okay?"

My stomach rumbled at the mention of food. I'd wolfed down a cereal bar at some point yesterday when I was in the kitchen retrieving Trevor's weekly mouse, but I hadn't eaten since. My mouth felt like the inside of a bowling shoe. Slowly, I flung my quilt aside and got up.

"Good girl," Nolan said, like I was a dog who'd done an impressive trick. He exchanged a victorious grin with Amber and then left to rustle me up some food.

I wondered if my mother had bothered to buy groceries this week. She hadn't been around all weekend, as far as I knew. Things with Latte Guy must have gotten serious or they'd broken up and she was back to her binge-drinking, game show-watching self and hiding out in her room like me.

In the bathroom, Amber started the shower and hung a fresh towel on the towel rack.

"I'm okay," I told her, even though the two-second

walk to the bathroom had turned my legs to jelly. "I can handle this myself."

She squeezed my arm and left the room, closing the door behind her. Feeling wobbly and slightly nauseated, I stripped off my wrinkly pajama pants and tank top and soaped myself under the heavenly spray. When the hot water ran out, I stepped out into the steamy air and brushed, flossed, and mouthwashed my nasty mouth. There. Almost human.

Back in my bedroom, Amber was adjusting my quilt over a clean set of sheets.

"Amber," I said, watching her. I wanted to tell her she didn't have to do that, but it was already done and the thoughtful gesture brought tears to my eyes. No wonder Nolan liked her enough to quit smoking for her.

"Feeling better?" she asked, flicking her bangs out of her eyes. Her streaky hair was loose, hanging smooth and straight to the middle of her back.

"Yeah. Thanks."

"I'll go up and check on Nolan while you get dressed." She moved past me to the door. "Meet us in the kitchen when you're ready?"

I nodded. When she was gone, I threw on a clean pair of yoga pants and a T-shirt and twisted my dripping hair into a messy knot at the back of my head. I checked my cell phone, which I'd turned down the day before when it wouldn't stop ringing and beeping. In the past twenty-four hours, I'd missed seven calls and twenty-three text messages. All the texts were from my friends, Nolan included, each one asking some variation of *Are you alive?* The missed calls were from Emily and Shelby, likely placed after I didn't answer their texts. No calls or texts from Tyler or Ben.

Oh God, I thought as Friday night slammed into me once again. *Ben.* He'd seen me loaded drunk and passed out on the floor like some raging, out of control alcoholic. And unless my listless mind was playing tricks on me, he'd also carried me out to Shelby's car. What if I'd said something embarrassing? Or worse, what if I'd said out loud the words that flooded my brain whenever I got close enough to him to breathe in his summery scent? I swear, if I'd actually said *Oh Ben you're so amazing I love you I want to marry you and have your babies*, I'd quit school and move to Bora Bora.

I made a mental note to call Emily later and find out exactly how much of an ass I'd made of myself. My stomach rolled just thinking about it.

Food. I tossed the phone onto my neatly made bed and went upstairs to the kitchen. A bowl of steaming hot chicken noodle soup rested on one of the placemats, along with a package of crackers and an unopened bottle of red Gatorade. We didn't buy Gatorade, so Nolan must have gotten it from his house or bought it at the convenience store around the corner.

"You're probably dehydrated," he said when he noticed me looking at it. "Drink the whole thing."

Normally I would have teased him about being bossy, but I felt too weak and ashamed to put up much of a fight. I sat down and tried a spoonful of the soup. The warm, savory broth felt good on my tender throat.

He sat down in the chair across from me. "Where's your mom?"

I shrugged and ripped the plastic off the top of the Gatorade bottle. "Haven't seen her since Friday evening. I think she came back for an hour or so yesterday after she got off work, but I didn't talk to her or anything."

"She didn't check on you to make sure you were okay?" Amber asked from the kitchen sink where she was rinsing out the soup pot. She sounded surprised. She didn't know my mother like Nolan and I did.

"She's probably with her new boyfriend." I gulped some Gatorade, which felt even better on my throat than the soup. I'd never been so thirsty in my life.

Amber finished cleaning up and sat down in the chair next to Nolan. They watched me eat for a minute, as if I was a toddler who might flip my bowl over or hide food under a napkin when they weren't looking. Their vigilance wasn't necessary; I devoured every drop and crumb, plus the entire bottle of Gatorade and two glasses of water. I felt a million times better, at least physically.

"Thanks. For the food and . . . just everything." I couldn't imagine any of my other friends barging into my room uninvited, threatening me into the shower, changing my foul sheets, and shoving soup and energy drinks down my throat.

"So what happened the other night?" Nolan fiddled with the salt shaker, sliding it back and forth across the table top. "We heard—"

"You heard what?" All that liquid sloshed in my stomach.

He glanced at Amber, who placed her elbows on the table and leaned toward me. Her bracelets slid down her arms, one by one. "My friend Brielle was there. At the party. All she said was you got really drunk and had to be carried out of the house by the student council president."

My cheeks blazed. "Is that really all she said?"

"Yeah. Well, she also mentioned it happened pretty late, after a lot of people had already left or passed out somewhere themselves. So I don't think many people saw you."

A small comfort. I sighed, wishing there was still soup in my bowl so I could drown myself in it. "Yep, that's pretty much what happened."

"Drinking yourself into oblivion at one of Dustin Sweeney's parties was a dumb move, Lexi," Nolan said, returning the salt shaker to its rightful place next to the pepper. "It's like a frat house over there."

I didn't know how he could know, never having been to one of Dustin's parties. I guess word got around. "My friends were there, too," I said defensively. *And a strong, angry, drug dealing bad boy, skulking in the shadows like a serial killer. . . .*

Nolan made a scoffing sound as if he didn't trust my friends to take care of a gerbil. "How could they let you get so drunk? And how long were you gone before they even noticed you were missing?"

"They found me and got me home safe, didn't they? I don't need my friends to monitor my alcohol consumption and stay with me at all times. I can take care of myself."

He raised an eyebrow as if to say *Oh really?* "I don't think getting drunk to the point of passing out and then staying in bed for two days afterward qualifies as taking care of yourself," he shot back. "It's not healthy and it's not normal. You should know that better than anyone."

I glared at him and then shot a quick glance at Amber, who was listening with an uneasy expression. No way was I going to discuss my mother in front of her or argue with Nolan about how I wasn't like my mother even though I may have acted like her sometimes. Besides, Nolan didn't even know the half of it. I could only imagine what he'd say about my relationship with Tyler, which was the epitome of unhealthy and abnormal. Nolan knew me better than anyone, knew my past and all my faults just like I knew his, but there were some things that needed to stay hidden, even between us.

"It's not like I make a regular habit of it," I said, ignoring his last statement. I'd save my indignation for later, when we were alone. Plus, I couldn't yell at someone who'd just made me soup. "I was just, you know, letting off some steam after a really hard week."

"I know you had a hard week," he said, calmer now. "But being in denial won't make everything go away. And it's not just you who's having a hard time, you know. My mom's been inconsolable all week."

"Nolan," I said through gritted teeth. "Can we talk about this later?" I flicked my eyes toward Amber, who bit her lip and shifted in her chair like it literally pained her to be sitting between us.

"Amber knows. I told her about your father and your fight with my mom and everything. It's nothing to be ashamed of, Lex."

But it was. Having a father who'd chosen drugs over you and then deliberately ignored you for most of your life was definitely something to be ashamed of, in my opinion. If I could help it, I'd rather people not perceive me as a poor, unwanted little stray.

"I won't tell anyone," Amber assured me. "Hey, if it makes you feel any better, my father sucks, too. He cheated on my mom with a woman half his age. I was thirteen when they got divorced and I've barely seen him since. Not that I want to. But yeah, I totally understand that punched-in-the-gut feeling."

Punched in the gut described it perfectly. I offered her a tiny smile. "Thanks."

"You have to face this shit with your dad," Nolan said, curling the corner of the placemat up and then letting it unroll again. "Have you Googled him yet?"

I shook my head. "I can't. I'm too . . . I don't know. Scared of what I might find. Or worried I won't find anything at all. Or something." *Or maybe he doesn't* want *me to find him.*

Nolan caught my gaze and held it. "Would you rather I did it?"

"I'll do it, Nolan. Eventually."

"What are you waiting for?"

I didn't have a good answer for this. Improvising, I said, "Courage?"

"You've always had that." His words erased any lingering hostility I felt toward him, just like that. He stretched his back and let out a yawn. "Come on, let's go Google him right now. Amber and I will stand behind you. Literally."

Amber nodded in agreement and they both stood up.

My heart slammed against my rib cage. *Whack.* "What, right now?"

Nolan gave the table a slight tap with his fist. "Right now. Got that paper my mom gave you with his info on it?"

I gazed up at the two of them, trying to soak in a bit of their shining optimism and strength. "Don't need it," I told him, and pulled myself to my feet. He was right. It was time to face this head-on. Get it over with. With them behind me, backing me up, maybe I'd finally have the guts to press ENTER and see what came up.

In the spare room, I sat at the desk and turned on the computer.

While it booted up, Amber distracted me with a painless, random question. "Why is your room downstairs when there are two bedrooms up here?"

I gestured around me. "This used to be my room. I moved downstairs when I was fourteen . . . for privacy." *And because my mother's boyfriend at the time often spent the night and the repulsive noises coming from across the hall made me want to barf,* I added silently, not wanting to scare Amber any more than I already had.

Nolan nudged my shoulder with his forearm and I turned my gaze back to the computer screen, which showed the Google homepage. "Okay. Plug in the deets."

I laughed nervously at his choice of words. My hands felt cold and sweaty. I wiped them on my pants and stared down at the keyboard. Okay. I could do this. Nolan and Amber stood on either side of me like supportive bookends, propping me up. *I can do this. I think.*

I positioned my fingers on the keys, then lowered them again. "What if his company doesn't even have a website? What if—"

"Lexi," Nolan said, prodding me with his arm again. "Type."

"Okay, okay." With stiff, shaking fingers, I typed everything I knew about my father into the search bar. I held my breath and tapped the ENTER key. Almost immediately, a full page of results appeared. For a moment, all I could do was stare at the screen, panicked and overwhelmed.

Nolan pointed at the third site. "That one. It's a website."

I clicked and he was right. It was a business website. A crappy business website, with scrolling text, blurred pictures of backhoes, and a vivid, seizure-inducing color scheme. It looked like one of those do-it-yourself jobs.

"It's a small town practically in the middle of nowhere," Nolan reminded me.

Our moms had both talked a lot about growing up in Alton, how sheltered and conservative it was. Even in this modern age, most businesses there probably wouldn't bother with websites at all. And if they did, they'd balk at anything complicated or fancy. Even the most prosperous Altoners, we'd learned, were modest, simple folk.

"Click on ABOUT," Amber suggested.

The ABOUT page consisted of a short, one-paragraph summary of the company's history, when it was founded and by whom (in the early seventies by Frank Davis, my grandfather). My breath caught when I glimpsed my father's name in the next sentence. He *had* taken over the company in January, just like Teresa said. Here was solid proof of his existence, right before our eyes in a hideous red font.

"Do we have the right guy?" Amber asked, leaning in to squint at the screen. "Maybe there's a picture somewhere."

I opened up the contact page, revealing words and numbers but no pictures. I let out a shaky breath, wondering if I should feel disappointed or relieved. In my mind, my father was young, slim, with a nice-looking, unlined face. Like in my pictures. Seeing him as he was now, his face likely fuller and creased with age, would be way too weird.

"It's him," I said, my gaze zeroed in on the contact information. *Eric Davis, Owner-Operator* it said, and underneath that, a phone number. The same phone number that was written on the paper Teresa had given me. All this time, I'd assumed it was his home number or his cell number. Was I supposed to call him at *work*? Or maybe this was the only number that Josie women was able to dig up. Evidently, Eric Davis liked his privacy, too.

"There's an email address," Nolan pointed out.

"Yeah." I'd seen it. In fact, it may as well have been neon and blinking.

He pressed on. "Are you going to contact him? I mean, I'm sure he'd get whatever email you sent to that address, even if it went through a receptionist or someone first. A bit easier than calling him, right?"

"Yeah," I said again.

"Yeah you're going to email him or yeah it's easier?"

"Nolan," Amber scolded softly. "Give the girl a minute to digest."

"What? I was just—"

"What are you kids doing in here?"

The three of us broke out of our huddle and whirled

around. My mother stood in the doorway, her face pinched in suspicion. For someone who'd been gone all weekend, doing God knows what, she looked fresh and well-rested in a pair of dark skinny jeans and a loose, gauzy white blouse. Due to the bickering bookends, I hadn't even heard her come home.

"Hi, Mom," I said in a much perkier voice than I usually used, causing her eyes to narrow even farther. My right hand, clutching the computer mouse, refused to obey my brain's directive to *move*. "We were just researching, um . . ."

"Magnets," Nolan said, furtively hitting a button on the keyboard and making my father's website disappear. "Electromagnetism. For our physics homework."

My mother shot him her special look, the one she held in reserve just for him. A look of pure contempt. A look that said, *You're one of them, one of those meddlesome Bruces, and I don't like you.* Guilt by association. That look was the reason why Nolan had only been in my house a handful of times in the past five years.

"Well, how about you research somewhere else," Mom said, her wary gaze on me now. "I need to catch up on some emails."

And some bills too, I hope. I stood up and ushered Nolan and Amber from the room. Hopefully, my mother wasn't aware that she could track my online activities by hitting Ctrl + H. I highly doubted it; she wasn't the computer savvy type. Note to self: delete browsing history later.

"Want to come over?" Nolan asked when we reached the top of the stairs. "We're doing burgers on the grill later."

"Please come," Amber begged. "It's always good to have an even male to female ratio."

I did want to go over and eat burgers with them, very

much, but after last week I wondered if I'd even be welcome.

Nolan saw the hesitation on my face. "Mom would love to see you." He lowered his voice, in case my mother was listening. "You really should talk to her, Lex. She has herself convinced you hate her and won't ever speak to her again, like your mother."

Damn it, he always knew precisely how to get to me. I sighed. "Fine. Just give me a few minutes. I have to return some calls first."

He nodded and swung open the front door. Sunshine poured into the entryway, along with the unseasonably warm breeze. All the slush and ice and leftover snow from last week had dissolved into water, trickling from rooftops and saturating the dead, parched grass.

"Hey, Nolan?" I said as he and Amber stepped outside.

They paused to look at me.

"Let your mom know I'm coming. And that I don't hate her. Okay?"

For the first time since he'd arrived at my house today, he smiled at me. "Okay."

In one way, at least, I wouldn't be like my mother.

Chapter Ten

Before school the next morning, it took every ounce of willpower I possessed to not smoke a cigarette. My nerves jangled just thinking about climbing into the backseat of Ben's car when he came to pick me up for school. When I'd returned Emily's call the day before, she'd sort of brushed off the whole party incident, even though I could tell she was disappointed in me for losing control of myself like that. But she'd said nothing about Ben's thoughts on the matter, and I couldn't ask. She *did* assure me that I hadn't said anything embarrassing, which eased my mind somewhat.

To offset my disgrace, I wore my best outfit, spent a half hour on my makeup, and styled my hair to perfection. I looked normal. Strong. In control. Too bad I didn't feel it, too.

Ben's Acura slid into place against my curb a few minutes later than usual. With my breakfast in my throat, I took my spot next to Emily in the backseat.

"Good morning," she said, leaning into me as if she was checking for the aroma of nicotine. Or alcohol. "How are you feeling?"

"Fine." I glanced at Ben, who was fiddling with the vents. Once they were all adjusted to his liking, he turned

and flashed me a small, tight-lipped smile. My muscles relaxed, but not all the way. Tori, sitting in the passenger
seat, didn't turn around or say anything to me at all. In
fact, the vibe I was getting from her was quite frosty. *Crap.*
I guess she didn't take too kindly to her boyfriend playing
Knight in Shining Armor for another girl.

The atmosphere was even frostier in first period math.
Throughout the entire class, I was hyper-aware of Tyler's
presence behind me, sensed him watching me, hating me.
I hadn't heard from him since he'd stormed away from me
on Friday night. Three days of no contact wasn't unusual,
but his behavior was. What had gotten into him lately? It
wasn't like either of us stopped seeing other people once
we'd started sleeping together. I knew he saw other girls,
probably had sex with them even, and he knew I went out
on the occasional date. Nothing serious, of course, because I would never become involved with one guy while
sleeping with another. I was a lot of things, but I wasn't a
cheater.

For some reason, seeing me with Dustin had offended
him, even though I hadn't kissed Dustin and didn't plan to.
This new possessive side of Tyler made me uneasy. The
reason I'd picked him in the first place was because of his
carefree, no-strings-attached reputation. Our casual relationship had always been enough for him. Or at least it
used to be.

Whatever was eating at him, I wished he'd get over it.
We'd only been apart for a few days, but already I missed
him in a purely physical way. My body craved his body,
just like my heart longed for Ben.

It would be nice if my heart and my body formed an al-
liance someday and started working together.

At lunch, I met up with Shelby and Emily in Ms. Hollis's classroom.

"Hey, everyone, it's the Tequila Queen," Shelby announced, applauding as I entered the room.

Being a good sport, I took my requisite bow and said, "I'm here all week."

"God, I hope not," Emily retorted. "Get buzzed, fine, but blacking out is just trashy."

I laughed, which wasn't easy, and sat down in a desk with my lunch. "Don't worry. I'm never drinking that much again."

"Why did you?" Shelby asked as she settled into the teacher's desk chair. Her stomach looked like it had ballooned another few inches over the weekend. "You never get smashed like that."

"Yeah," Emily agreed. "You were a little off all night. Upset about something."

I concentrated on picking a green pepper off my cold pizza slice. *If only they knew the truth,* I thought. If only I could tell them about my father without the fear of being judged or pitied. If only I could share with them my feelings of confusion and rejection and the tiny spark of excitement that sometimes popped up when I thought of that email address, neatly copied onto the paper in my snake book. For the past two years, I thought my father was gone, dead. Admitting that he'd abandoned me would make me look even worse than I had on Friday night. I could never let myself come across as vulnerable. Not around them. The only person I trusted with the real, raw part of me was Nolan, and only because we'd grown up together, constant bystanders in each other's lives. He had seen every side of me—the good, the bad, the authentic, the fake, and everything in between—and I'd never once feared losing him as my friend.

I'd also never feared losing Teresa. Even after a week of stubborn silence on my part, she'd welcomed me back with open arms—literally—when I arrived at her house yesterday afternoon. She had my forgiveness immediately, especially after I found out she'd called Josie back during the week to gather more intel on my father. Just in case I ever wanted to know more, she'd said.

I'd been surprised to discover that I did want to know more. Curiosity chipped away at my denial, making way for a torrent of questions. Most had to do with my mysterious half-siblings, whose existence fascinated me. After gobbling down burgers, Teresa and I had sat alone together on the back deck while she told me what she knew about them. My mind drifted back to our conversation.

"Josie wasn't sure about their names," Teresa said. "But she said they were young, preteen age. A girl and a boy. She also mentioned that the girl looked just like the mother."

The mother. My stepmother. "What's she like? His . . . wife."

"Josie said she seems friendly. Her name is Renee. She works at the backhoe company, too, doing the books."

"And my father's father . . . my, um, grandfather." It felt weird, assigning these familiar titles to people I didn't know at all. "You said he died. How . . . ?"

"A heart attack. It was really bad."

"And his wife? My grandmother?"

Teresa reached down to stroke Gus, who'd stretched out in the sun beside her patio chair. "She died years ago. Breast cancer."

I thought of the quilt she'd made for me, its colorful squares of fabric so carefully sewn together. The quilt's presence in my room now suggested that I must have been attached to it even at age four, when my mother or I packed it away in a suitcase and carried it three thousand miles from Alton to Oakfield.

I waited until Teresa stopped petting Gus and then looked her square in the eye. "Do you think my mother knows any of this?"

She blinked a few times, but held my gaze. "I don't know, sweetie. Maybe. Josie hasn't spoken to her, but I'm sure there are people in Alton who do."

"Why wouldn't she tell me?"

"For the same reason I didn't, I imagine. She wants to protect you and she thinks you're probably better off not knowing him. He was such a mess back then, Lexi. The drugs . . . " She trailed off, shaking her head. "But hey, maybe he's a different man now. People change."

That, I doubted. If he'd changed, become a better man, why hadn't he contacted me even once in thirteen years? Why didn't he want me back in his life, now that he'd presumably gotten his shit together? Was it because he had a new family now, one that wouldn't up and leave him one day, so he'd decided to just cut his losses and forget me? It was what I believed, but all I said to Teresa was, "Yeah. Sometimes."

As I sat in Ms. Hollis's room picking the mushy toppings off my lunch, I felt my friends watching me, waiting for me to open myself up and give them a glimpse inside. Instead, I gave them my stock response to pretty much any inquiry on my life or current mindset. "Everything's fine."

If only.

The warm weather continued for the rest of the week. On Thursday evening, I went to Grace's. We were going to the playground while her parents labored over their taxes at the kitchen table.

"Mommy and Daddy have to finish the taxis before the deadwine," Grace informed me when I dropped by to pick her up.

"You're a godsend, Lexi," Rachel said, securing a pint-size Barbie backpack on Grace's shoulders. "If you can keep her out for about an hour, that would be great."

"No problem."

The park and playground were a ten minute walk away. The whole way there, Grace prattled on about what she wanted to do first when we got there. By the time we arrived, she'd settled on swings first, then slide, then "rock climbing," which was just a six-foot-tall, plastic structure with footholds.

"Push me, Wexi," Grace said, running ahead to the swings. I quickened my pace and followed her.

Only a handful of people were there, two parents sitting on a bench and three little kids racing each other down the biggest slide. When I reached Grace, she handed me her backpack and scrambled into one of the saucer-shaped swings, the kind you can lie down on if you're small enough. Grace leaned back, her sneakered feet hanging off one end, and ordered me again to push her, adding, "Pwease."

I pushed her, slow at first and then high enough to make her grab onto the edges of the swing and shriek. "Higher!" she shouted. Little adrenaline junkie.

"It doesn't go any higher, Gracie."

After a few minutes of this, she got bored and bolted over to the slides. The family was packing up to leave, the mom securing the smallest kid in a stroller and the dad seizing the hand of the slightly bigger kid, who was wailing. I sat down on the bench they'd just vacated and pulled out my cell phone, scanning it quickly for messages. None. Ten days. It had been *ten days* since Tyler last climbed through my window. Sure, I'd told him a million times in the past seven months that we should stop seeing each other, but I was obviously bluffing. He'd never taken the suggestion to heart before. We rarely went this long without having sex and it was starting to really get to me. Why wasn't he answering my texts and calls? How mad *was* he, exactly? Mad enough to get back at me somehow? His silence made me nervous.

"Wexi!" Grace called from the top of the twisty slide. "Watch me!"

I stuffed my phone into my pocket and watched her spiral down the slide and pop out the other end, landing on her butt in the gravel. "You okay?"

"Yep." She got to her feet, brushed off the back of her pants, and headed for the ladder again. Not much discouraged Grace.

Forty-five minutes later, after she'd gone on every piece of equipment at least five times, had a drink of water and a pack of Goldfish, and chased a squirrel through the trees near the soccer field, I figured it was safe to head back. When I called to Grace that we needed to leave, her lip quivered for a second and then she shuffled, ever so slowly, over to me. I took her hand and we trekked up the grassy incline to the sidewalk. Disappointment swiftly forgotten, she started belting out the chorus of what sounded like a Disney movie song.

When we rounded the corner onto Sprucewood Drive, Grace suddenly stopped singing. "Who's that man?"

Instinctively, I pulled her closer to my side, peering across the street and then behind us. "What man?"

She pointed straight ahead. "That one, at the store."

I looked in the direction of the convenience store a few yards ahead of us and saw Tyler out front in the tiny parking lot, standing beside his car. His right hand rested on the driver's side door handle while his left clutched an unopened pack of cigarettes. He was looking right at us. Even from several feet away, I could see surprise with a hint of panic flash across his face. My first thought was *When did he get his car back and how?* Followed quickly by *Oh God, we have to walk past him to get home.* Hopefully he wouldn't get into his car, shift into reverse, and run me over. Grace would be traumatized for life.

"That's not a man," I told her as we continued walking. "It's a boy."

Grace studied him as he let go of the door handle and just stood there, nervously glancing around as if he was contemplating running. "He's big and tall like a man," she said, kicking a rock with the toe of her sneaker. "And he has whiskers on his face wike my daddy."

We slowed down as we approached him. When we were almost at the parking lot, Tyler quit fidgeting like a criminal who'd just robbed the place, eager to make a clean getaway, and sort of slumped against the door of his black Impala. My mouth watered at the sight of him, though I wasn't sure if it was because he was hot and I wanted him or because he was holding a brand new, tantalizing pack of smokes. Probably both.

Grace and I detoured into the parking lot and stopped about a foot away from the Impala's dented back bumper.

"Hi," I said, taking comfort from Grace's grimy hand in mine. He'd probably refrain from acting like a jackass in front of a small child. "You got your car back early."

"Yep," Tyler replied, sliding the cigarettes into his back pocket. The unseasonably warm air always turned chilly in the evenings, reminding us it was still only April, but he was dressed in a thin T-shirt and jeans. The skin on his arms, I noticed, had sprouted goose bumps. "I'm very persuasive."

"Yes, I'm aware."

Grace, never one to be shy, gazed up at him. "What's your name?"

"Tyler. What's yours?"

"Gwace Madison Cwarke."

His mouth twitched when he heard her pronunciation. I'd mentioned Grace to him once or twice, the way she spoke and the cute things she said, but he tended to zone out during casual conversation. Especially when he was high. "Nice to meet you, Grace Madison Clarke. How's it going?"

"We went to the park because my mommy and daddy are busy doing taxis."

"Oh." His gaze flicked to me for a moment. "Cool."

"Did you buy some candy in the store?"

He laughed. "Kind of."

Grace tugged on my hand. "Can we go in and buy some candy, too, Wexi?"

"Um, not right now," I replied, which unleashed a series of whiny pweases.

"Grace," I said, giving her a stern look. "I didn't bring any money with me. We'll get a treat next time, I promise."

"But I want a wing pop," she insisted.

Tyler dug in his front pocket, brought out a tattered five dollar bill, and held it out to me. "Here."

I shook my head, refusing to take it, so he bypassed me and handed it to Grace. Her face lit up.

Perfect. I was sure Grace's parents would be thrilled to know that I bought their three-year-old a ring pop with drug money. "Thanks," I said, feigning politeness for Grace's sake. "You shouldn't have."

He smirked at me, which set off a warm, unsettled feeling in my stomach. "The poor kid just wants a ring pop." He leaned in close, his minty breath tickling the side of my face. "Unlike you, Lexi, I'm not made of stone."

The warmth instantly dispersed as if my body was a furnace and he knew just the right buttons to press to control the temperature.

When he pulled away, I caught his steely gaze and held it. "Are you going to tell?" I asked under my breath.

A look of disdain flitted across his face and I knew he got what I meant. He knew all about my crippling fear of being exposed for who I really was. "And ruin your spotless reputation?" He gave an exaggerated shudder. "God forbid."

We glared at each other for a few seconds before I broke the gaze and turned away. "Come on, Gracie," I said, leading her toward the entrance of the store. "Let's go get some candy."

"Yay!" She jumped up and down, her Barbie bag thumping against her back. "Can I get M&M's *and* a wing pop?"

"Sure."

I looked back at Tyler, watching as he climbed into his car and slammed the door, clearly finished with me. A few seconds later his engine roared to life, along with the top-of-the-line stereo he likely stole out of someone else's car. The pounding bass shook every window in the vicinity and scared the hell out of an elderly lady walking her Shih Tzu on the sidewalk behind him. He waited for her to pass and then, barely looking, he backed out of the parking lot and peeled down the street like the cops were chasing him. If he kept driving like that, they would be very soon.

"Is that boy your boyfwiend?" Grace asked, giggling.

My gaze followed the car until it disappeared around the corner. Then I turned back to her, shifting my focus to her sweet, innocent face. "No. Definitely not."

Chapter Eleven

Latte Guy liked to talk about himself. I realized this around ten minutes into our "getting to know each other" dinner. Before my linguine carbonara was even half gone, I knew all about his job (marketing manager for an IT company), his travels (he'd been all over the world for work and pleasure, and spoke three different languages), and his political views (like I cared). Why a young, successful, cultured man like this would be interested in a thirty-nine-year-old massage therapist with a teenage daughter was a total mystery to me.

Instead of letting my mother go to the trouble of cooking a meal at our house, Jesse had insisted on taking us out to dinner. His treat. He chose a casual Italian restaurant in the city, a place neither of us had ever tried. He'd had to call a few days ahead for Sunday evening reservations, and once we got our dishes I knew why. The food was authentic and amazing.

During dessert—an amaretto tiramisu that made my knees buckle—he finally moved off the topic of himself and turned his attention to me. His gray eyes rested on my face so intently, I wondered if I had food on my chin. "So, what's *Lexi* short for? Alexis? Alexandra?"

I took a sip of my coffee, which was so rich and delicious I didn't care that it would keep me up all night. "It's just Lexi. Not short for anything."

He looked over at my mother, the brain child behind my name.

She shrugged. "I thought it was cute," she explained.

"It is cute," he agreed, his eyes once again fastened on me. He smiled, revealing teeth even whiter than Mom's. "It suits her."

I answered his smile with a weak one of my own and glanced at Mom, who stared into her cup like she was wishing it contained wine instead of coffee. Earlier, during the main course, she'd looked happier and prettier than I'd ever remembered seeing her. She'd hung on Jesse's every word, glowed under his attention, touched his arm whenever they spoke. But as she picked at her dessert, she looked older, defeated, the light from the centerpiece candle accentuating every blemish and line on her skin.

I knew I'd pay, eventually, for Jesse's compliment, even if it had been innocent. She always blamed me whenever her boyfriends were overly nice to me or looked at me too long, which started happening around the time I turned fourteen and developed breasts a full cup size bigger than hers. Like it was my fault some of the guys she dated were disgusting pervs.

Our waitress appeared then, carafe in hand. "More coffee?" she asked, shattering the awkward silence that had descended upon our table.

Jesse glanced at Mom, who was studying the young, curvaceous waitress with an expression bordering on hostile. "No, thank you," she said tersely.

I declined too, and Jesse fixed his confident grin on our pretty server and requested the check. As she walked away, he didn't even attempt to hide the fact that he was ogling her ass.

Right about then I decided that, restaurant tastes aside, the guy was a total dick.

When the check arrived, he paid for it on his Visa and we got up to leave. Mom's mood seemed to improve when he helped her on with her coat, brushing her hair aside as he settled it across her shoulders. I stuffed my arms into my own jacket as fast as I could and walked ahead to the exit.

Outside on the sidewalk, I dutifully thanked him for dinner.

"You're very welcome, Lexi," he said, squeezing my hand and holding it a beat too long. "I enjoyed getting to know you."

"Same here," I replied, even though he hadn't asked me anything beyond my age, grade, and the query about my name. But I was just as adept as he was at faking sincerity. It took one to know one.

"I'll be back late. Don't wait up," my mother told me as she and Jesse headed in the direction of his Lexus, parked half a block away.

I almost laughed. Never, in our entire history as mother and daughter, had we waited up for each other. Bullshit was going around like a virus tonight.

"Are you sure you don't want to go to the movie with us, Lexi?" Jesse called over his shoulder as Mom tugged him away.

I didn't even have to look at her to know she was frowning, silently imploring me to say no. She was like a teenage girl, begging her mom for some unsupervised time alone with her boyfriend.

"I can't." I backed away, eager to get into our little red Ford—which I'd driven—and head home to a blissfully empty house. "I have to study. Math test tomorrow."

They waved and continued on their way. I went in the opposite direction, making eye contact with no one as I wove through the confusing city streets to my car. Just as I pulled onto the street, my hands already sweating at the thought of navigating through the congested traffic, my cell phone beeped with a new text. In Oakfield, I would have reached over, dug the phone out of my purse, and read the text while driving, but doing the same thing in the city would have been suicide. Whoever it was would have to wait.

Fifteen death-defying minutes later, I was safely on the highway, zooming toward Oakfield with the radio on low. My phone beeped again, testing my patience, as I turned onto the exit for home. Temporarily disregarding the horror stories I'd heard in driver's ed about texting and driving, I slid the phone out of my purse while paused at a red light and checked the texts. My pulse quickened when I saw they were from Tyler.

can i come over later?
need help with math

Math? After ignoring me for almost two weeks, he needed my help with *math*? What the hell? I was about to tap out a response when the person in the car behind me honked the horn, alerting me that the light was now green. I stuck my phone in the center console and left it there until I reached my house. In the driveway, I killed the engine and picked up the phone again, all ready to tell him where he could stick his math book. Instead, my thumb formed the words Come over now. My mom's not home so knock on basement door.

Weak. I was so goddamn weak.

Inside, I brushed and rinsed away my garlic breath and then puttered around my room, changing Trevor's water and stuffing dirty clothes in the hamper. I didn't bother making my bed.

After twenty minutes, I heard a faint tapping at the basement door. I let Tyler in and pushed the door closed behind him, wincing at the loud bang it made. This door was the reason why he used my window whenever my mother was home; it shook the entire house when it shut.

"Hey," I said, drinking him in. When my gaze reached his face, I raised my eyebrows and added, "Where's your math book?"

He opened his mouth as if to answer me, then shut it again and stepped closer, weaving his fingers into the hair at the nape of my neck. Warmth pooled in my stomach and I swallowed, my eyes glued to his, expectant. After what felt like an eternity, he finally put me out of my misery and kissed me, hard. Hands still twisted in my hair, he backed me out of the laundry room, through the family room, and straight toward my bedroom, lips never leaving mine.

Once in my room, Tyler kicked the door shut and backed me up against it, our bodies colliding with enough force to rattle the door frame. His hand slid down to grip the back of my thigh, lifting my leg until it hooked around his hip. I dug my fingers into his lower back and pressed him even closer. I wasn't sure if it was because we were completely alone in the house, or if it was because we hadn't been together in a while, but I was frantic, almost crazed, to feel him against me. Inside me.

Tyler obviously felt the same. He positioned my other leg until they both circled his waist and carried me over to the bed. We sank into the quilt together, tangled and breathless. By this point, I'd forgotten all about his lack of study material.

Afterward, we didn't get dressed right away. We just lay under my sheets, not touching. I felt vaguely ashamed, especially when I caught the expression on his face. He glowered at the ceiling, disgusted with himself. Apparently, I wasn't the only one who had trouble making clean breaks. One weak person was bad enough . . . two weak people meant a never-ending cycle, always leading back to the same bad habits.

Several minutes passed without either of us speaking. The longer he stayed quiet, the angrier and more self-conscious I felt. The anger mounted in me, rising up my body to my throat until finally, it escaped through my mouth. "Why are you even here? It's obvious you don't want to be."

He didn't look at me, just continued his staring contest with my ceiling. "Beats me."

"Then do me a favor and leave. God." I turned on my side, yanking the sheet up over my shoulder.

Once again, silence yawned between us. He didn't move, didn't speak, didn't even acknowledge that I was a mere six inches away from him, seething.

I flopped onto my back again and blinked into the darkness. I would not cry in front of him. Or over him. I would not. "You are such a hypocrite," I hissed at his profile.

That brought him to life. "What?" he said, turning his head toward me.

"Friday after school, I saw you and Skyler Thomas in the parking lot next to your car, practically feeling each other up. And you get pissy at *me* for letting Dustin Sweeney kiss my neck while we're both drunk at a party? You're a total hypocrite, Tyler."

"*I'm* a hypocrite? You're in love with that Ben guy."

Damn. How I wished I'd never admitted my crush when Tyler had accused me of liking Ben months ago. I sat up, dragging the sheet with me, and glared. "Yeah, well, at least I'm not sleeping with him."

"Who says I'm sleeping with Skyler? Who says I've slept with anyone since we started doing whatever the hell it is we're doing?"

I barked out a laugh. "Yeah, sure. Tyler Flynn engaging in a monogamous relationship? Tell me another one."

Roughly, he flung the sheet aside and sat up, reaching down to the floor for his clothes. In the dark, his grim reaper tattoo looked like an amorphous stain against his skin. "Face it, Lexi," he said as he pulled on his boxers and then his jeans. "You don't really know me at all."

He gathered the rest of his clothes and, before I had time to hurl a comeback at him, he was gone. A few seconds later, the walls shuddered as the basement door slammed shut.

Sighing, I fell back on the mattress. This marked the third time in the span of nine days that he'd stormed away from me. What the hell was his problem? What happened to cocky, easygoing Tyler, the one who'd sneaked happily through my window for the first time back in September? When did things get so complicated?

I don't need this, I thought as I got up and threw on a pair of pajama pants and an oversized T-shirt. *I don't need him.*

But Tyler's recent fondness for temper tantrums was something I'd have to deal with later. It was time to take advantage of my mother's absence and finish the email I'd been agonizing over for the past three days.

It wasn't one specific thing that provoked my decision to email my father. Rather, it was a combination of things. The sky-blue eyes identical to mine, peering out from the pictures in my snake book. The draw of those little half-siblings. The promise of a whole new family, a family I didn't know but was connected to, irrevocably, by blood. And, underneath all that, a powerful sense of good old-fashioned curiosity. I needed to reach out to this man, to connect, even if it turned out horribly. I had to know.

In the spare room office, I sat down in the computer

chair and brought up my email account. The letter I'd spent so long creating was waiting for me in the drafts folder.

Dear Eric,

No way would I ever call him Dad.

I know this email will probably come as a shock to you. It shocks me, too, and I'm the one writing it. But I feel like it's about time we got in touch.

When my mother and I left, fourteen years ago this August, everyone (including you, I assume) called me Lexi Claire. Now I'm just Lexi. I'm seventeen, turning eighteen in June, and I'm a senior in high school. Mom and I are still living in Oakfield. She works as a massage therapist and has never married. It's always been just us.

I'm not sure what, if anything, you might want to know about me. I like math. I have your blue eyes and curly hair that I hate. My best friend is my neighbor, Nolan Bruce. His mother, Teresa, was the one who told me about you. She found out about you through her friend Josie, who lives in Alton. I was very surprised to hear about your life there. To be honest, all these years I thought you were dead.

That was as far as I'd gotten. I reread my words three times, searching my brain for an appropriate ending. What did you say to a man who ignored the fact that you'd been born? Who might read your words and instantly hit DELETE, pretending they were never there? I took a deep breath and touched my fingertips to the keys.

If you don't email me back, I'll understand. Please know that I'm not writing to you because I need something from you or because I want to disrupt your life. All I want is an explanation, maybe, for why, at age seventeen, I have no idea who my father is or why he let me go. Then I can move on with my life and you can move on with yours, and it'll end there. If I don't get an answer from you, I'll know you want things to stay the same. If that's the case, I'll never bug you again.

I hope this email reaches you, and I look forward to hearing from you soon.

Thanks,
Lexi Shaw

I scanned the email a few more times, but my attention kept getting stuck on that last line. *I look forward to hearing from you.* Like I was closing out a cover letter to a prospective employer or something. What a crock. When it came to me and my father, looking forward was as pointless as looking back. We didn't have much of a past and it was probably too late for a future.

I clicked to that line, intending to change it to something less misleading. Instead, I sat there and watched the cursor blink over and over until the text surrounding it grew distorted. Then, with my heart hammering in my ears and the scent of Tyler still on my skin, I shifted the mouse forward and pressed SEND.

Chapter Twelve

"**W**ell, I did it," I told Nolan at the end of physics class the next day. "I emailed him. Last night."

He paused with his textbook halfway into his backpack and gaped at me. "Really? Holy shit. What did you say to him?"

I gave him a brief overview as we walked out of the classroom together. "What do you think? Too much? Not enough? Just enough?"

"Sounds good for an introductory email. I think you said everything that needed to be said. When do you think you'll hear back from him?"

We darted toward the stairs leading to the main floor and my locker. "Who knows? It's a business email, so he probably won't even see it until today. And there's a three hour time difference between us."

"Oh right." He glanced at his watch. "It's only nine a.m. in Alton right now. Maybe he's reading it right this second. Or his receptionist is."

Imagining that, my heart rate accelerated. "Do you think he'll, like, freak out?"

He shrugged. "I think it would be quite the mindfuck, hearing from you after all these years."

Mindfuck. Nolan always knew the perfect term to use.

Emily and Shelby were at their lockers when we

rounded the corner. As we approached, Emily looked at Nolan and wrinkled her nose like she'd caught a whiff of rotten meat. I looked over at him, too, taking in today's outfit of old frayed jeans and a *Super Mario* T-shirt with holes in the collar. *Sloppy*, my friends liked to call him behind his back. But to me, he just looked comfortable. Like Nolan.

"Hey, Lexi," Emily said, joining me at my locker.

Instead of taking off to wherever he usually went at lunch, Nolan lingered for a few minutes, leaning against the locker next to mine like he enjoyed making my friends uncomfortable—which he did.

"Hey," I replied, exchanging my backpack for my lunch bag. "Going to lunch today?"

"No. I have a deadline." She shifted from one foot to the other, like she was nervous. "I was wondering," she began, and suddenly I knew what was coming next. "Can you maybe give me a hand with some edits? I hate to ask, but I'm *so* swamped."

"Edits?" I said, and Nolan snickered softly beside me. I was about as talented at editing words as I was at printing them. "Um, I guess so?"

She closed her eyes and let out a breath. "Thank you. You're a true friend, Lexi."

"And what am I, an artificial one?" Shelby stopped in front of us, her hands pressed to the underside of her bulge, holding it up. "I'm pretty sure I helped you last time you asked."

"Yeah, after ten minutes of begging."

I shut my locker and glanced over at Nolan, who mouthed the word *sucker* at me.

Shelby, catching the exchange, let out an amused snort. Then she gazed at Nolan's shirt and started humming the *Super Mario* theme song under her breath, complete with the coin-collecting *ding* sounds. It made him smile. Of all my friends, Shelby was the one he tolerated best. And she, having learned over the past few months what it felt like to be ridiculed and judged, had grown more charitable toward people in general.

"Let's go," Emily said, urging me forward.

I waved good-bye to Shelby and Nolan and let Emily drag me through the halls to the newspaper office, which was just a small room off the main office area. As we passed the receptionist's desk, the door behind her opened and I saw Mrs. Moncrief, the school vice-principal, her hand gripping the door knob as she spoke firmly to someone inside her office. A few seconds later, Tyler appeared in the doorway, his facial expression a mixture of pissed off and bored as he listened to the end of her lecture.

"You're running out of chances, Mr. Flynn," I heard her say as Tyler turned to leave her office, his teeth clenched like he was struggling to keep from telling her to go to hell.

Emily had paused to listen, too, and we watched as Tyler bolted toward the main doors and shoved them open with enough force to rattle the glass. Outside, he brushed past a cluster of onlookers and then disappeared from my line of sight.

Beside me, Emily muttered, "He's such a skeeze."

"Yeah," I agreed as Mrs. Moncrief slipped back into her office and shut the door.

By Friday of that week, Tyler and I were no longer speaking, let alone anything else, and I still hadn't heard back from my father. I'd pretty much given up on the last one ever happening. Clearly, he didn't want anything to do with me, but that was nothing new. Tyler's silence, however, was.

Not only were we no longer speaking, I also hadn't seen him around school all week. Asking questions wasn't an option, of course, so I kept my ears open. Soon, I started hearing the words *week-long suspension* and *fight* being uttered in conjunction with his name. He'd been suspended for hitting someone on school grounds. Wouldn't be the first time. Finally, I knew what Mrs. Moncrief had meant when she'd told him he was almost out of chances. After so many suspensions, the next step was expulsion. To be expelled two months before graduation did not bode well for his future.

I asked myself why I even *cared* about Tyler's future. Like he'd said the last time I'd seen him, I didn't really know him at all. Our relationship was based purely on a physical connection, not an emotional one, so we'd never had any revealing, heart-to-heart conversations about our lives. He didn't know anything about my father, or what growing up with my mother was like, or how I feared every day that my friends would uncover the real me and throw me back into the dark, lonely pit of unpopularity.

And I knew nothing about his life, aside from the basics. Two parents who worked a lot and basically ignored him unless they were punishing him for one of his many transgressions. An older brother who'd made the Dean's List at college three years in a row, a feat that drew constant comparisons between the two of them from their family and the teachers at Oakfield High who'd had the older Flynn brother in one of their classes. In a nutshell, all I knew about Tyler's personal life was that he felt disregarded, angry, and severely lacking—which was why, I suppose, I'd been drawn to him. We'd sensed a deficiency in each other, an emptiness begging to be filled. In those moments together in my room, we'd found relief.

But not anymore. Without Tyler, I'd had to find my relief in other ways, like by overeating and spending entirely too much time over at the Bruces' house, being coddled by Teresa. Or both at the same time.

Friday evening, I'd gone across the street to return a DVD Nolan had lent me weeks ago and found the family in the middle of their customary Friday night take-out pizza dinner. Feeling a little like a homeless person, I joined them at their request and proceeded to demolish three slices. Teresa was one of those moms who loved to see people eat (she was one-fourth Italian), so she didn't mind my gluttony.

After dinner, Nolan and Landon went out—Nolan to meet Amber for a movie and Landon to the middle school dance. It occurred to me that Teresa might like to enjoy the empty house, but always sensitive to my moods, she insisted that I stay. So I sat on the living room couch and sifted through the box of pictures that were kept in the antique chest they used as a coffee table. Looking at old pictures was something I did when I felt restless and adrift. Evoking happy memories anchored me.

"This one's blackmail material," I said to Teresa, who'd settled next to me with a cup of tea.

She leaned over to see the picture I was holding. Nolan and me, age four, were sitting in a kiddie pool in the Bruces' backyard, both of us topless and grinning. She laughed. "You two were so cute. Your mom and I always used to joke that you guys would end up married someday."

Sometimes I thought Teresa still wished for that. She loved Amber, but she loved me more and couldn't quite accept that a romance between us would never happen. Nolan and I knew it all too well, because our one and only try at being more than friends had been a complete and epic fail.

Our families and friends had no idea we'd been each other's first kiss. It was one of our many little secrets, stored away and never mentioned. We were twelve when it happened. We'd been lounging in his cool family room, hiding from a brutal summer heat wave and bored silly. The experimental kiss was my idea, an attempt to break up the monotony of another long, sweaty day. Plus, I was curious. Nolan apparently was, too, because he'd agreed readily enough. So, after a few false starts, we pressed our lips together like we'd seen people do on TV. The kiss lasted approximately five seconds, but it was long enough to determine that the two of us kissing felt *wrong*. Almost incestuous.

"It's like I kissed my sister," Nolan had said as he'd wiped his mouth afterward, and I'd known what he meant. We had zero romantic chemistry, then or now, and we liked it that way. Kept things simple.

"Oh, I remember this day," Teresa said, plucking another picture from the box. It showed the four of us at the beach—Nolan and me in the foreground, building sandcastles while our moms looked on from their lounge chairs. Mom and Teresa were laughing like they'd just shared a private joke. They looked so young. Happy.

"Who took this?" I asked.

"If I remember correctly, we asked some guy walking by to take it." She placed the picture on her knee and ran a finger over it. After studying it for a few moments, she sighed and shook her head. Her eyes shone with tears. "I miss Stacey a lot," she said when she noticed me watching her.

"I know," I said, taking the picture and replacing it in the box. "She misses you, too. But you know how she is. Stubborn. She doesn't like to admit when she's wrong."

"Yes," Teresa said softly. "She's always been proud, your mom."

"And pigheaded."

She didn't disagree. It would be hard to. "Speaking of proud"—she set her hand, warm from the mug of tea, on my forearm—"did I mention how proud I am of you for sending that email to your father? Sweetie, that took guts."

I shrugged. "A lot of good it did me."

"Oh, don't give up yet. There might be a very good reason why he hasn't replied." Teresa sounded like Shelby when she made excuses for her deadbeat baby daddy.

"Or he could just be denying my existence, like usual."

Teresa deposited her empty mug on the coffee table. "You know, I didn't really know your father when I lived in Alton, but I knew *of* him. When your mom called to tell me she was dating him, I wasn't surprised. She always had a thing for those tattooed, wild types."

I squirmed on the couch. Why, out of all the traits I could have inherited from my mother, did I have to get stuck with that one?

"Anyway," she went on. "He seemed *nice*, you know? Your mom was happy, really happy, for a long time."

"Then the drugs," I cut in.

She gave me a cautious look. "Stacey . . . did some drugs, too. With him. But she stopped when she got pregnant with you."

"And he didn't." I'd heard all this before, my whole life. She was stronger than he was, she grew up, she made sacrifices, she was a better parent, a better person. She saved me from him and for that, I should be grateful.

"He didn't," Teresa agreed, idly sliding another picture from the box. A Bruce family picture, circa about fourteen years ago when Landon was a tiny baby. Rocking a shoulder-length, layered hairstyle, she held baby Landon in her arms while four-year-old Nolan stood in front of his father, both of them dressed in suits. Malcolm's meaty hand rested on his son's small shoulder. All four of them smiled for the camera, a nice, normal family captured for posterity.

"My point is," she continued, putting the picture back, "he wasn't a horrible person, even then. Troubled, yes, but not totally incorrigible. He had good qualities, too, and I'm sure they eventually resurfaced. That's why I decided to tell you what I knew about him. It's also why I think he'll do the right thing and email you back. If he's as brave as his daughter."

My eyes felt damp. Like her son, Teresa always knew the right thing to say. I might have inherited the worst of my mother, but Nolan had gotten the best of his.

Chapter Thirteen

In the end, like so many other things, the email arrived only after I'd stopped thinking about it.

I definitely wasn't thinking about it Saturday night, when a bunch of us went out to dinner to celebrate our college acceptance letters, which we'd begun receiving in the past week. I'd gotten into my first choice, Benton, a small college about a six-hour drive from home. Student loans would cover tuition, books, and residence, the last of which I was extremely excited about. Rooming with a perfect stranger would surely be an improvement over living with my mother.

I wasn't thinking about it Sunday morning either, when I stayed in bed past noon, alternately dozing and thinking about Ben. He'd been accepted into Avery, a prestigious college located several hundred miles away from mine. If I was ever going to gather the courage to let him know how I felt about him, it would have to happen within the next five months. This deadline made me feel even more desperate to get close to him. Tori must have sensed it, the way sharks sense weakness, because she'd been acting incredibly bitchy lately.

I still wasn't thinking about it on Sunday afternoon—exactly a week to the day since I'd sent the email—when I sat down at the computer and typed in my password like

I'd done a million times since then—which was why it took me a few seconds to register that it was there, finally. An answer.

Dear Lexi,

I can't even put into words how stunned I felt when I read your email yesterday. It was very unexpected. My wife Renee read it first and called me. I was an hour away, securing a deal on a new cat (the excavating kind, not the furry kind), and I came back as fast as I could. A letter from you was the last thing we were expecting to see in the three pages of emails we'd missed since our emailing system crapped out two weeks ago. We just got back online yesterday, so I apologize for the delay.

Renee is helping me write this email because honestly, I'm finding it hard to express in words how happy I am to hear from you. I'm not much of a writer. Like you, I'm more of a numbers person, which makes me wonder what else we have in common. I knew you had my eyes and blond, curly hair just like your mother's. She always hated her curls, too.

A lot has changed for me in the past thirteen years. I don't know what you've been told about my past, from your mother or from this Josie person (who for the life of me I can't place, though Renee tells me she works at our bank), but I spent most of my twenties putting every cent I earned into my arms, up my nose, and down my throat. At present, I am twelve years sober. It hasn't been easy. Ten years ago I married Renee, who somehow still puts up with me. We have two kids, Willow (8) and Jonah (6).

There's so much I want to say to you, Lexi, but I'm not sure how much I can get across to you in a letter. Just know that I'm so incredibly pleased that you contacted me. I'd like us to try, if you're willing, to start building a relationship. I'll understand if you don't want to. It's been almost fourteen years since I've been any kind of father to you. Every day, I regret those lost years. I think of you often and I hope it's not too late for another chance.

The ball is in your court now. I'll leave you with my home phone number, just in case you ever want to talk. No expectations, no pressure.

Eric

P.S. I'd love to see a current picture of you.

My first reaction was relief. An email system failure, not a lack of interest, was the reason for his week-long delay. He was happy, not dismayed, to hear from me. Great.

My second reaction was rage. *I'm not much of a writer?* This was his excuse as to why he didn't mention once, not *once* in his entire email, *why* he'd failed to reach out to me all my life? *Start building a relationship?* Why? So he could drop out of my life all over again whenever it suited him? How could I build a relationship with someone who'd basically abandoned me and let me grow up with a crazy woman? How was I supposed to get past that? How did he expect me to ever trust him again?

I let myself fume for a few minutes, then forced myself to calm down and read the email again. Different things popped out: My siblings now had names and ages to go with the images I'd concocted in my head. He was kind of funny, like when he said "the excavating kind, not the furry kind" about the new cat he'd bought. He'd acknowledged his nonexistent parenting and expressed feelings of regret. He hoped for another chance. Okay. So maybe, like Teresa said, he wasn't *all* bad.

I moved the mouse until the arrow hovered over REPLY. The ball was in my court. No expectations, no pressure. *Click.*

My answering email was brief. Partly because I could hear my mother on the other side of the door, banging around the bathroom, and partly because one sentence was all I was able to give him.

Eric,
No promises, but I'm willing to try.
Lexi

When I walked into math class the next morning, Tyler wasn't in his usual seat at the back of the room. For a second, I wondered if his suspension had been extended, but as I sat down I noticed him sitting at one of the tables in front. The one right beside mine and Emily's, in fact. Terrific. Cranston must have moved him. Skyler Thomas, still at the back of the room, looked disappointed with the change. It was hard to stare at or flirt with someone who was three tables ahead with his back to you.

Several feet—and Emily—separated us, but it was like Tyler and I were connected by invisible strings. Each time he moved, I noticed. He never so much as glanced at me, as far as I knew, but I still felt warm and self-conscious, like he was aware of my every move, too. I must have been acting weird because Emily shot me a couple confused looks, and at the end of class she asked if I'd had one too many chai lattes this morning.

"You keep fidgeting," she said, beaming again at her graded test paper. For once, she'd beaten my score.

It was no surprise to me; it was the test we'd written last Monday, the morning after my spur-of-the-moment "study session" with Tyler, minus the books. Between the sex and the fighting, I hadn't exactly gotten much studying done. "Yeah, caffeine overdose," I lied as we left the classroom together.

At lunch, we convened in Ms. Hollis's room, even Emily, who chose to eat instead of douse fires in the newspaper office like she did most days. The April issue was done and ready to go to print. It was the one time of the month she allowed herself to partially relax, if only for a day or two. I wasn't sure why she still bothered to overachieve. It was senior year, and we'd already been accepted to college. She was going to Avery, like Ben. Apparently, they had a great journalism program there. I could picture her conducting interviews and covering breaking news stories just as easily as I pictured him in politics. The two of them radiated competence.

While we ate, Emily and I discussed college and our plans, topics we'd been understandably stuck on lately. Shelby stayed quiet and focused on her sandwich, ripping the bread off in tiny pieces and popping them in her mouth. I knew she felt excluded whenever college came up. She'd applied with the rest of us back in the fall, when she still thought she and Evan were going to be a happy little family, but since then she'd decided to take a year off. Piper would need her, she reasoned, especially at the infant stage. College could wait. Clearly, listening to us talk about our futures made her all the more aware that hers would be entirely different. While we were surviving freshman orientation and sitting in class, she'd be enduring night feedings and changing poopy diapers. Most likely by herself.

Emily, noticing Shelby's uncharacteristic silence, changed the subject to something more universal—our contempt for Evan. Recently, he'd started giving Shelby the cold shoulder, ignoring her calls and avoiding her at school. He was like a soap bubble, fragile and erratic, liable to vanish completely with the slightest hint of pressure.

"Did that boy come crawling back to you on his hands and knees yet?" Emily asked.

Shelby tossed her mangled sandwich back into her lunch bag and shrugged. "He'll come around. He has to, right? I mean, it's his daughter."

Right. Like the title of *daughter* or *son* meant anything to some parents. Like the sharing of genes and chromosomes yielded instant connection and love. He might come around, but there was no guarantee he'd stay.

I wasn't about to deflate Shelby any further, so I agreed. "True."

"He'd better get his head out of his ass soon," Emily said, stretching her legs out into the aisle. "Or he'll miss out on his kid's life and end up with a boatload of regrets."

Exactly, I thought, but I kept my firsthand experiences to myself and ate my chicken wrap.

"He's acting like Tyler Flynn," Emily muttered. "Going around knocking girls up and then dodging responsibility."

I took another huge bite of wrap, knowing better than to refute that stupid rumor. Emily would believe what she wanted to believe.

"Speaking of Tyler Flynn," Shelby said, desperate for a topic that didn't involve her flaky boyfriend.

My heart leaped into my throat.

"Did you hear why he and Brody Wilhelm got into that fight?"

"I heard it was over drugs," Emily said.

I relaxed a little. I'd heard the same. Brody Wilhelm was Tyler's competition, a fellow dealer who didn't mind pushing heavier stuff in order to get an edge in the business.

Tyler had had more than one run-in with him over the past two years.

"No," Shelby said, shaking her head. "It was over a *girl*. Apparently, Brody made a comment about some girl and Tyler didn't like it. So he went nuts and punched Brody in the face."

"What girl?" Emily asked.

"Don't know. There were a few witnesses, but none of them heard a name. And Brody's not talking."

Emily snorted. "Probably some slut he's banging."

Luckily, I'd already swallowed the food in my mouth because my lungs constricted in an involuntary gasp. Before anyone noticed, I covered it up with a cough. Still, I could feel Emily's eyes on me again, assessing. My skin felt hot, itchy. What if Brody had said something about *me*? I couldn't imagine what he'd say. We barely knew each other. But a crack about, say, Skyler Thomas wouldn't have set Tyler off like that. I'd made fun of her plenty when he and I were alone together and he never once got mad. He didn't care about Skyler. At one point, I would have said he didn't care about me. But his behavior over the past month or so suggested otherwise.

Instead of missing him like before, I felt grateful that our relationship seemed to be fading out. Things were getting way too messy. I didn't want to be the slut Tyler Flynn was banging. And I certainly didn't want to be the one girl he cared enough about to defend.

Chapter Fourteen

My mother was so preoccupied with Jesse lately, she failed to notice the sudden frequency of my visits to the spare room. Or maybe she thought I was in there playing Solitaire or writing my memoirs for hours at a time. No way in hell would I ever tell her I was actually emailing back and forth with my father.

In the four days since his reply, a total of nine emails had been exchanged between us. For me, it became easier after that second one. We didn't talk about anything too heavy. Mostly, I wanted to know about Willow and Jonah.

Do they know about me?

I'd asked that in my third email. He said they did, and they knew about my recent contact, too. Apparently, they were as curious about me as I was about them. So, in my fourth email, I'd attached a current picture of myself. Eric answered an hour later with his own picture, a shot of the four of them posing in front of a Christmas tree.

The young father from my pictures had turned into someone who looked like my friends' dads. His hair was short now, and darker, and lines bracketed his eyes and smile. Long sleeves covered the tattoos I assumed were still there. He looked healthy and handsome and genuinely pleased with life. Renee had shoulder-length, honey blond hair (real blond, by the looks of it, not dyed like Mom's) and a pleasant, heart-shaped face. The girl, Willow, was her clone. But the boy, he looked a lot like his father . . . and me. Different color hair, but the same sky-blue eyes, same pointy chin, same oval face with a dusting of freckles. Looking at them, my brother and sister, I felt a new kind of stirring in my chest. A kinship with people I'd never even met. A belonging. Family. Each time I studied their faces, my defenses weakened just a little bit more.

When I couldn't risk using the computer at home, I checked and sent email—slowly and laboriously—on my phone. I'd had to resort to this method on Thursday afternoon because my mother was at home with a horrible cold. Being sick bored her, so she'd probably be camped out at the computer when I got home, trolling Jesse's Facebook page or searching his name to see if it popped up on any dating sites. I'd figured I'd better get my email-checking out of the way after school.

A couple crotchety, anti-technology teachers known to confiscate phones and iPods—even outside of school hours—had been prowling around, so just to be on the safe side, I'd found a quiet little alcove near the service elevator and settled on the floor.

Just as I turned my phone on, the sound of footsteps echoed through the empty hallway. I leaned sideways until my head was sticking slightly out of the alcove. When I saw the source of the footsteps, I yanked myself back into hiding. Ben and Tori stood several feet away from me in the middle of the hallway, facing each other and talking. Actually, it sounded more like *fighting*. Uh-oh. I pressed my back against the cinderblock wall behind me and kept perfectly still. Neither of them could see me.

" . . . so sick of this." Tori's words were sharp with anger. "You always make me feel so . . ."

The next few words were too low to hear, but I did catch the deeper murmur of Ben's voice, seemingly placating her.

Then Tori's voice came again, loud and clear, easily reaching my ears. "Stop telling me what to do, Ben. You aren't my father, okay? God, you're such a—"

When her words broke off into a sob, I couldn't stop myself from taking a peek. They were still in the same spot, facing each other. Ben's face was close to hers. He held her forearm and spoke to her softly, firmly, his expression stoic and controlled. Even from where I sat, I could plainly see Tori's face darkening more and more with each of his words, until finally, she snapped.

"Leave . . . me . . . *alone!*" she screamed, and quick as a flash, her hand flew up and connected with Ben's nose.

He yelped and jerked away from her, his hand moving up to his face, while she turned and stormed off down the hall, her back to both of us. I sat there on the floor, looking at him, looking at her, too stunned to even move.

Tori is *psycho*, I thought when Ben took his hand away and gaped down at his palm, eyes wide with shock. Bright red blood covered his hand and the lower half of his face. I wondered if it was the first time someone had ever hit him.

Without thinking, I threw my phone in my backpack and scrambled to my feet. Ben was still planted in the middle of the hallway, staring at his hand, as I approached him. When he heard me coming, he glanced up, on guard like he thought Tori had returned to finish him off. He relaxed slightly when he saw it was me.

"Are you okay?" I asked stupidly. Clearly, he wasn't. Blood was dripping onto his shirt, staining the white fabric with circular red dots.

"I think she broke my nose," he said, sounding amazed by the possibility.

I slung my backpack over my shoulder and stepped closer to him. "Let me see."

He kept very still as I examined him, not even flinching when I pressed my fingers to his nose, feeling for anything abnormal. My nose had been broken during a game of volleyball in fifth grade, so I knew what one looked and felt like. Aside from some swelling that would surely get worse, Ben's nose seemed intact.

"I think it's fine, but maybe you should go to the office. I'm sure someone is still there."

He shook his head quickly. He was embarrassed, obviously, about taking a hit from a girl half his size. "Did you, uh"—he looked sideways at me—"witness that whole thing?"

"Some of it. She's got a mean right hook."

He laughed, releasing another trickle of blood. We needed to stop the flow before he bled to death or something.

"I'll go get some damp paper towels."

He nodded, and I noticed how pale he'd become in the last few minutes. I did not want to come back to find him passed out and bleeding on the just-buffed floor, so I took his non-bloody hand and towed him toward the nearest girls' washroom.

"Seriously?" I said when he hesitated at the door. "It's four o'clock. Almost everyone has gone home. There's no one in here. Look, I'll even check." Leaving him there, I slipped inside and peered under each stall, then opened the door again. "Empty," I assured him. He walked in, slowly, glancing around like he was expecting tampons to drop from the ceiling.

I ripped off several lengths of paper towel and held them under cold water until they were just partially wet. As I did this, Ben leaned over one of the sinks, examining the damage in the mirror.

"Damn," he said to his reflection. He did look rough. Like he'd just been smashed in the face with a frying pan. Tori really did have quite the arm on her.

I waited while he scrubbed the blood off his hand and then ordered him to turn around. When he obeyed, I pressed the cold paper towels to his nose. He flinched. It was starting to swell. I wished the bathroom had an ice machine alongside the feminine hygiene dispensers.

"Hold that there," I said, and his hand replaced mine on the wad of towels. I soaked another batch and used it to wipe away the blood on his mouth and chin. Soon, his skin was clean enough so I could make out the fine blond stubble on his jaws.

"I used to get nose bleeds sometimes when I was a kid," he said, sounding like he had the world's worst cold.

"Yeah?" I rinsed the bloody paper towel under the tap, squeezing until the water was no longer pink. "Hopefully they weren't caused by blunt force trauma like this one."

Again, he laughed, but without the red trickle. We'd staunched it, finally. "No, they just happened randomly. I'd have to sit with my head tilted forward and pinch my nose until it stopped."

I told him about my run-in with the volleyball in fifth grade. "I needed to wear a splint," I said as I used the clean towel to wash off the rest of the blood. "And I had two black eyes. I looked like a prizefighter."

"Really." His eyes flicked over my face and focused on my nose, which still had a small, telltale bump on the bridge. "Well, you healed perfectly."

My skin tingled and all of a sudden I realized how close we were standing to each other. My chest grazed his bicep with each swipe of the soggy brown towel and my hair brushed against his shoulder. The freshness of summer mixed with the metallic tang of blood surrounded me, making me feel dizzy. Clearing my throat, I drew back and gently pulled the other clump of paper towel out of his hand. "I'll make this cold again." I turned on the freezing water, wishing I could splash some on my burning cheeks.

I made sure to leave a few inches between us as I pressed the fresh, folded paper towel to his nose. Ben lifted his hand, and just as I was about to let go so he could take over, he wrapped his fingers around my wrist and held me there. Startled, I stared first at his hand and then shifted my gaze to his eyes. The expression in them—admiration mingled with a trace of surprise—made my heart race, then stumble, then race again, like a clumsy sprinter. He'd never looked at me like that before.

"Lexi," he said softly.

I couldn't tear my eyes from his, even as he slowly slid his hand down my arm, ran his fingertips along the crease of my elbow, and then reached up to touch my hair. "We've been friends for so long," he said, taking the paper towel off his face, "sometimes it slips my mind that you're beautiful. Then you do something nice like this and I remember."

My mouth felt like the dental hygienist had vacuumed it for hours with her suction wand thing. Ben Dorsey had just called me beautiful. In a disgusting school bathroom on a Thursday afternoon with the smell of disinfectant in the air and blood-streaked paper towels all around us. It was the most romantic moment of my life.

When I didn't say anything, he let go of my hair and turned away, his cheeks reddening to match his nose.

Oh crap. He thought he'd *offended* me. As if. As if I hadn't been waiting for him to say something like that for two years. I thought again about how he was leaving for college in the fall. Time was ticking. In less than five months, we'd be in different places, living separate lives. It was now or never.

Desperate, I blurted out, "I've had a crush on you since tenth grade."

To my relief, he turned back to me, intrigued. His nose had stopped bleeding, but the swelling kept getting worse, making his features seem slightly unbalanced. Somehow, it made him look even more adorable.

"Really?" he asked with a faint smile.

I nodded, biting my lip. Had I really just said those words out loud? In the girls' washroom? To a boy who'd just gotten his nose busted by his girlfriend? To a boy who possibly still *had* a girlfriend?

"Well," he said.

"Yeah," I replied.

He started to grin, but it quickly changed into a wince as the muscles under his nose attempted to stretch. "Ugh."

I sincerely hoped the *ugh* was in response to his pain and not to my declaration of love. Or crush, as it were. "Does it hurt?" I asked. Captain Obvious strikes again.

"Not anymore."

All of a sudden, I had a flash of him lifting me off Dustin Sweeney's laundry room floor and carrying me all the way to the street and Shelby's car. He'd helped me when I was vulnerable, and now I'd helped him. Karma. We were square.

"So." He tossed the paper towel into the sink behind him, his hazel eyes never leaving mine. "Can I drive you home?"

Just by the way he asked, I knew his offer meant something beyond a simple drive home. The question felt loaded with possibility. "Sure. That sounds great."

Chapter Fifteen

The next day, Ben and Tori were officially over. A week later, I took her place in the passenger seat of Ben's Acura TL. I had arrived. Again.

Waiting a week before publically "coming out" was all Ben's idea. And the reason behind it was purely logical and practical, like Ben himself. He thought it might look bad for him to be seen with another girl only a day or two after a break-up. I understood, even though it killed me to spend an entire week pretending nothing had happened between us and worrying he'd change his mind. Still, I did it. For him. In Ben's world, seven days was an acceptable period of time between girlfriends. Any sooner, he explained, and the cheating rumors would start circulating. But as it turned out, in our case, a million years probably wouldn't be long enough to satisfy the more imaginative busybodies.

The first time we walked into school together, hand in hand, the rumors quickly grew rampant. In one, Tori had hit Ben because she'd found out he was cheating on her with me. In another, Tori and I were involved in a catfight and Ben had intervened, taking an errant punch to the face. And the most ridiculous one, *I* hit Ben in a jealous rage because seeing him with Tori had driven me over the edge.

None of it even fazed me. My head had been stuck in the clouds since our little moment in the girls' washroom. After Ben drove me home that afternoon, we'd ended up sitting in my driveway for over an hour talking about us. About why we'd never tried dating before, and if we should.

"I just never really saw you that way and I thought you didn't see me that way either," he'd said.

I told him the truth, that I'd hidden my feelings because I was so intimidated by him. Hearing this, he shook his head in amazement. He was totally unaware of the effect he had on people. Namely me.

By the end of the conversation, it was decided. If I was willing, he'd like to try being more than friends. See how it went. *If I was willing.* I felt like laughing from the absurdity of his comment and the sheer joy that erupted at the thought of me, Lexi Claire Shaw, dating wonderful, perfect Ben Dorsey. Being his girlfriend. *Me.*

Between the recent developments in my love life and the fragile-but-steady progress with my father, I was feeling pretty good about life for once. Confident, even. So when Ben and I made our official debut as a couple, I tried to copy his indifference to the raised eyebrows and stares we were garnering. I also tried not to feel insulted by the occasional expression of shock. Okay, so I wasn't Ben's usual type, but circumstances changed. People changed. Right then and there, with his warm fingers entwined with mine, I vowed to prove all the doubters wrong and be the best damn girlfriend he ever had.

Of course, being the best damn girlfriend ever came with some sacrifices, and one of them involved revealing my new relationship status to my mother.

"You're shitting me," she said when I told her the news on Friday evening, the day after the public unveiling.

"I can assure you, I'm not." *Jeez.* It wasn't a good sign

when my own mother found it hard to believe that Ben would deign to go out with me.

She leaned into the bathroom mirror and made her open-mouthed, bug-eyed mascara face, the one that always used to amuse me as a child when I watched her get ready for dates. In fact, it still amused me. "The blond boy," she clarified as she swiped on her first coat of mascara. "Rick Dorsey's son."

"Yes."

Blinking, she moved back to admire her lashes, then dug through her makeup bag for her blush. My mother's makeup routine ran longer than some of her dates. Earlier, when I'd walked in and sat down on the edge of the tub, she'd already been at it for twenty minutes, concealing and plucking and smoothing the years away.

"Well," she said, dabbing at her cheeks with a tissue. "If he's anything like his father, you're in for a world of hurt. Rick Dorsey is a womanizer. Ever since his wife died, he's been running around with a bunch of twenty-year-old gold digging bimbos. It's pathetic. He's older than *me*," she added as she spackled on another layer of under-eye concealer.

"Ben isn't a womanizer." I was pretty confident on that. Whenever he dated someone, he focused all his attention and energy on her and her alone. After two days with him, I already felt like the only girl in the world when we were together. "He's sweet and respectful."

Mom smiled at her reflection, checking her teeth for lipstick smudges. "Sounds like Jesse."

I pressed my lips together to keep from laughing. Her hypocrisy and lack of awareness astounded me sometimes. She'd called Ben's father a womanizer, yet she was dating the biggest letch around. My mother was delusional.

"Okay, I'm leaving," she said airily as she zipped up her makeup bag and gave her hair one last fluff. "I'm staying at Jesse's tonight, so I'll just go to work from there in the morning. Have fun, say no to drugs, don't do anything I wouldn't do and all that jazz." With this parting wisdom, she blew me a kiss and flounced out of the bathroom.

Well. That had gone . . . exactly as I'd expected. My mother never did care much about the guys I dated. She'd taken me to her doctor to get birth control pills when I was fifteen and that was pretty much the extent of her input into my sexual health. She probably wouldn't even care if she found out about Tyler and me having sex in my room. In fact, the main reason I'd insisted he enter my house through the window instead of the front door wasn't because I thought she'd disapprove, but because I'd spent most of my life waking up to drunk male voices at three a.m. and watching strange men doing the walk of shame past our kitchen in the morning. I didn't want my mother to think I was anything like her.

But I didn't have to worry about that anymore. Tyler was history, and for the first time ever, I was a normal girl in a normal relationship I could proudly share with the world. With a boy everyone loved. Well, almost everyone. Ben *had* left a lengthy trail of bitter ex-girlfriends behind, most recently Tori, who'd quit student council and practically ran the other way when she saw Ben in the halls. And Kyla, the girl before her, who'd brushed past me yesterday after school as I stood alone at my locker and muttered, "Good luck, honey." And most notably, Shelby, who seemed less than thrilled about Ben and me getting together. She kept her Ben-bashing to a minimum around Emily, but I'd heard enough over the past year or so to know where each of them stood. Their break-up had been messy, and Shelby getting knocked up by Evan a few months later didn't exactly help matters. Basically, they avoided each other at all costs, and I worried that my new relationship with Ben might affect my friendship with Shelby.

"I'm fine with it, Lexi," she'd assured me when I voiced my concern to her. "Ben wasn't right for me, but he might be right for you. Besides, maybe he's changed."

Or maybe, I thought as I got ready for my own date, *he's just been waiting for someone like me.*

For our first official date, Ben and I made plans to go to a movie and then hang out at a coffee shop or somewhere afterward. The prospect of being alone with him for several hours in a row made me insanely nervous. After Mom left, I spent a half hour in her closet, looking for a top Ben hadn't already seen me in a million times. Finally, I chose the gauzy white blouse she'd worn the day she caught Nolan, Amber, and me on the computer in the spare room. It was loose on her, but on me it fit like a glove. I figured Ben wouldn't be opposed to some cleavage.

The doorbell rang while I was working on my makeup. *Oh crap.* He was fifteen minutes early. I swung open the front door, my face still partially naked, and then relaxed when I saw it was just Nolan.

"Did I leave my Jenga game over here?" he asked. "Amber just told me she's never lost a game of Jenga, like, ever. So naturally I have to test her claim."

I vaguely remembered borrowing his Jenga game a few months ago because Grace saw a commercial for it on TV and wanted to play. "Um, I don't know. I'm kind of in the middle of getting ready to go out, but feel free to search my room if you want. It's either there or buried in the family room somewhere."

"Cool." He came inside, taking in my half-done makeup job as he brushed past me to the stairs. "Where are you off to?"

"The movies with Ben."

"Ah," he said, nodding, and then he continued downstairs without another word. Nolan was trying his best to act indifferent about me dating Ben. He didn't really like him, but he knew how I felt about him and wanted me to be happy. For the most part he kept his opinions to himself, aside from one subtle dig when he first heard the news. "Good thing we quit smoking," he'd said, reminding me of the incident a few weeks ago when Ben had thrown my pack of cigarettes in the trash and Nolan dug them out. Come to think of it, Nolan never did give me back that pack.

The doorbell rang again five minutes later. It was Ben . . . ten minutes early. I still hadn't finished my face, so I told him to come in.

"You have freckles," he said, sounding surprised.

I resisted the urge to cover my face with my hand. He'd never seen me without my trusty armor of liquid foundation. "They're dorky, I know."

"No, they're cute. I like them."

I smiled. He looked pretty cute himself. The swelling around his nose had faded completely, and he wore jeans and a light blue Oxford-style shirt under a plain black jacket. I couldn't recall ever seeing him in a T-shirt or hoodie or anything wrinkled.

"Is your mother home?" he asked as I led him up to the kitchen.

"No." I gestured to the fridge. "Can I get you something? I'll just be another five minutes or so."

Instead of answering, he moved closer to me and placed a hand on my hip. My cheeks burned, because he was seeing my freckles up close and because he was staring at my lips like he wanted to kiss them. For the first time ever. Here. Now. In my kitchen. Did *all* our romantic moments have to take place in utterly unromantic locations?

"I didn't want to wait until the end of the night to do this," he said, leaning in. I closed my eyes in anticipation, but all I got was the tease of his breath on my lips before the sound of heavy footsteps clomping up the basement stairs broke through the silence. Ben reeled back in surprise.

"Found it!" Nolan called from the entryway, and then the front door closed with a bang.

I'm going to kill him, I thought. *I hope his Jenga tower collapses on his head and buries him alive.*

Ben regained his composure and glanced toward the doorway. "Was that . . . ?"

"Nolan. Yeah. He just came over to get something."

"Oh."

I looked at Ben expectantly, waiting for him to come close again so we could pick up where we'd left off when Nolan had so loudly interrupted. But he stayed where he was, a small frown on his lips. "The movie starts in twenty minutes."

I blinked. *Awk-ward.* "Right. Um, I'll just . . . finish getting ready. Be back in a sec."

Our town wasn't big enough for its own movie theater, so we drove into the city. Ben was a little quieter than usual on the way, probably because he was disappointed with our failed attempt at a first kiss. I knew I was. I'd only been dreaming of that moment since I was fifteen years old. Nolan barging in, however inadvertently, had never been part of my fantasies.

Ben seemed to perk up as we waited in line to buy movie tickets. He held my hand, and kept holding it all through the movie. It wasn't as good as a kiss, but it was something. I had a feeling the physical aspect of our relationship would progress very slowly, which was fine. After Tyler, I could do with a slow, sweet romance. Fast and fiery hadn't worked out so well for me.

After the movie, we walked down several blocks until we came across a cute little coffee shop called Jitters. Inside, we bought hot chocolate from the tall, black-haired girl behind the counter and sat down at the only vacant table in the room. The place was bustling with caffeine addicts of all ages and types, waiting out the chilly rain that had recently begun to fall.

Ben and I talked about the movie for a while, and then the hot chocolate, which was positively sinful compared to the sludge they sold at the chain coffee place in Oakfield. That evolved into a conversation involving the importance of supporting local businesses over large corporations. Once we'd exhausted that subject, Ben steered the conversation to my friendship with Nolan.

"You've known each other a long time, right?" he asked, sliding his empty mug to the side of the table.

"Since we were four," I replied, wondering where he was going with this. Nolan was an odd topic of discussion for a first date. Or any date, really.

"You guys have never gone out?"

I shook my head. A curious, tentative kiss when we were twelve did not count as going out. "We're just friends."

The frown from earlier made another appearance. "So he just sort of . . . drops in at your house? Whenever?"

"Sure," I said with a shrug. "We drop in and hang out at each other's houses all the time. Like I said, we're friends. He has a girlfriend," I added when Ben's frown deepened. I nudged his knee with mine and smiled. "What, you don't believe a guy and a girl can be just friends?"

"No," he said, his gaze steady on mine. "I don't."

My smile held on, quickly turning plastic. "*We* were just friends for two years," I pointed out.

"Yeah, but you said you were attracted to me the entire time. See what I mean? I don't think males and females can be friends without at least one of them wanting more. Usually it's the guy who wants more from the girl though."

"I've never been attracted to Nolan."

The corner of his mouth lifted into a slight smirk. "I can understand that, but I'd bet anything he's at least a tiny bit attracted to you. I mean, look at you." His eyes traveled from my crossed legs to my cleavage to my face, which was probably tinged with pink. "Just because I've never asked you out before now doesn't mean I didn't admire your"—he cleared his throat—"uh, attributes."

I laughed and flushed harder, letting his opinions on male-female platonic relationships—opinions I disagreed with wholeheartedly—slip by without comment. We'd have plenty of time for debating later. At the moment, all I wanted to do was get the hell out of the crowded coffee shop.

We slowly made our way through the light rain back to Ben's car, not talking much. A cacophony of honking horns, loud voices, and screeching brakes filled the quiet spaces between us, making our frequent pauses seem less awkward. At the car, Ben unlocked the doors and held mine open for me, always the gentleman. As I brushed past him to get inside, I purposely let my "attributes" skim along his arm. He paused, noticing, and I was sure he was going to grab me right then and there and mash his mouth into mine. Instead, he waited for me to get in the car and then shut the door behind me.

He didn't say a word as we left the city behind and veered onto the highway that would take us home. I didn't say a word either, not then and not when he suddenly turned off at the wrong exit and pulled into the parking lot of an elementary school, dark and deserted for the weekend. There, he shut off the car and, still not saying a word, leaned over the center console and kissed me.

And it was . . . nice. He was a good kisser. No, a *great* kisser. Even so, everything about it was sweet and chocolaty and nice. No fireworks, no heat, no magnetic, uncontrollable pull between our bodies. Just a normal kiss with a respectable boy. Just like I'd always wanted.

When I looked at it that way, it was easy to convince myself that I was exactly where I was supposed to be.

Chapter Sixteen

My father and I had been emailing each other for a lit-tle over a month when he broached the possibility of a phone call.

At first, I was reluctant. Hearing his voice, talking to him, would make him seem even more real. Email felt safer. But curiosity trumped my denial once again, and on a Friday evening in mid-May, while I was at the Bruces' house and safely out of earshot of my mother, I shut my-self up in Nolan's room with my cell. Exactly at seven o'clock, the time we'd agreed upon in our last email, my phone buzzed with a long-distance call.

"Lexi?" His voice sounded as clear as if he was in the next room instead of three thousand miles west.

"Hi," I said, sitting down on Nolan's bed. "It's me."

"It is you. Wow, I can't believe—you sound like a young woman."

I laughed nervously and reached over to pet Hugo, who was curled up in the middle of the bed on a discarded sweatshirt. "Well, I am."

"True," he said, laughing, too. "It's just the last time I saw you, you were learning how to print your name and ride a tricycle. That's how I remember you, I guess."

I swallowed. It was so weird. He remembered lots of things about me but I had only a vague recollection of him. As he spoke, I listened for something in his voice, a certain tone or inflection that might strike me as familiar. But he just sounded like some man I'd never heard before, a stranger whose DNA happened to match mine.

"Are you—?" I said at the exact same moment he said, "I'm really—" We both stopped talking and laughed again.

"Sorry," he tried again. "I'm really nervous. What were you going to say?"

A bead of sweat rolled down my back, reminding me that I was nervous, too. Extremely. "I was going to ask if you were busy with work. I know it's only four there."

"No, not really. I mean, I'm always busy with work, but my partner Gil is running things this afternoon. I'm at home, actually, by myself for once. The kids . . . they're in a million after-school activities, it seems like. Willow's at dance class and Renee took Jonah to soccer."

Hearing that, I felt a strange, almost-jealous pang in my gut. He knew where *those* kids were at all times. He was their dad, and had been their dad all their lives. They had no idea what it felt like to not have him around, paying for classes and sports and just being there, at home, waiting for them. In fourteen years, had he ever cared where *I* was? When did he stop waiting for me to come home?

"Lexi?"

His voice brought me back to the present and Nolan's messy room. I focused on the poster on the closed closet door across from me. Batman in comic book form, his black cape billowing out around him. I looked at his muscular arms, his pointy black ears, the familiar symbol emblazoned across his huge chest. Easy distractions to override the hot anger simmering in my throat.

"Lexi," Eric repeated when I failed to answer. "Look, you don't have to say anything, okay? I know this is a lot to take in. Talking to me after so long." He sighed. "You have every right to be angry with me. I missed a huge chunk of your life. The most important chunk. But Lexi, you need to understand something. In the year before you moved away, things had gotten so bad. I was . . . my addiction ruled me. I wasn't fit to be a parent. Your mother did the right thing, taking you away from me."

That surprised me, but I stayed silent and waited, listening to the tiny crackles of static on the line as he thought about what to say next.

"I missed you," he went on, his voice thick. "Every day, I thought about you. But no, I didn't fight it when your mom moved you so far away. I didn't deserve to be your dad. Even after I got sober and met Renee, I still felt the same. Like it was too late, like I'd lost you for good and it was all my fault. It took Renee almost two years to talk me into having more kids. I was so scared it would happen again. And when they were babies, all I could think about was you at that age. Especially when Jonah came along, because he looked so much like you."

Batman turned blurry and I closed my eyes, wishing the deep, sorrowful voice would just stop. Stop talking, before I said something I might regret. But he didn't stop, and I kept listening.

"That you reached out to me even after I screwed everything up . . . blows my mind every day. I feel selfish asking for more, but it would mean a lot to me if you'd give me the opportunity to explain my side someday. Not today, but someday. Soon. I'd really appreciate the chance to be in your life again."

I opened my eyes and tried to focus, but all I saw was red. "I didn't reach out for *you*," I told him, resentment seeping into my voice. "I did it for me. So I can get some answers. That's all."

He was silent. Obviously, after all those civil, almost-formal emails, he wasn't expecting me to be so bitter.

Finally, after a long, awkward pause, I managed to say, "I have to go."

"Oh. Of course. Well, you have my cell number. Feel free to call or text anytime. Okay?" His voice took on a hopeful, careful tone. "I'd love to hear more about your college plans and this new boyfriend you mentioned in your email a few days ago."

Over email, it had been so easy to tell him about Ben and my recent college acceptance. Eric's delight over both pieces of news had left me with a quiet, pleased feeling. My mother, who I lived and interacted with in person on a daily basis, hadn't been nearly as interested or proud. But on the phone with my father, with my head whirling with everything he'd just said, hearing his pride and interest was like one more drop in an already overflowing bucket.

He had no right to act like a proud father. He'd done nothing to earn that role.

"I have to go," I said again and hung up before he could say anything else.

I stayed in Nolan's room for a long time, stroking Hugo's silky fur and going over the entire phone call in my head. I knew Nolan was out there, waiting to hear how it went, and that Ben would be at my house in forty minutes to pick me up, but I couldn't seem to move. My body felt sapped. Heavy.

A few minutes later, Nolan knocked on the door and then stuck his head in the room. "How'd it go?"

I was still sprawled on the bed, cell phone back in my pocket. I sat up, dangling my legs over the side of the mattress. "Fine."

When I didn't say anything more, he came into the room and shut the door behind him. At the sight of him, Hugo rolled over onto his back and started to purr. Nolan gave him a brief scratch on the belly as he sat down next to me, his gaze never leaving my face. "No, really, how'd it go? You're white as a sheet."

"It was fine," I repeated. Then, remembering I was talking to someone who never took *fine* for an answer, I added, "Kind of weird. I think I'm more pissed at him than I realized. It's going to take me a while to feel comfortable with him, you know?"

He nodded and wrapped his arm around me, squeezing my shoulder with his hand. It was a gesture he'd made a thousand times before, in comfort or just because, and it had never once bothered me. But for some reason, this time it made me feel uneasy. I thought of Ben and the conversation we'd had on our first date, the one about Nolan and me, our friendship. It was a topic that had been revisited a couple times in the two weeks since, and Ben's position hadn't budged. My relationship with Nolan, he insisted, was odd. Now here we were, Nolan and I, sitting on his bed, alone in his room with the door closed. And all I could think about was how it would look to Ben.

What would Ben think? was a question I'd been asking myself a lot lately. If I hung out with Nolan at his house, if I wore a top that showed too much skin, if I had a few drinks at a party, if I talked to this guy or that guy, if I didn't take school seriously enough, if I didn't live up to his expectations . . . what would Ben think of me? Would he come to his senses, realize he was too good for me, and dump me like trash?

Ben's disapproval, subtle as it was, made me extremely anxious. I could not afford to mess it up. With Ben, I felt important. Respected. Even envied. We did nice, normal couple things, like going to movies and bowling and out to dinner with other couples. He held my hand and opened doors for me and kissed me on the cheek after walking me to my classes. He drove carefully and always kept his cool. He didn't smoke or get drunk or do drugs. He was smart and ambitious and well-liked. All these good qualities more than made up for the few faults I'd uncovered. He could be moody sometimes, and critical, and maybe even a tiny bit arrogant. And after two weeks of steady dating, making out with him still hadn't progressed past *nice*.

Still, the possibility of upsetting him stressed me out so much, I found myself becoming hyper-aware of everything I did and said. Even at times when he wasn't anywhere near.

"Wow, it's getting late," I said, glancing at my watch as I slid out from underneath Nolan's arm. "I'd better go get ready. Ben's picking me up at eight."

"Okay," Nolan said, seemingly unaware of my discomfort. "I heard there's a party at Dustin Sweeney's house tonight. You going?" When I nodded, he smirked. "Try not to pass out in the laundry room this time, okay?"

"Don't worry. My days of passing out in laundry rooms are over."

By the time we arrived at Dustin's house an hour later, I was in dire need of a drink or two. The mental exhaustion from my first phone call with my father compounded with the pressure of being with Ben was almost too much to endure while stone-cold sober. Honestly, I wouldn't even have been at the party if Ben hadn't insisted on going. It seemed like we were *always* in public, seeing people, being seen. Sometimes I just wanted to hang out at my house and watch a movie or something, but that kind of thing didn't interest him. He was exceptionally social. Pretty much the only time we were ever truly alone together was when we were in his car, going somewhere. But I'd never complain.

"Stay put. I'll be right back," Ben told me, leaving me

in the kitchen with Emily, who was sitting on the counter by the sink, pounding back a bottle of neon-blue cooler.

With each swallow, she shivered at the sweetness. "Lexi, you have to help me drink these. I bought way too many and if I drink them all, I'm going to be puking blue all night."

"Um." My last party at Dustin's house had not ended well. Then again, rum coolers were much less potent than tequila.

"Oh come on." She glanced in the direction in which Ben had disappeared. "Forget Ben. He's my cousin and everything, but he's a freaking stick-in-the-mud sometimes. Always has been."

I laughed. I liked Emily best when she had a few drinks in her. It loosened her up, made her more fun to be around. "Just one," I said.

She cheered. "They're in the fridge, bottom shelf on the right."

I squeezed by a group of girls who were hugging each other and squealing and yanked open the fridge. The interior, virtually free of food and bursting with bottles and cans of all colors, suddenly reminded me of my own fridge. When I'd opened it earlier in the evening to get grape jam for my PB&J dinner, I'd been greeted by some old friends. A box of wine, already half gone, sat on the bottom shelf beside several bottles of beer and an unopened bottle of Bailey's. *Mom's drinking again,* I thought as I got my jam. She was drinking and she was still with Jesse, a recovering alcoholic. *What the hell?*

A hand slid across the small of my back. I jumped, almost dropping the bottle of cooler on the ceramic tile.

"What are you doing?" Ben asked as I straightened up and shut the fridge door.

I repeated my earlier words. "Just one."

"Hope so," he replied, narrowing his eyes at the bottle

in my hand. "I'm not really in the mood to peel you off
the floor again."

He kind of smiled after he said it, but I still felt like I'd
been chastised. Then again, after what happened last year
with Shelby and Evan, I could understand why Ben was
wary of his girlfriends drinking at parties. The last thing I
wanted to do was run the risk of embarrassing myself—or
him—so I sipped the syrupy cooler slowly, making it last.

Ben and I spent most of the night on the couch in the
living room, talking to Dustin's friend Colin Hewitt and
Colin's longtime girlfriend Mara, both of whom I didn't
particularly like because they acted like a boring old married couple. But I didn't dare get up and leave. While not
exactly clingy, Ben preferred to have me nearby while we
were around our friends. I didn't mind, of course—how
many times had I envied Kyla or Tori or whatever girl was
by his side?—but sometimes I felt like I was on stage, au-
ditioning for a part in a play. Ben's girlfriend, as portrayed
by Lexi Shaw. Let's see how she stacks up against the actresses before her. Let's see if she falls on her face.

Luckily, I'd already had years of practice at pretending
to be someone I wasn't.

That solitary cooler did nothing to relax me, and by
eleven I was feeling more than a little on edge. I wanted
to go outside, but all I could think about was the last time
I'd roamed around Dustin's yard. All night I'd felt para-
noid, wondering if Tyler was going to show up at some
point with his baggies of pot. What would he do when he
saw me with Ben? The way he'd been acting lately, I
wouldn't put it past him to expose our secret relationship
in a fit of rage to the entire party. Seeing me with Dustin
had made him angry enough, and I'd never crushed on
Dustin or even dated him really. But Tyler knew how I felt
about Ben.

"Let's go in the hot tub," I suggested once Mara and

Colin moved off and Ben and I were semi-alone on the living room couch. I felt claustrophobic, desperate for fresh air, and the back deck was the only place I could think of to go without worrying about Tyler lurking nearby.

"I don't have a swimsuit," Ben said.

"I have mine. I brought my bikini."

That intrigued him, and he actually looked like he was considering it for a second, proper swimwear or not. Then he shook his head. "No. Let's just stay here."

My mind flashed on my last party at Dustin's and seeing Tori standing beside Ben in the kitchen, looking totally pissed. At the moment, I could almost relate. "Fine," I said, standing up.

Ben raised his blond brows at me.

"I'm just going to the bathroom," I assured him in my sweetest voice, the one I used on my mother when I was trying to convince her that I wasn't really the demon child she believed me to be.

On my way back from the washroom, I passed Dustin going the other way down the hallway. On impulse, I grabbed his arm. "Hey, Dustin."

"Lexi," he said, happy to see me. "What's going on?"

Glancing around, I hastily dropped his arm. A few people had witnessed him practically groping me on his basement couch a few weeks ago, and I didn't want anyone to think we were about to do it again. Especially with my new boyfriend a mere few feet away. Carefully, I leaned in just close enough to be heard over the music. "Is Tyler Flynn coming here tonight?"

He pulled back and looked at me, confused. He'd been so drunk last time, he probably didn't even remember that Tyler had been here. "No," he said, and then a light blinked on in his eyes as he caught on. "He doesn't do that anymore."

"He doesn't? Since when?"

"I don't know. A couple weeks, maybe?" Dustin's dimples appeared. "Why? You want something? Because I know another guy who can—"

"No," I said, backing away from him. "I was just wondering."

Relieved, I went back to Ben, who was still stationed on the couch, talking to a new set of admirers. I took my place next to him, and he reached out to encase my hand securely in his, holding me there.

Chapter Seventeen

Shortly after I found the stash of liquor in the fridge, my mother started coming home with wine on her breath again. By the end of May, she and Jesse had begun spending an excessive amount of time lounging around our house, watching TV and drinking and who knows what else. I wasn't sure who'd fallen off the wagon first, or if they'd tumbled off together, but I wasn't about to stick around and figure it out. Dating someone with an extremely active social life came with some advantages. I was always on the go, rarely home.

Ben had reasons to avoid his house, too. His father's new girlfriend, a ditzy party-girl type who was just five years older than Ben, had started spending weekends at their house. Ben couldn't stand the girlfriend or her miniature Yorkie dog, which she insisted on bringing with her even though it yipped constantly and wasn't quite house-trained. Ben and I, both only children of immature parents, shared a common goal—escape our houses as often as possible until college.

We had plenty of excuses to get out. Final exams were creeping up, and since neither of us could get much studying done at home, we spent hours in the local library, sprawled out on the plush sofas with our books. I loved to watch Ben study, loved the little crease that appeared between his eyebrows when he was puzzling over a particularly tough math problem. He never noticed my staring; Ben worked the same way Nolan drew—viciously focused and totally in the zone.

When we weren't hitting the books, we were hanging out with friends or participating in fundraising activities for student council. Always busy, always moving, always surrounded by people. On the rare occasion we did manage to squeeze in some private downtime, we spent it in his parked car. Just as I'd predicted, the physical side of our relationship was moving at a snail's pace, likely because I'd somehow given Ben the impression that I was sexually inexperienced. It wasn't deliberate . . . he'd just never asked, and there never seemed to be a good time to set him straight. As far as he had witnessed over the years, I'd dated occasionally but hadn't been involved in any serious, long-lasting relationships. Because of that, he assumed I was selective with guys. And possibly a virgin. I didn't correct him. In fact, I found myself perpetuating the idea, even going so far as to stop him when his hands started exploring. I kind of enjoyed playing the part of the chaste, innocent girl, and it was surprisingly easy for me to slam the brakes with Ben. Brakes had been nonexistent with Tyler, and even if they had existed, I would have been too preoccupied to notice them, let alone slam them.

I tried not to think about how it had been with Tyler. Every thought of him was like a stick poking a sleeping animal inside me, rousing it, making it stretch and growl and try to claw its way out. Back when I'd loved Ben from afar, I'd been so sure that if we ever got together he'd be enough for me, that I'd no longer crave the release of those moments in my bedroom with Tyler. But I never stopped craving, and the pressure kept building. I missed the exhilaration and buzz I felt around him, even when we were fighting. With Tyler, even conflict was satisfying, in a way.

Conflict with Ben, on the other hand, was entirely different. Fighting with him left me feeling small. Stupid. *Wrong*. His eyes didn't burn when he was angry; they cut. Winning an argument against him was virtually impossible. He never yelled or lost control of his emotions. Instead, he acted infuriatingly calm and rational, which made his opponent seem like a crazy person in comparison. He'd learned this tactic during his two years on our school's debate team, and he'd never lost a debate. Not one.

Ninety-nine percent of our arguments had something to do with Nolan. The amount of time we spent together, how we acted with each other, how we looked to others. For example, one day in the first week of June, I made the grievous mistake of flaunting my friendship with him in the school hallways for everyone to see. Meaning, he walked me to my locker after physics class, like always. Ben was at my locker waiting for me and saw us together, laughing over a private joke and looking—at least to Ben—entirely too chummy. It wasn't that he was possessive, exactly. It was more that he was acutely aware of how others viewed him. He was popular and visible, which made me popular and visible. Therefore, whatever I did reflected upon him. And the spectacle of his girlfriend walking and talking and giggling with a misfit loser like Nolan Bruce did not reflect well on Ben at all. Or on me, for that matter.

As for Nolan, he knew exactly what Ben was thinking as we approached him at my locker, but Ben's opinions had zero impact on Nolan. He behaved as usual, squeezing my shoulder and saying, "Catch you later, Lex" before disappearing down the hall.

Beside me, Ben quietly seethed. "Do you even care," he said calmly, "that it bothers me?"

Things had been so much easier when Ben spent his lunch hour in various meetings. Now that senior year was winding down, most clubs had disbanded for the year. The abundance of free time meant he'd shifted his full attention to me.

I shoved my books in my locker, feigning ignorance. "What bothers you?"

Ben never rolled his eyes when annoyed or impatient. Instead, his face and neck turned pink and blotchy, as if he'd suddenly broken out in hives. An allergic reaction to cluelessness. "You and him." Each word was slow and deliberate.

"There is no 'me and him.' We've gone over this a million times already."

I spotted Shelby over his shoulder, standing in front of her open locker and watching us, one hand on her protruding belly. Our eyes met and she gave me a brief, sympathetic smile, reminding me she'd been on the receiving end of Ben's discontent once or twice, too. *But this is different,* I thought, flicking my eyes back to Ben's. He'd dumped Shelby for getting drunk and dirty dancing with Evan. I'd done nothing but spend time with my best friend.

"Be reasonable, Lexi," Ben said. *Be reasonable* was his go-to phrase, a precursor to whatever well-thought-out, valid point he was about to make. "The guy hates me. He's always hated me, and now I know why. He's jealous."

I shut my locker and bent over the combination lock, letting my hair cover my face as I snapped the lock into place and spun the dial. Ben wasn't used to being disliked, so naturally he assumed the fault must lie with Nolan, but jealousy had nothing to do with why he didn't like Ben. He thought Ben was a phony. Nolan thought the same about Emily . . . and me too, when I was with them. He tolerated my school image only because I'd never let it spill over into my relationship with him. He endured the other Lexi with the made-up face and altered reality because he knew, deep down, she only had one true friend and he was it.

But that wasn't the Nolan Ben knew. The Nolan Ben knew was distorted by two years of bumming rides and deliberately antagonizing and the fact that he shared a long, anonymous past with me. Those were his crimes, and Nolan had been tried and convicted for them.

"People say things about you two," Ben went on, his voice low and close in my ear. "Everyone thinks your friendship is weird. Everyone. They think something's going on between you guys and that I'm just too blind to see it. But I do see it. I see the way he looks at you, Lexi. And I don't like it." He reached up and tugged on one of my curls, just like Tyler used to do.

I felt myself soften.

"Maybe it's me who's jealous," Ben said, lowering his hand. His fingers brushed against my cheek, light as air.

I looked up at his beautiful face, the face I used to gaze at and dream about and wish I could kiss whenever I wanted. Now I could. The pressure inside me dissolved, along with all the words I longed to fling at him, words about my life and my past and everything I'd been through, and how Nolan and his parents had been there for me the entire time, supporting me, the only family I knew.

But Ben wouldn't fully trust me, I realized, until I showed that I trusted *him*. So later, when we were alone in his car together after school and I felt the pressure start building again, secrets straining to get out, I set one free. I told him everything I knew about my father.

"Lexi? Hi. Thanks for calling me back."

"Sure." It was crazy, how I was starting to get used to Eric's voice. We'd spoken on the phone four times, and like the emails, each time it got a little easier. The animosity I felt toward him was always there, lingering in the background and sometimes surfacing in my tone, but that never seemed to discourage him. He just kept calling, kept trying.

"I know last night wasn't one of our scheduled calls," he continued. "But Renee and I had a discussion yesterday and I have something I want to run by you."

He sounded nervous, like a young boy gathering the courage to ask a girl to dance. I leaned back on the couch, waiting. I was at Nolan's house again, but I was in the family room instead of his bedroom. Less private, yes, but also less weird. And instead of Hugo in the room with me, I had Gus, who was snoring away on the blanket-covered couch cushion beside me.

"Okay," I said after a long pause.

"So we had an idea. Well, Renee had an idea and I agreed with it. That's usually how it works with us. She's the brains in this marriage. But anyway." He cleared his throat.

My father, I'd learned, tended to ramble.

"How would you feel about coming to visit us this summer?"

I bolted upright. A visit? Actually *see* him? I was still getting used to talking to him on the phone. A visit would be too much. Too soon. I wasn't sure how to respond. Ironically, even though I felt bitter toward him, I didn't want to hurt his feelings or disappoint him, this man who'd let me down over and over my entire life. What the hell was wrong with me? Low self-esteem and need for approval, Emily would tell me, another nugget of wisdom from her psych teacher mom.

Answer. He wanted an answer. After a few moments, I finally settled on, "I don't think so."

He let out a breath. "I understand if you're not ready for that. No pressure. Just throwing it out there. But it's a standing offer, okay? If you ever change your mind, just let me know and I'll send you a plane ticket right away. Anytime. I'd love to see you."

He dropped the subject, and we talked about other things for a few minutes before hanging up. Our phone calls might have been getting easier, but my body still felt depleted afterward, like a battery drained of its voltage. While I waited to recharge, I flopped back on the couch pillows and reached for Nolan's sketch pad, which was on the end table next to me, and started idly flipping through it.

Faces peered back at me, some smiling, some not, each of them an almost perfect replica of the subject. A couple were newer ones of me wearing expressions Nolan had taken notice of and felt the need to recreate on paper. Me with a serious, haunted look in my eyes. Me with my lips gently curving up, cautiously happy. And with freckles. Always with my freckles.

I turned a few more pages, pinching the far corner of the paper so I wouldn't smudge anything, until I came to some older sketches at the back of the book. One was of Shelby, her face way less bloated than it was these days, and several of Amber with shorter hair. When I flipped the page again, another familiar face greeted me, a face I hadn't seen up close in a while and certainly didn't expect to ever see in Nolan's sketch pad. I stared at it, my tired body suddenly zinging to life.

Footsteps pounded down the stairs and Nolan appeared in the family room, his eyes bloodshot from studying all day. Exams started next week. "You done?" he asked, sitting on the other side of Gus. He gaze flicked to his sketch pad, which I held facedown against my chest, before settling on my face. "What'd he say this time? You look really pale again."

"He wants me to visit him in Alton this summer," I said without looking at Nolan.

"Really?" He paused, digesting this news. "Are you going to?"

I glanced at him and shook my head. "I still feel like I barely know the guy."

He nodded in understanding. "He can't expect you to trust him right off. He has a lot of years to make up for."

I looked away, my fingers clutching either side of the pad. Nolan was undoubtedly wondering why I had it, but he said nothing. Gus's snores grew louder, and out of the corner of my eye I could see Nolan's fingertips, smudged with graphite like usual, sliding along the dog's shiny coat. *Trust*, I thought. Nolan could do anything to that dog, even dress him up in tight, itchy sweaters, and Gus would never lash out. He trusted his owner that much.

"Nolan," I said quietly as I turned the sketch pad over and tilted it toward him. "What's this?"

He glanced at the page and then back down at Gus. "It's a sketch of Tyler Flynn. Good, right? I added a copy of that one to my portfolio when I applied to art school. I needed to show I could draw entire people and not just faces."

"I *know* it's a sketch of Tyler Flynn," I said. "My question is *why* do you have a sketch of Tyler Flynn? And like this?"

Nolan cocked his head at the drawing, scrutinizing it. I didn't have to look at it again. It was already tattooed into my brain. Tyler in a crouching position on a dead patch of grass, elbows resting on his knees, face angled downward, dark eyes gazing at something unseen at ground level. The background was shaded to represent nighttime, but Tyler himself appeared to be illuminated, as if he'd been caught in the beam of a flashlight. Or the glow of a nearby window. In the foreground stood a desolate lilac tree, its branches spindly and bare. Just like the one in my front yard, before it sprouted flowers.

The sketch *was* good. Amazing, in fact. It wasn't hard to see why Nolan had been accepted into a local art school, even with his so-so grades. What *was* hard to understand, at least for me, was why he'd drawn a picture of Tyler Flynn outside my bedroom window. Nolan only drew things he'd observed with his own two eyes.

"I just thought it was interesting," he said, raising his eyebrows at me.

I dropped the sketch pad on the coffee table in front of us. "How long have you known about this?"

"About you and Tyler Flynn? Since November, I guess. One night I couldn't sleep so I took Gus out for a walk. I saw him just like that," he said, gesturing to the sketch. "At first, I thought he was breaking into your house and I almost called the cops, but then I saw you opening the window for him."

"Why didn't you ever mention it to me?"

"What was I supposed to say? 'Hey Lexi, it's come to my attention that you're having a secret affair with the school drug dealer?' " He shrugged. "I assumed you had your reasons for keeping quiet about it, even though I don't get why you would."

I studied the sketch again. A depiction of Tyler through Nolan's eyes, captured from an angle I'd never seen. He was the *one thing* I'd managed to keep hidden from everyone in my life, even my closest friend. Or so I'd thought. And now my secret was exposed, literally documented in black and white.

"You know why, Nolan," I said, my tone harsh and impatient. I rarely spoke to him that way, but it seemed like he was being purposely obtuse. He went to Oakfield High. He was aware of the social hierarchy there, how tenuous it could be. He refused to play the game, but he still knew the score. "How could you draw this?"

He stopped petting Gus and stared at me. "What's the

big deal? *You're* not in the picture. No one would ever connect it with you."

"That's not the point. It's—" I sat up straight, head throbbing as my blood—along with everything that had transpired in the last half hour—rushed to my head, overwhelming me. "It *feels* like I'm in it. To me. You must've known how embarrassing it would be for me to see this sketch. To find out you . . . know what you know."

"So what if I know? It's me, remember? I'm not gonna shun you for hooking up with someone who's not on the A-list."

I knew that. Knew Nolan would never judge me for Tyler. Still, it made me uncomfortable at times, how easily he saw through me. The Lexi he saw was still the same girl I'd spent the last three years trying to transform. A girl who ran to him for security and trusted him with her sad, ugly truths. A girl whose shame and weaknesses were so strong, they sometimes leaked through her perfect veneer and claimed her, reminding her of who she really was. A girl I hated.

Nolan's sketch pad was just loaded with that girl. I picked it up, making Tyler disappear as I turned to the newest sketch of me. Why did he draw me like this? No makeup, frizzy hair. He'd even added the zit I'd had on my forehead at the time. Did he *try* to make me look awful?

"I draw you the way I see you," he said as if I'd asked those questions out loud.

"Well." I tossed the sketch pad back on the table and looked at him, sitting there in his blue OPTIMUS FOR PRESIDENT *Transformers* T-shirt, watching my expression carefully, storing it away for future reference like always. "Maybe I don't like the way you see me. I've changed, Nolan. I'm not the same pathetic girl who used to sit around playing video games with you all night. I have a life now. Friends, a boyfriend." Ben's face filled my mind, and my next words popped out as if the image of him had possessed my vocal chords. "And while we're on the subject, Ben doesn't like the way you see me either."

A flicker of disbelief crossed Nolan's face and then his eyes went flat. "Please tell me you're not implying what I think you're implying."

I didn't answer. He continued to watch me, unwavering, until I finally looked away.

"Wow," he said dully. "I thought it would take at least six months for Ben to turn you into a pretentious asshole like him, but it's only been what? A little over a month? Impressive."

I wasn't sure what it was that surged through me then, anger or guilt or a bit of both, but it propelled me off the couch and toward the basement door. Just as I touched the doorknob, I retraced my steps and grabbed the sketch pad off the coffee table. I found the drawing of Tyler and tore it out, the sound of the paper ripping loud in my ears. Once it was free, I folded it up until it was small enough to fit into my pocket.

"Don't draw him again," I said firmly to Nolan, who was looking at me like he wasn't quite sure who I was. Or what I'd become. "Or me," I added for good measure, and then I left his house and went home.

Like the note Teresa had given me so many weeks ago, I was so sure I'd destroy that sketch the first chance I got. But somehow, it too ended up in *Corn Snakes: An Owner's Guide*, which was so full of my secrets by now, I could barely get it to stay closed.

Chapter Eighteen

Due to her obsession with Disney princesses, Grace was adamant about seeing me in my prom dress before I took off for the prom.

"You wook wike Pwincess Awowa in Sweeping Beauty!" she exclaimed when she and her mom reached our front yard, where Ben and I stood in front of the lilac bush, posing for pictures.

"Thanks," I said, smoothing my dress—a long, pink, shimmering halter-style with an empire waist and open back.

"And Ben looks like Prince Philip, huh?" Rachel prompted.

Grace frowned. "No. Pwince Phiwip has bwown hair."

We all laughed, even Mom. She always acted cheerful and friendly around Rachel, who was a bubbly, proficient Supermom type. As if they had enough in common to be friends. "Okay, just a couple more," Mom said, holding up the digital camera.

I gritted my teeth and smiled. It was brutally hot outside and my dress, despite appearing light and airy, actually made me feel like a tightly encased sausage. A sausage that was currently being fried. I needed shade or air-conditioning before my makeup melted or my hair frizzed up, ruining an hour's worth of torture with the straightener. Somehow, Ben seemed completely cool and unaffected in his tux as if he was immune to sweat. It wouldn't have surprised me.

It still amazed me, even as we stood there all dressed up, that I was going to the senior prom with Ben Dorsey. I'd fantasized about that moment for years, played it out in my head as I lay in bed or sat in class, never expecting it to actually happen. In my fantasies, he would pick me up in a limo, present me with a gorgeous corsage, all the while gazing at me lovingly. Then we would dance all night, kiss under the stars, spend the entire summer together before going off to college—also together—and get married in our mid-twenties and have a litter of kids. That was my frivolous fifteen-year-old-girl dream. As a newly-minted eighteen-year-old adult, my dreams for the future were more realistic. Unlike Princess Aurora, I probably wouldn't get a spell-breaking kiss and a happily ever after with my prince.

Ben and I had spent most of June fighting. Not screaming, storm-away-from-each-other fighting, but long, drawn-out disagreements that left me teary-eyed and frustrated. At some point, fantasy had turned into reality and the shine began to fade. Shelby was right about some things. Ben was inflexible in his opinions. Unforgiving of mistakes, his own and other people's. He wasn't as perfect as he appeared from afar. In fact, he was almost as flawed as I was, a realization that consistently surprised me. The only difference was, I accepted his faults while he barely tolerated mine.

Any other girl would have walked away a long time ago, but I couldn't seem to let go of the idea that this was where I was supposed to be, who I was supposed to be, and who I was supposed to be with. As for Ben, he seemed to thrive on that kind of unbalanced relationship. He was happiest when he was winning, and with me it was easy. I rarely challenged him, even when it came to Nolan.

"He's not coming over here, is he?" Ben asked in an undertone after the photo shoot was done and my mother was busy showing the various shots to Rachel and Grace.

"Who? Nolan?" I knew very well who Ben meant; he must have caught me sneaking peeks over at the Bruces' house between poses. "No. Why would he? I was already over there earlier, before you got here."

The moment those last few words vacated my mouth, I felt like kicking myself with one of my high-heeled sandals. Ben had been so pleased, so smugly vindicated, when Nolan and I quit speaking to each other after our fight a couple weeks ago. I couldn't tell Ben why we'd fought, of course, but he didn't really care about details, anyway. All that mattered was that Nolan and I weren't spending time together anymore, either alone or in public. He didn't seem bothered that I was completely miserable over it. Nolan and I had argued before, and even stopped speaking to each other once or twice, but never for this long and never over something so significant. Our fighting upset Teresa too; she was the one who'd insisted I come over earlier, using her desire to see me in my dress as an excuse. I knew Nolan would be around, but I swallowed my stupid pride and went anyway. It wasn't fair to punish Teresa just because her son and I were on the outs.

But Ben didn't see it that way. He saw only my defiance. "You went over there?" Telltale blotches emerged on his skin.

"His parents wanted to see me in my dress," I explained. God, it was hot in the sun. I shifted to the right, trying to find relief in the patchy shade of the lilac bush. The night hadn't even started and already I wanted to go inside and stick my head in the freezer.

"I bet he wanted to see you in that dress, too," Ben muttered, his gaze traveling over my curves. "He's not—"

"No," I cut him off, already knowing exactly what he was going to ask. "He's not going tonight. I told you that." Nolan and Amber were both anti-prom, anti-formal wear, anti-anything to do with school tradition. They'd probably spend the whole night watching movies and eating popcorn in the family room. For a moment, I envied them.

Ben's face relaxed slightly and the blotches disappeared. He reached out and took my hand, easing me back over to his side. "You look so beautiful," he murmured against my hair.

I turned my face toward him, touching my lips to his the way he expected me to do. The scent of summer was all around me, on Ben's skin and in the air, genuine mixed with synthetic. It reminded me of before our relationship changed, before I knew the different sides to him. Back when we were just friends, my vision was tunneled, blurred, never seeing beyond surface-deep. Now, my eyes were clear and wide open.

"Wexi?" Grace tugged on my hand as Ben and I got ready to leave. "Don't forget my birfday party, okay?"

As if I could forget. Grace had spoken of little else for the past month. For her fourth birthday, she was having a fancy princess party at her house, complete with tiaras and gowns and a giant pink princess cake. It was tomorrow afternoon and I'd promised her I'd go.

Bending down to her level, I whispered, "I'll be there with a *big* present for the birthday girl."

She grinned. "What is it?"

"It's a secret. You'll have to wait and see." I straightened up and watched her skip over to her mom, who was still chatting with mine. Grace threw her arms around her mother's waist and Rachel's hand came down to stroke her hair. The easy, unconscious way she did it, like a mother cat nuzzling her kittens, set off a familiar twinge in my chest. Longing. Family.

"Ready?" Ben asked.

His voice snapped me out of my trance and I turned to him, a shiver rippling through me in spite of the heat. When I nodded, he reclaimed my hand and led me away.

Ben waited until after ten o'clock, just when the prom itself was wrapping up, to spring his big plan on me. "I got us a room upstairs," he said in my ear as we slow-danced to the last ballad of the night.

"What?" I pulled back to look at him.

He was smiling, proud of his ingenuity. Our prom was being held in the ballroom of a huge hotel, and a few other seniors had gotten the bright idea to reserve rooms for partying afterward. But this wasn't our plan. Our plan was to head directly to Leila Acker's party, which was taking place at her family's summer cottage on the lake. I barely knew Leila, but the lure of bonfires, barbecue, and a couple jumbo-sized kegs guaranteed that most of the graduating class would end up there.

"I got us a room," Ben repeated, running his palms over my hips. He'd been covertly exploring my pelvic area all night, delighting in the fact that the taut, smooth fit of my dress required me to go commando.

"What about the party?"

"Who cares about the stupid party?"

"But . . ." My mind was whirling. Sex with Ben. I'd fantasized about that too, of course. A lot. And I knew it would be nice, just like making out with him was nice. The problem was, he still thought I was sexually inexperienced. Naive. I could fake a lot of things, but I wasn't quite talented enough to fake virginity.

"But what?" he said with a trace of impatience. "You don't want to?"

"I just . . ." My hands felt sweaty against the heavy fabric of his tux. Turning him down would definitely widen the already gaping rift between us, but for once I didn't care. Just the thought of spending the entire night with him, sustaining the charade for hours, exhausted me to my core. "I really want to go to the party," I finished lamely.

"Fine." His hands slid back to my waist. "We'll go to the party."

I knew from experience that I wasn't forgiven, not really. The latest offense would simply join the ones before it, piling up like Nolan's Jenga blocks, towering and wobbly, always threatening to fall.

Leila Acker's cottage was tiny and rundown, but the massive back deck overlooking the lake made up for any shortcomings. By the time we arrived at eleven-thirty, the grill was hot, the kegs were tapped, and several people were already well on their way to smashed.

"Beer?" I suggested the minute we emerged into the clearing where the cottage stood, quaint and cozy-looking in the darkness. A line-up of around two dozen people trickled up the yard and onto the deck, where I assumed the kegs were located.

"Who owns this cottage again?" Emily asked as she threaded her arm through Dustin Sweeney's and started in the direction of the beer line. Ever since Dustin had asked her to the prom last month, Emily kept insisting they were going as friends, but I'd caught them holding hands several times. Colin Hewitt and his girlfriend Mara followed closely behind them, and Ben and I brought up the rear, neither speaking nor touching, the gloomy finish to an otherwise cheerful convoy.

A lot of people had changed out of their formal clothes and into shorts and T-shirts at some point between the prom and the cabin, but the three of us still wore our dresses. Mara, stunning in a long, ice blue strapless gown and Emily in the short white dress with the sweetheart neckline that Shelby and I had helped her pick out last winter. I wished Shelby could see her in it, but she'd skipped the prom for several reasons—she couldn't find a dress to fit, Evan was still being an ass, and her due date was less than two weeks away and she didn't want to risk having the baby at the prom. *How cliché*, she'd exclaimed.

"Leila Acker," I answered Emily as we got in line. "You know, the girl with the curly brown hair who hangs out with Bianca Sykes."

Her nose wrinkled. Bianca Sykes had a reputation for being—in Emily's words—"a total skank." Meaning, she went through guys like Kleenex and shamelessly slept around. She was the female version of Tyler, who, predictably, she'd gone out with a few times last year.

When it was my turn at the keg, I filled my red plastic cup to the brim and immediately started downing it. When it was gone, I got back in line for another. I knew Ben would disapprove, but he was already pissed at me so I thought what the hell, I'd have two beers. Maybe even three. It was prom night, after all, and he was off somewhere anyway, probably practicing his valedictorian speech for an audience of unsuspecting squirrels in the woods.

The second beer shot straight to my bladder, so I went inside in search of a bathroom. Of course there was only one, and of course there was a line for that too, even longer than the keg line. When I was finally done in the washroom, I made sure my dress was positioned properly on my hips and returned to the kitchen, hoping for a glass of water. But instead of water, I got something else I'd been thirsting for: Tyler Flynn.

You have got *to be kidding me*, I thought when I turned the corner and saw him leaning against the ancient yellow-gold stove and talking to some guy with a lip ring I'd seen around but didn't know. They both glanced up as I entered the room, and then the guy turned back to Tyler and continued talking, oblivious to the abrupt shift in atmosphere. Tyler regarded me with the same deer-in-headlights look he'd worn in the convenience store parking lot a couple months ago.

I should have turned around and walked away right then, but dammit, I was thirsty. So I squared my shoulders, dug out a plastic cup from the bag on the counter, and filled it at the sink. The entire time I could feel Tyler just a couple of feet away, his eyes searing my skin. After another minute or so of one-sided conversation, Lip Ring Guy excused himself and departed through the sliding doors to the deck, leaving us alone in the kitchen.

My water was lukewarm and slightly bitter, but I kept drinking, drinking, soothing my parched throat and filling my stomach with a sloshy heaviness. When my cup was completely drained, I suppressed a burp and looked over at Tyler, who was watching me with a mixture of amusement and apprehension.

"What are you doing here?" I asked, depositing my cup in the sink. "You weren't even at the prom."

"I don't do proms," he said, moving closer to me. The base of my spine tingled when I caught his scent. The simple act of standing near him produced more of a reaction in my body than when I was full-on making out with Ben. "But I *do* do after-prom parties."

"Oh?" I crossed my arms over my chest and pretended not to notice when his eyes dropped to the swell of my breasts. "Someone told me you, uh . . . stopped being an entrepreneur."

His lips curled at the reminder of our rum-and-coke-fueled banter on my bed a while back. "I did stop," he said, stuffing his hands into the pockets of his shorts. He and Ben were a study in contrasts—Ben, stiff and formal in a tux, face clean-shaven, hair neatly combed, Tyler, relaxed and casual in a T-shirt and shorts, jaws bristly with stubble, hair tousled as usual. Light, dark; good, bad; summer, winter. Opposites in every way.

"Why?" I asked. "Too many late nights? Long hours? Sucky benefits?"

"Not exactly." He leaned around me to flick an ant off the counter and for one dizzying moment I was surrounded by the familiar scents of smoke and beer and maleness. "I just thought, you know, unless I want to do another shitty year at that shitty school, I'd better get my act together and focus on graduating."

"And you are, right? Graduating on Tuesday?"

He smirked. "Well, I'm not *valedictorian* or anything, but yeah, I managed to squeak by."

Teasing me about Ben, just like old times. I let myself smile. "Good."

We stood silently for a moment, our bodies angled toward the kitchen window, which faced out onto the lake. The moon was big and bright, reflecting on the calm, inky water below. A drunk, laughing couple, both stripped down to just their underwear, danced clumsily together on the edge of the wharf, prom clothes in a messy heap beside them. They looked happy. Free.

"Lexi."

I tore my gaze away from the couple and focused on Tyler's face. *I miss kissing you*, I thought. *I miss the scuff of your cheek against mine and the delicious weight of your body as you brace yourself above me.* "What?" I said, the word squeezing past my throat.

"I like your hair like this." He reached up, captured a smooth, flat strand between his fingers.

Heat bubbled in my stomach, the water inside rising to a boil.

"But I like the curls better," he said, burying his fingers deeper until they made contact with my scalp. I closed my eyes as my body slanted toward him, caught in his magnetic pull.

Thwack. The screen door flew open and Emily stumbled in, drunk off her ass. I jerked away from Tyler, but not before my friend saw how close we'd been standing to each other, Tyler's hand tangled in my hair.

"Oh my God. Oh my *God.*" She slapped a hand over her mouth, her body swaying a little to the side. "I knew it," she said, taking her hand away. She looked like she'd just walked in on her parents having sex. Horrified. "I freaking *knew* it. The way you always stare at him at school . . . I *knew* there was something going on between you two, just like I knew you had a crush on Ben since, like, forever. Oh my God."

"It's not—" I started to explain, but the words had barely left my mouth before Emily straightened to her full height and strode purposefully to the door and outside, slamming the screen behind her. "Oh shit," I muttered. I knew exactly what she was doing and exactly who she was getting. I slumped against the counter.

"It's okay," Tyler told me just as the screen door slid open again and Emily marched back in, followed by an utterly perplexed Ben.

It was so *not* okay.

"What the hell is going on?" Ben asked no one in particular. His gaze skipped between each of our faces and then landed squarely on Tyler, who stood motionless beside me, hands back in his pockets. "*This* guy?" Ben's confusion morphed into disgust as he looked back to me. "You're cheating on me with a fucking *drug dealer*?"

The crowd from the bathroom line had steadily begun seeping toward the kitchen, hungry for drama. Ben so rarely raised his voice or showed any emotion other than calm, poised confidence, obviously something big must have been going down. From the corner of my eye, I could see Tyler's body stiffen at Ben's words, but he kept his hands in his pockets and to himself. He was dead serious about not messing with his chance at graduation.

"I'm not cheating on you, Ben," I said, shooting a look at Emily.

She sneered back at me, sobered up and out for blood. She'd suspected me for months, saw right through my lies and duplicity, and it was finally time to see justice served.

"I've never cheated on you. God, I haven't been with Tyler since the beginning of April, *weeks* before you and I started dating. I swear."

"Wait. So you *were* with him at one point?" Ben let out a short laugh and shoved both hands through his hair, messing it up. "Seriously, Lexi? Jesus."

"Well, there's definitely something going on," Emily piped up before I could respond. "I mean, he freaking punched Brody Wilhelm in the face because he made some crude remark about Lexi's ass when she walked past them. Why else would he do that?" When everyone looked at her, she shrugged and added, "Dustin told me."

Ben frowned at that news, and I could almost see the pieces clicking together in his brain. He listened to school gossip. He was aware of Tyler's reputation, he knew a girl didn't just "spend time" with a guy like him without sex being involved somehow. Obviously, I wasn't the inexperienced little virgin I'd portrayed myself to be. I wasn't *anything* I'd portrayed myself to be.

"So . . . what? You had sex with him?" He actually looked kind of hurt. "Is that it? Or are you 'just friends' with him, too?"

It was strange the way they kept referring to Tyler like he wasn't even in the room. They did the same thing whenever Nolan was around. Like he wasn't good enough for a simple acknowledgment. Like he was below them. Trash.

I looked down at the well-worn floor, avoiding the many sets of eyes on me. It seemed as if the entire party was lurking by the kitchen, watching us like we were the night's entertainment. Once again, I felt the sensation of being on a stage, acting out a role in a play. Only my costume was being ripped from my body in front of everyone, my nakedness revealed for all to see. The girl buried beneath all those layers had finally been exposed, and half the senior class had a front row seat.

And then Ben, taking my silence as confirmation, decided my public unveiling wasn't quite done yet. "I guess it makes sense, you being attracted to a piece of shit like him. Your mother has a thing for douchebags too, right? It's in your genes."

My head snapped up and I gaped at him, imploring him with my eyes to shut up.

He ignored me. Ignored everyone. For the first time since I'd known him, he didn't seem to care that people were watching. Humiliation had blinded him. "Crackhead father," he continued as my eyes filled with hot tears.

He'd promised . . . *swore* he wouldn't tell anyone.

"Lets his kid move across the country instead of raising her like a real man . . . then ignores her for thirteen years while he goes off and starts a new family. What a winner." Ben made a scoffing sound in his throat. "And you let everyone believe he was *dead*. You let *me* believe he was dead. Like we had this huge thing in common. Dead parents. Nice, right?"

I looked away, swiping a thumb under my eyes. His contempt for me was a physical ache; I could feel it in my bones like a flu virus. Beside me, Tyler resembled a marble statue, his body tensed and rigid in his effort to control himself.

Ben moved a few inches closer to me, his face flushed an angry red. The room was deathly quiet, a collective holding of breath. Waiting. "You're not the person I thought you were, Lexi. Turns out you're an even bigger whore than your friend Shelby."

Tyler lost it then. He lunged toward Ben, fists clenched and ready. I quickly stepped between them, pressing a palm against Tyler's chest. Luckily, it was enough to stop him. I couldn't let them fight. Tyler would get in trouble and possibly spend graduation day in jail, and Ben would most likely end up in the emergency room, nose broken for real.

"Tyler." I pushed against his chest, trying to get him to focus on me. But his eyes were glued to Ben, who glared back at him in a *Try it, I dare you* kind of way. "Tyler, stop. Just leave the room, okay? Walk away. Please."

The *please* seemed to snap him out of his all-consuming rage. He backed away, hands raised, and then turned and slipped through the door to outside. A tremor went through the floor beneath us as he pounded across the deck and down the stairs at the side of the house. Once he was gone, probably heading for the woods to punch a tree, the room seemed to exhale in relief.

Ben left next, choosing an alternative route through the living room. Emily fled shortly after, too appalled and disappointed to even look my way as she walked past me to the kitchen door. Excitement over, the gawkers began dispersing, too, murmuring amongst themselves as if discussing a movie they'd just seen.

Shaky and exhausted, I escaped to one of the cottage's tiny bedrooms and lay down on the narrow, musty bed. I hid out for an hour or so, alternately crying and panicking, and then tentatively made my way back outside. After a while, I found a designated driver, a girl named Destiny from my English class who hadn't witnessed the fiasco in the kitchen, and hitched a ride back to Oakfield with her.

My house was a mess when I walked in—beer cans everywhere, pizza congealing on the counter, drawers hanging open—but none of it really registered. Down-stairs in my room, I peeled off my prom dress until it was nothing but a shiny pink puddle on the floor and then climbed under my quilt.

Chapter Nineteen

I didn't have Nolan anymore to barge in my house and force-feed me soup, so I stayed in bed well past noon the next day. My cell had started dinging at around ten and didn't stop for the next several hours, texts from people wanting the dirt on last night. Just like the last time I'd crashed, I couldn't bear to face the morning-after consequences.

The only reason I got out of bed at all was because I needed to defrost a mouse for Trevor. Also, my prom dress couldn't stay balled up on the floor. After throwing on some clothes, I walked over to it, intending to hang it up and try to smooth out the wrinkles. But I didn't. Instead, I used my bare foot to kick it across the room. It slid under my bed, joining millions of dust bunnies and a few misplaced socks. *Good*, I thought, and headed upstairs.

The kitchen was still a disaster area. Mom hadn't bothered to clean it before she left for work and God only knew where Jesse was. He'd practically moved in near the middle of June, always popping up at the breakfast table or in front of the TV, his creepy eyes following me whenever I passed. Being around him made me want to bathe in scalding hot water mixed with bleach, so the rare times I was home, I'd taken to hiding in my room for hours on end. That had afforded me plenty of time to cram for my exams, and I'd wound up with straight A's as a result. Self-imposed imprisonment could be a very effective study method.

But exams were over, as was high school, and for that I was grateful. In September, I'd be gone, living somewhere else, meeting new people. People who didn't know about me. At Benton, I could reinvent myself yet again, erase the Oakfield High Lexi and hope that others erased her, too. Time held the power to do that—obliterate the past, wash it away.

Ignoring the mess, I opened the freezer and sifted through its contents until I spotted a "rodent coffin," as my mother called the little boxes of frozen mice. As my fingers closed around it, something on the freezer door caught my eye. A frosty, half-full bottle of vodka.

Even though I wasn't dehydrated from a hangover, I suddenly felt incredibly thirsty. Thirstier than last night in the kitchen with Tyler. Thirstier than I'd ever been before. Plain water wouldn't be enough to quench that kind of dry, persistent need. It required something more. Something strong enough to dull the ache.

It's in your genes, Ben had said. He was right—it was.

I placed the mouse on the counter to thaw and gathered up the bottle of vodka, a carton of orange juice, and a tall glass, carrying all three to the living room. Making sure the blinds were tightly closed, I flicked on the TV and proceeded to mix myself a drink at the coffee table. Mom worked late on Saturdays; I knew she wouldn't be home for at least six hours, and Jesse wasn't quite pathetic enough to hang around while she wasn't there. I had all the time in the world to watch sitcom reruns and get ripping drunk.

When I came to a few hours later, the living room was spinning and Grace was standing near my head, bawling her head off.

What the hell? I thought as I squinted up at her. She was wearing a shiny pink dress and a silver tiara, like a miniature prom queen. For a moment, I thought I was back at the cottage, being scowled at by the princesses from hell.

Princesses. Oh shit.

"I c-couldn't w-wake you up," Grace said through her sobs. "I was shaking you f-fowever."

Guilt sliced through me, the strength of it propelling my body into a sitting position. My head throbbed and my stomach threatened to blow, but I tried to focus on Grace and the puzzling fact that she was in my living room instead of at her house, enjoying the spoils of her birthday party. The party I'd missed because I was a horrible babysitter and a despicable person.

"Grace," I said, wincing at the pain that resulted from simply moving my lips to speak. "How did you get here?"

She sniffled and wiped her nose with her hand. Her fingers were adorned with plastic jewels. "I walked."

"By yourself?"

She nodded.

"Do your parents know you're here?"

A head shake. No.

Dammit. Rachel and Todd were probably frantic, looking for her. She could have gotten lost or kidnapped or hit by a car, and it would be all my fault.

"Why didn't you come?" Grace asked me as I glanced around the room for the phone. "You said you were coming."

I looked at her standing there in her pretty princess dress with her mouth smeared with pink frosting, and I wanted to jump off the nearest bridge. How could I have forgotten? How could I have done this to her? Grace loved me unconditionally, trusted me completely, and she didn't deserve this. She was just a child, pure and innocent.

"I'm so sorry, Gracie," I said, taking both her hands in mine. "I didn't mean to miss your party. I was just . . . I didn't feel well and I fell asleep on the couch."

She nodded, accepting this, and another wave of shame crashed through me. They were my mother's words, the same lame excuses she'd used on me when I was Grace's age and found her facedown on the couch or bed or even on the floor. *I didn't feel well. I was sick. I fell asleep.* I sounded just like her.

The phone rang then, startling us both. I knew before I even picked it up that it was Rachel, and it was. She let out a huge sigh of relief when I assured her Grace was safe at my house. I wanted to apologize to her, too, but it wasn't the time. Todd was coming to pick up Grace and I still had to dig out her present.

But first, I got rid of the vodka bottle and shoved a few sticks of gum in my mouth. Then I jogged down the stairs to my room to get Grace's gift. All those fast, jerky movements made my head pound even harder, but that was fine. I deserved a lot worse.

Luckily, Todd wasn't the observant type and accepted my "sick" excuse without question. Grace left happy, her little arms hugging the giant stuffed unicorn I'd chosen for her. They thought the world of me, all of them, and I'd screwed up. I'd screwed everything up. For years I'd had all these different personas warring inside me—good, bad, popular, pariah, real, fake—each of them vying for control. After last night, when that control was stripped away, I'd immediately lapsed into the one persona I knew inside and out. The persona that existed in my blood, my genes—a drinking, lying, unresponsive lump. I'd become my mother.

The realization sent me to the toilet, where I purged my stomach of the last few hours, and then to the shower, where I scrubbed myself raw. Then it pushed me across the street to Nolan's house, where I pounded on the door until it swung open.

Nolan stood on the other side, wearing a shirt that said KEEP OUT OF DIRECT SUNLIGHT and peering cautiously at me. "Yeah?" he said, not ready to be friendly.

"Can I come in?"

He shrugged and held open the door. "Suit yourself."

I stepped in and he closed the door behind me. The house was quiet. *Saturday,* I thought. Malcolm was away for work, Teresa was showing houses, and Landon had baseball. I knew their schedules and routines as well as I knew my own.

"I was just sketching," Nolan mumbled as we descended the stairs to the family room. He sat on the couch and picked up his sketch pad. I followed, perching on the edge of the cushion beside him.

"Who is that?" I asked, peeking at his drawing. I didn't recognize the face, but she was gorgeous, whoever she was.

"My dental hygienist."

I snorted. I couldn't help it. Nolan always went to the dentist willingly, hadn't missed a cleaning in years. Now I knew why. I wondered if Amber had seen the sketch.

"Shut up," he said, but not unkindly. In fact, it appeared as though he was trying not to laugh.

His expression made *me* laugh. God, I'd missed hanging out with him. Despite my splitting headache and severe indigestion, I was struck with an amazing sense of clarity. How could I have jeopardized our friendship? And for *Ben*?

"I'm an idiot," I said softly. "And a bitch. And a pretentious asshole."

Nolan continued to sketch, sliding his pencil over Hottie Hygienist's lips.

"I'm really sorry," I went on, knowing he was listening. "For everything. Fighting with you sucks. I don't want us to be like our moms, too stubborn and proud to forgive each other."

He glanced at me, eyebrows cocked, calling bullshit on my last statement. His mom had tried to mend fences, many times. It was *my* mom who was stubborn and proud. "I don't want to be like my mom," I amended.

He went back to his drawing. "You're not like your mom, Lex."

But I was, and to prove it I proceeded to tell him everything that had happened in the past twenty-four hours. Everything. And through it all, he kept drawing, shading, blending, letting me unload.

"It's over with Ben," I said in conclusion, "but that's not why I'm here right now, apologizing to you. It was long overdue. I never should have let him get into my head like that. I deceived him, I get that. I own it. But he's not the person I thought he was, either."

Nolan stayed quiet for a few minutes. When he did speak, he didn't say a word about Ben, didn't crow that he'd told me so even though he had the right. He didn't even comment on my catastrophe of a prom night or my vodka pity party in the living room. He just nodded his forgiveness and asked, "Can I still draw you?"

"Uh . . . sure."

"With freckles?"

"Naturally," I quipped.

"Can I draw Tyler Flynn hitting Ben?"

I shot him a look. *Don't push it.*

He grew serious for a moment. "You're part of my family, Lex," he said, catching my gaze and holding it, making sure I heard and understood his next words. "We all love you, but none of us are *in* love with you. Got it?"

"Got it." I'd never let myself doubt it again.

★ ★ ★

That night in my room, I picked up my phone and started scrolling through the dozens of texts it had accumulated in the past twelve hours. Just as I'd thought, most of them were from curious classmates wondering what had happened. A few were mean, one word texts from girls I didn't even know. *Bitch. Slut.* Nastygrams from Tyler's admirers, I assumed. Or Ben's sympathizers. I deleted those. Obviously, there was nothing from Emily or Ben, both of whom hated my guts at the moment. The thing I'd feared since tenth grade was actually happening—I'd fallen to the bottom of the food chain, vulnerable and reviled, unworthy of a simple acknowledgment.

Just as I was about to give up and hit DELETE ALL, I came across a text from Shelby.

Heard about last night. Not mad at you. Shit happens, I understand. Em & Ben aren't perfect, either. Remember that.

Tears stinging my eyes, I sent a quick response. Thanks.

Out of the three of them, I valued Shelby's friendship the most. It felt good to know I hadn't lost her, too.

"Pssst. Lexi."

I dropped my phone and let out a little shriek. *My walls are talking to me,* I thought inanely. *I'm losing it.*

But no, the voice was coming from the direction of my open window. Heart in my throat, I crawled off my bed and peeked outside. Tyler was crouched on the grass, his face angled toward the window. Nolan's drawing come to life.

"Why do you insist on scaring the hell out of me?" I hissed at him.

"Sorry. Can I come in? I want to talk to you."

Sighing, I pushed the little levers that held my screen in

place and then popped it off. Tyler shimmied in, landing with a soft thud beside me. I immediately replaced the screen so as not to let in the mosquitoes. My screen kept out insects and wildlife just fine, but apparently it didn't work on teenage boys.

"What is it, Tyler?" I said, flopping back on the bed. I was so tired, so done with all the drama. My nerves felt like old rubber bands, stretched tight and thin. Ready to snap.

He started pacing my room, walking back and forth between my dresser and the bed. I'd never seen him so agitated. "I feel bad about last night," he said, coming to a stop in front of Trevor's tank, his back to me. "Responsible."

I just stared at him. Tyler Flynn, remorseful? Taking responsibility? What planet was I on?

"It's my fault," I told him. "Not yours. It was bound to come out eventually. It's just too bad it had to happen on prom night in front of a few dozen witnesses."

"I still feel bad." He peered in at Trevor, his face inches from the glass. "I know you were embarrassed."

"Well, yeah. Weren't you?"

He flicked a glance over his shoulder. "I was never ashamed of us. That was you."

I opened my mouth to deny it but shut it again. He was right. I was ashamed of what we'd done. Ashamed of myself. Of him. In some ways, I was no better than my ex-friends.

"I never would have told anyone, you know," he said. "About us, I mean. No matter how pissed off you made me."

"I know." If he'd proven anything to me over the last nine months, it was his commitment to keeping our secret. My secret. "I'm sorry for how I treated you. For using you like that. It wasn't fair."

His shoulders lifted in a shrug. "It wasn't exactly torture for me."

I could hear the smirk in his voice, that old Tyler cockiness. Impulsively, I slid off the bed and joined him in front of the tank. Together, we watched Trevor slither along his Astroturf, raising his head every few moments like he was expecting us to pet him. That was when I remembered. His mouse was still on the kitchen counter, probably at room temperature by now. With all the craziness of today, I'd forgotten to feed the poor guy. "I'll be back in a second." I dashed out of my room and up the stairs.

Someone had cleaned up the kitchen. Garbage was thrown away, drawers shut, counters cleaned. And no mouse.

Shit, I thought when I realized it wasn't where I'd put it. What had she done with it? Mom would never touch a dead mouse, even one securely enclosed in a box. It had to be somewhere. I searched under papers, behind the toaster, in the fridge . . . no mouse. With a resigned sigh, I flipped open the garbage can and started gingerly sifting through the stuff on top.

"Looking for something?"

I whirled around, the garbage can lid slamming as my foot slid off the pedal. Jesse stood in the kitchen doorway, watching me, arms folded over his bare chest. I hadn't even heard him approaching.

"Yeah," I said, suddenly regretting my outfit of tiny cotton shorts and a skimpy tank top. "My, um, dead mouse. For my snake. Have you seen it?"

He uncrossed his arms and moved farther into the room, not stopping until he was about a foot in front of me. Too close. The smell of liquor wafted off him like a nauseating mist. "Hmm, let's see," he said, his bloodshot eyes roving down my body. "You gotta ask yourself, 'If I was a dead mouse, where would I be?' "

I tried to step back, put some space between us, but there was nowhere to go. The backs of my legs hit the stainless steel garbage can, sliding it against the side of the counter. Jesse noticed the movement and laughed, amused by my revulsion. The cold deadness in his eyes made my heart thump with panic.

"Your mom made me throw it out," he whispered, like he was confessing a secret. "Said it made her want to puke. She's a real hag, isn't she? Your mom?" He shifted closer to me, one hand reaching up to touch my bare shoulder. "You're a lot sweeter. Sexier, too."

Adrenaline coursed through me and I jolted to the side, intending to skirt around him and make a break for it. But he stepped in front of me, blocking my way, and then maneuvered me back to where I'd been. My legs knocked against the trash can again, causing it to skate sideways along the floor until it smashed against the wall a couple feet away. The reverberation was loud . . . definitely loud enough for the entire house to hear.

"Not so fast," he murmured as he backed me into the edge of the counter. He was so close, I could feel the heat from his skin. "I've been waiting months for this." His fingers brushed the bottom hem of my tank top and slid underneath, skimming along the skin above my waist band. "Wonder what you've got hiding under here."

My body was paralyzed. Helpless. I wanted to shove him away, knee him in the balls, but my limbs refused to cooperate. I was in shock, unable to fully comprehend what was happening. Months of being creeped out by this guy, of carefully avoiding his presence, had somehow culminated in him attacking me in my very own kitchen while my mother slept off a bender just a few doors away. This could not be happening.

I started to cry.

"Hey," he snapped, grabbing my chin roughly and forcing me to look at him. "This is what happens to little cock teases like you. So stop the blubbering and—"

The kitchen exploded, the flurry of sounds almost deafening in my ears. A surprised yell, hard bones connecting with flesh. Chairs scraping and then clattering to the floor. Garbage can toppling, its contents scattering in the sudden swirl of air. The dull thud of a man colliding with a wall. And the uneven panting of a younger, stronger man, who was using his forearm to exert pressure on my assailant's throat, pinning him to the wall as he struggled to escape.

There was no stopping Tyler, no stepping in between him and his target. He was too far gone and truthfully, I wanted him to hurt Jesse. Wanted to watch his face turn purple as he panicked and fought for air. That was what the vengeful, animalistic side of me craved. But the other side, the lucid, practical one, knew it had to end before someone got seriously hurt or ended up in prison. No lives would be ruined over me.

As it turned out, I didn't need to intervene because my mother stumbled into the kitchen, her sudden presence snapping Tyler out of his wild rage. He let go of Jesse and walked over to me, his eyes blazing with hatred and blood-lust and underneath all that, concern for me.

"Are you okay?" he asked, loosening my fingers from the lip of the countertop.

I hadn't even realized I was gripping it. Unable to speak, I nodded quickly, my eyes still on my mother.

"What the hell happened in here?" she demanded, her sleepy gaze moving from the upended kitchen chair to the heap of trash on the floor to Jesse, clutching his throat and gasping for breath. "Jesse?"

"That guy tried to strangle me," he croaked, tilting his head toward Tyler.

"Because you were sexually harassing a teenage girl, you sick son of a bitch," Tyler snarled at him.

"*She* came on to *me*, Stacey, I swear," Jesse inserted quickly. "I was just trying to fend her off, and the next thing I knew this maniac had me by the throat."

Tyler dropped my hand and started toward him again, but I yanked him back and held on tight. He complied and stayed put, albeit reluctantly. I looked back at my mother, watched her face harden as she slowly pieced together what had happened. When it finally clicked, she turned to stare at me.

"What did you do?" she asked me quietly. When I didn't answer right away, she repeated her question with volume.

"N-nothing," I replied, stunned. She was seriously blaming *me*? Tyler stepped closer and squeezed my hand, keeping us both in check.

Mom blinked at him, confused, as if she was just now noticing his presence. "Who the hell are you?" she barked at him. "Why are you in my house? Get out of here before I call the police and have you arrested for assault."

"No!" I told her, and then said in a softer voice to Tyler, "She means it. Go."

He shook his head. "I'm not leaving until he does."

Mom ignored him and shifted her disdain back to me. "I should have known," she said, voice dripping with venom. "I see how you act around Jesse. I'm not stupid. Always flirting with him, parading around the house half-naked. You can't stand to see me happy, can you?"

"What the hell are you talking about?" I yelled back at her. "How can you believe him over me? I'm your *daughter*. He attacked me, Mom. *He's* the one who should be arrested for assault." I snatched the cordless phone off the counter and held it out to her. "Fine, go ahead. Call the police. I'll tell them *exactly* what happened."

"To hell with this shit," Jesse muttered, and then he stormed out of the kitchen and down the hall to Mom's bedroom.

Mom followed him, pleading with him not to go as he gathered up his stuff and made tracks for the front door, ignoring her all the way. Once he was gone, zooming off in his fancy SUV, she returned to the kitchen, her cheeks wet with tears. "Thanks, Lexi," she spit at me. "Thanks a lot." Then she turned and went back to her room, slamming the door behind her like a bratty little girl.

The adrenaline had worn off and I was shaking uncontrollably, just like I'd done the night Keith Langley had beaten Mom to a pulp and I threw a can of vegetables at his head. The night Teresa threatened to have me taken away. What I'd never told her, or anyone else, was that sometimes I wished Keith had come back, just so she'd have to follow through on her warning.

Tyler wrapped his arms around me and I muffled my sobs in his shirt for what felt like hours. When the sobs tapered off into sniffles, he led me down to my room, helped me into bed, and tucked my quilt around me. Then he locked my bedroom door and slid in beside me, curving his body around mine. "Just in case he comes back."

Less than five minutes later, I was asleep.

Just after dawn the next morning, I leaned over Tyler's sleeping form, grabbed my cell phone off the nightstand, and quietly tapped out a text to my father.

If the offer still stands, I'd like to come and visit you.

Six hours later, a plane ticket arrived in my inbox. Three days later, the morning after graduation, I woke up

at four a.m. and got dressed in the dark. I called a cab and
wrote a note for my mother.

> *I'm on my way to Alton to see my father. We've been
> in contact for months. When I get back next week, I'll
> be staying at the Bruces' house for the rest of the
> summer. I'm an adult now, which means you no longer
> have any say in what I do or who I see.*
>
> *Nolan will be dropping by every morning while
> you're at work to change Trevor's water. He has my
> house key and trip info, so if there's an emergency and
> you need to contact me, you'll have to ask him or
> Teresa.*
>
> *Lexi*

Chapter Twenty

At first I thought he'd forgotten about me. Minutes dragged by as I stood in the baggage claim area, sweaty hands clutching the straps of my backpack and eyes darting through the crowd, scanning for a possible match. The airport was enormous. How was I supposed to find someone I hadn't seen in person since my preschool days?

Just as I was about to veer right toward baggage claim, I saw him. The man from my pictures, approaching me head-on with a small, expectant smile on his tanned face. He wore a plaid shirt with the sleeves rolled up, faded jeans, and cowboy boots—an interesting complement to the intricate tattoos covering both his arms.

My father's an inked-up cowboy, I thought as I slapped on my own version of a smile, letting him know he'd found the right girl.

"Lexi," he said when he reached me, grinning wide. "I knew it was you just from your profile. It's almost identical to your mother's. You have her nose."

I smoothed back my hair, which felt frizzy and tangled, and looked up at him. He wasn't as tall as I remembered, even though he was a full head above my five-foot-six. To four-year-old me, he must have seemed like a giant. At a loss for words, I managed to squeeze out a weak "Hi."

"Look at you." His bright blue eyes—identical to my

own—drank in my features. "You're even prettier in person than you are in your pictures. I just . . . I can't believe you're actually standing in front of me right now." He shook his head in awe and then hesitantly lifted both arms as though he was getting ready to hug me.

I felt myself stiffen, but I relaxed a little when he met my eyes first, silently asking permission. In response, I took a step forward and waited for him to fold me into his arms. When he did, I even hugged him back, desperate for a glimmer of connection. Up close, he smelled like a mix of Irish Spring soap and motor oil. Unfamiliar. I felt a pang of homesickness and wondered if I'd made a huge mistake in coming. This man was still a stranger to me. He was still the same guy who'd willingly let me go almost fourteen years ago, and one week with him wasn't going to change that.

We pulled away at the same time and just looked at each other awkwardly for a few moments.

"Let's go get your luggage," he suggested brightly.

I nodded and turned away, pretending not to notice the tears in his eyes.

"We're almost there."

My eyes popped open and I glanced around, disoriented and thinking I was still on the plane. At some point during the two-hour drive, I'd completely passed out. "Hmm?" I said, my brain sluggishly playing catch up.

"Next exit," the voice said.

I looked to my left and saw a plaid shirt and tattoos and a kind, open face. *Right,* I thought as I sat up straight and rubbed my sore, grainy eyes. My father and I were sitting in his gigantic, heavy-duty pickup truck, tooling down the rain-slicked highway toward Alton. It hit me at that moment how little I really knew this man. Sure, he'd seemed nice over the phone, and so far he seemed nice in person too. But still . . . I was encased in a moving vehicle with a virtual stranger on my way to spend a week at his house with people I'd never met before in my life. Everything about it felt surreal.

"I didn't mean to doze off," I said, stifling a yawn.

"No problem. You must be beat." He took a drink from the bottle of water he'd bought back at the airport.

I glanced at his tanned, calloused hand as it curled around the bottle, trying to reconcile it with the warm hand that enveloped mine in my memories. I wondered if he remembered those walks in the woods as clearly as I did.

"Hey," he said, and I returned my gaze to his face. "I meant to ask you before . . . how was graduation yesterday?"

Well, my own mother—who hasn't spoken to me in days— didn't even bother to show up, people were whispering about prom night, and I spent the entire ceremony wondering if my ex-friends were going to throw rotten tomatoes at me when it was my turn to cross the stage. Other than that, fantastic. "It was fine," I told him.

"Wish I could have been there."

I didn't respond because honestly, he'd missed the vast majority of my life's milestones, so why should he get to witness that one? Eric seemed to be experiencing similar thoughts because he got really quiet and the air between us grew heavy with tension. Thankfully, the sign for Alton was just up ahead because I could hardly wait to be out of the truck. Within minutes, we were off the highway and cruising along the town's main street.

"I guess you wouldn't remember much of this," Eric said. He was back to smiling, the tension diffused.

"No," I agreed, peering out my rain-smeared window as we passed a gas station, a convenience store, a grocery store, a drug store, and three restaurants. Alton was even smaller than Oakfield, quaint and quiet, just like Mom and Teresa had described. Nothing about it triggered any memories, not even when Eric started pointing things out to me.

"That's where you used to go to daycare," he said as we drove by a small used clothing store. "I mean, back when it was a daycare. And right up there, that's the playground you used to play on. You loved the swings the most."

Like Grace, I thought with another stab of homesickness. What had I been thinking, coming here? I picked up my backpack and held it to my chest, longing for something familiar.

"And down here," my father said, veering off into a residential section of town, "is our house."

Obviously, it was the newer, more elite part of town. The houses were all big and modern, each of them endowed with a one or two-car garage. Less than a minute later, we pulled into the wide, paved driveway of a large, two-story brick house. Wordlessly, we climbed out of the truck.

Thunder rumbled in the distance as Eric carried my suitcase to the front door. I stood off to the side as he turned the knob and nudged open the door with his hip. The moment we stepped inside the airy foyer, a small figure darted past and I heard a loud whisper.

"Mommy, she's *here*."

Eric placed my suitcase on the floor and laughed. "That would be Jonah."

Before I had a chance to process it all, a thin, blond woman emerged from the hallway in front of us, her hand resting on the shoulder of a cute brown-haired boy. The boy—my little brother Jonah—stared at me unabashedly for a moment and then presented me with a wide, gap-toothed smile. I couldn't help but smile back.

"This is Lexi," my father said just as a little blond girl

inched into the foyer and sidled up to her mom, half hiding behind her.

Willow. I smiled at her, too, but unlike her brother, she preferred to hold back and assess me from afar.

"Lexi, this is Renee, Willow, and Jonah. They've been waiting a long time to meet you."

Renee squeezed her son's shoulder and walked over to me. "It's so nice to meet you, Lexi," she said, hugging me briefly and then pulling back to stare at my face.

It had to be weird for her, seeing her husband's features on some girl she'd never met. Some girl who had previously existed only in his past. And a sordid past, at that. Still, she seemed genuinely happy to have me in her house.

"Will we give her the tour?" Eric asked, and Jonah started jumping up and down.

This one's a little firecracker, I thought as he grabbed my hand and tugged me toward the hallway. He was the tour guide, apparently.

We covered the main floor first, trekking through each room as if the house was for sale and we were prospective buyers. The inside was just like the outside—neat and tasteful and modern, yet comfortable and homey. Next, Jonah led us downstairs to the finished basement, which was less neat but still impressive. The family room was a total kid zone, toys and video games and beanbag chairs scattered everywhere.

"Why don't we show her where she'll be sleeping?" Renee suggested.

Jonah bounced ahead to the next door and pushed it open. "This is the guest room," he said, catapulting himself onto the queen-size bed. "You sleep here because you're our guest."

The room was small, but like the rest of the house, it was pretty and tastefully decorated. In addition to the bed, which was covered in a velvety gray comforter, there was also a dresser and a decent-sized window facing the backyard. I looked outside and caught a glimpse of the deck and the big round swimming pool I'd noticed when we were upstairs in the kitchen.

Turning away from the window, I caught all four of them staring at me. "Um, is there somewhere I can freshen up?" I asked, directing the question at the wall because I wasn't sure who to ask.

"Oh! Of course!" Renee said, waving a hand for me to follow her. "There's a bathroom right across the hall."

Eric brought me my suitcase, and I shut myself up in the bathroom while the three of them headed upstairs. Evidently, both my father and Renee sensed my need for a few minutes alone.

All of it was just too much. Only three short months ago, I'd found out I had a living, sober father, a stepmother, and two siblings—a whole other family I'd known nothing about. And now I was three thousand miles from home and standing in their house. It was extremely weird and overwhelming.

After a shower, a change of clothes, and a hefty dollop of mousse in my hair, I felt somewhat better. Unable to stall any longer, I headed back upstairs.

"You're looking more awake," Eric said when I appeared in the kitchen. He and Renee stood at the counter, transferring different foods from Tupperware containers to serving dishes. Willow was in the adjacent dining room, sitting at the big cherry wood table and shyly watching me as she pretended to read a book. Jonah sat cross-legged by the door to the deck, slamming two action figures together in what looked like an ultra-violent wrestling match.

"Your natural curls are so pretty, Lexi," Renee said, smoothing down her own sleek bob. She looked like the women Nolan sometimes referred to as "soccer moms." I could picture her behind the wheel of a minivan, Venti latte in hand as she transported her kids to their various activities.

"Thanks," I said in response to both their comments.

Lunch was an interesting mix of salads and multigrain breads, all fresh and unrefined. Apparently, they were a healthy living kind of family. Afterward, I helped clean up, even though I'd been told to relax. But I couldn't relax, not yet. Possibly not ever. So instead, I helped my father store leftovers.

"We're not total health nuts," he assured me as if I'd complained about our all-natural lunch. "We started cutting out sugar and processed stuff a couple years ago because of Jonah. Our family doctor suggested we change his diet to see if it would help with his hyperactivity." Eric chuckled. "It didn't, as you can see, but by then we were sort of hooked."

I watched him as he cheerfully spooned leftover cucumber tahini salad into a container. I felt a surge of frustration. I wasn't there to discuss health food or my curly hair or where I used to go to daycare; I was there to get answers. The truth. All my life, I'd assumed my father was dead, in jail, or living on a street corner somewhere, begging for spare change. Seeing him in his nice, big house with his nice, normal family, laughing and eating quinoa, made me feel like I'd been deceived. Not only by my mother, but by him, too. All along, he'd been living a brand new life. And he'd never once tried to make room in it for me.

Chapter Twenty-one

My first day in Alton was the longest. By the end of it, I was more tired than I ever remembered being in my life. So tired, I assumed I'd fall asleep the second my head hit the pillow. But it didn't happen that way. Instead, I lay awake for hours, listening to the thunder that had been shaking the house on and off all day and wishing I was home.

I'd left Oakfield less than a day ago, but it felt like I'd been gone for weeks. I missed Nolan and Teresa. I missed Trevor. I missed my bed, even though it was slightly less comfortable than the one in the guest room. I missed almost everything about home, missed it so much my entire body ached with it.

But more than anything or anyone else, I missed Tyler.

Our relationship had been changing and evolving for weeks, and the incidents with Ben and Jesse seemed to have altered it even more. We were no longer just two people who used each other for release. I wasn't entirely sure *what* we were. All I knew was that during the past week, the subtle shift between us had become a radical transformation.

Jesse never showed his face at my house again, but Tyler stayed with me on Sunday night, too, stroking my back while I drifted off to sleep. And sleep was all we did. But the next night, when he once again wriggled through my window and curled up in bed with me "just in case," I turned to him, laced my fingers through the hair at the nape of his neck, and pressed my lips against his. He returned the kiss for a minute and then pulled back to ask me if I was sure. Instead of answering with words, I sat up, yanked my T-shirt over my head, and tossed it on the floor. After that, he forgot about being cautious and restrained.

Alone and restless in the cozy guest bed, those were the moments that kept coming back to me. Not the whispers or the gossip or the painful humiliation of losing half my friends. Not the bitter smell of Jesse's alcohol breath or the loathing and betrayal on my mother's face. Just that last night with Tyler, his hands slow and gentle on my skin as if he was afraid he might break me. As if it was my first time. Our first time. In a way, that was exactly how it felt.

Those moments, those memories, were the main reason why I chose to pick up my phone instead of escaping out the window, stealing a car, and hightailing it back to the airport. If anyone understood the allure of robbery and fleeing a scene, it was Tyler.

"Yeah," he answered on the first ring. Even though it was three a.m. in Oakfield, he sounded alert and capable, a skill he'd perfected during his two years of dealing with random phone calls from "clients" in the middle of the night. He'd stopped selling, but old habits die hard.

"It's me." I kept my voice down, even though I was pretty sure everyone was asleep and no one would hear me all the way downstairs anyway. "Did I wake you?"

"No. Yes. Kind of. But I don't mind. What time is it?"

I told him. "I'm sorry for calling you so late. It's just . . . I needed to hear a familiar voice."

"I don't mind," he said again. He sounded a bit more

awake, conscious enough to detect the sadness in my tone. "How's it going? What are they like?"

I ran my hand over the smooth comforter, wishing for the dips and grooves of my quilt. "They're . . . I don't know. Nice. Normal. They're trying to make me feel comfortable and welcome and everything but it's all so *weird*. I . . . I don't know if I can do this."

"Do you want to come home?"

I squeezed my eyes shut but it was no use; tears leaked out and dripped onto the pillow beneath my head. The pillow that smelled like lemons and sunshine instead of dryer sheets and Tyler, like mine did at home. Nothing felt right. "Yes," I said, wiping my eyes. "But I won't. I'm staying. I have to."

"Okay," he replied, and we fell silent for a while. Just as I was starting to wonder if he'd nodded off again, he said, "I miss sleeping beside you."

I rolled over on my side and snuggled into the comforter, the phone pressed to my ear. Outside, the storm was finally beginning to wind down, the lightning weakening to an irregular flicker. "I miss it too," I said, letting my body relax and my eyes drift shut. Seconds later, I was out.

I woke the next morning to the sounds of giggling and splashing. For a moment I wondered if I was in the middle of some weird dream, then I heard Jonah.

"Cannonball!" he bellowed, and another huge splash followed. I turned toward the open window and caught the scent of chlorine and warm air. The air smelled different, dry and sharp, nothing like the fresh, salty ocean air I took for granted back in Oakfield.

The position of the sun, bright and far up in the sky, told me I'd likely snoozed the morning away. My watch—

still set to Oakfield time—said ten after two, so it was after eleven. *Oops.* I slipped on a pair of shorts and a tank top, washed my face, and headed upstairs to the empty kitchen. I could see Jonah and Willow through the glass door, zipping around the pool and squealing. My father sat a few feet away at the patio table, facing the pool and talking into his cell phone. Work, I assumed. He and Renee had taken time off for my visit, but owning the business meant being on call, even during vacation. I pushed open the door to the deck and stepped outside.

"Hi, Lexi!" Jonah called, waving at me as he attempted to mount an inflatable alligator. I waved back at him and went to join Eric, who was still sitting at the glass-topped table with the phone glued to his ear. Seeing me, he quickly wrapped up his call and hung up.

"Sleep well?" he asked as I sat across from him. Luckily, the giant umbrella above us provided lots of shade because my skin always burned in about ten seconds and I wasn't wearing any sunscreen.

"A little too well," I said, glancing at the kids. I couldn't seem to take my eyes off them. Growing up I'd always wanted a sibling, and now I had two of them. Just like that. "I didn't mean to sleep so late."

"It's okay," Eric said, folding his arms on the table.

Since yesterday, I'd been furtively examining his tattoos, trying to make sense of the designs. So far I'd picked out a skull, some flowers, and some kind of tribal pattern. Most of them, I'd already seen in the old pictures I had of him. I wondered how long it took to get full sleeves like that, and if he regretted them.

"So," he said, and my eyes flicked up to meet his. "Are you looking forward to college?"

Just as I was about to answer him, a sprinkle of cold water hit my ankle. "Daddy, I need help," Jonah said from the side of the pool. "My alligator is leaking."

"Sounds like a serious dilemma," Eric said, standing up. "Bring him over and I'll check him for holes."

As Jonah doubled back to retrieve his leaky gator, Eric crouched by the edge of the pool, waiting. It wasn't until he stood up again, alligator in hand, that I noticed the tattoo on the outside of his left calf. It was a red and black cobra snake, its head rising above its tightly coiled tail, forked tongue protruding. Seeing it, something in my brain went *ping*—an ancient, long-buried memory fighting to emerge.

"When did you get that?" I asked, trying to sound casual. Instead, I ended up sounding alarmed, causing Eric to glance back at me. "The snake tattoo on your leg," I clarified.

"Oh." He looked down at it. "Let me see . . . I got it right around the time I joined my band. So . . . about twenty-one years ago, I guess. Why? Are you terrified of snakes, too? Renee is. Come to think of it, so was your mother."

"I like them," Jonah piped up. "I think they're cool."

"I . . . I love snakes," I said. "I have one. A corn snake."

"No way!" Jonah said, gazing at me in awe.

Eric handed the re-inflated alligator to Jonah and returned to his chair. "It's funny," he said to me. "When you were little you used to love that tattoo. As soon as you could crawl, you'd come over and sit at my feet and sort of pet my leg like the snake was alive. I just thought you liked the bright colors, but maybe it was the snake itself."

Was it possible, I wondered, for a single image to implant itself in a small child's brain and then remain there, in her subconscious, for the next several years? Or was it just a coincidence? My whole life, I'd felt inexplicably drawn to snakes. For me, they represented grace and peace and beauty. Holding Trevor in my hands gave me a feeling of comfort. Security. But after seeing Eric's tattoo and hearing that story, I couldn't help but wonder if the comfort and security I got from snakes were somehow connected to how I'd once felt around him. Those same feelings emerged whenever my mind flashed on that crystal clear memory of us walking in the woods together, hand in hand. At one time, we'd shared a bond.

It didn't make any sense, but I knew without question he'd loved me back then. It was like I carried it in my bones, or in a tiny corner of my heart. And I'd loved him back. Our connection was evident in the one picture of us that I owned, blowing out the candles on my birthday cake. We'd been close. The same kind of closeness he shared with Willow and Jonah, the kind that made them want to run to him for scraped knees and closet monsters and deflating alligators. The kind that made me want to crawl to him and sit at his feet as a baby or walk with him beneath the trees and hunt for bugs. Despite everything I'd heard all my life, despite the inexorable hold his addiction had had on him, he'd once been my dad.

What had changed? Why had he decided letting me go was easier than getting well for me? Being with him and his happy, much-loved children allowed me to see exactly what I'd missed out on—a loving, involved parent who put his children first, a priority. Clearly, I'd never been a priority to him. Instead of choosing me, he'd withdrawn into his addiction, shattered the bond between us, started all over again with a brand new family, and become the kind of father he'd never been strong enough to be for me.

I'd loved that tattoo not because it was a snake, but because it was a reliable, permanent part of him. A benchmark. And that image—along with the feelings it evoked—had stuck with me, long after he'd tried to rip it away.

"Lexi, are you coming in?"

I looked over at Jonah's bright, freckled face and then beyond him to Willow, who was watching me with an insightfulness that was well beyond her years, as if she could read my innermost thoughts, the way Emily used to do. Obviously, the real me wasn't concealed as well as I'd always thought.

"No, I think I'll—" I stood up quickly, banging my shin on the table leg. Ignoring the pain, I started toward the doors. I couldn't do this. Couldn't let myself love him or get close to him again. Couldn't let myself get attached to his family. It was too much of a risk. "I need to go to the store," I said, not looking back. "I forgot to pack something."

Luckily, Renee was nowhere to be seen as I passed through the kitchen to the basement stairs. In the guest room, I grabbed my backpack and carried it upstairs and through the front door. I didn't care that I wasn't entirely sure how to get downtown. I didn't care that my skin would surely fry on the way there. All I cared about was getting away.

As it turned out, the main street was only a ten-minute walk from the house and easy to find. *I could leave*, I thought as I passed a vacant taxi parked alongside the curb in front of a convenience store. I pictured myself in the backseat of that taxi, following the same route I'd taken almost fourteen years ago with my mother. I wondered if she'd looked back as we left Alton, or felt a pang of regret during that two-hour drive to the airport, or questioned her decision as we stepped onto the plane that would take us to our new home. I wondered if she'd been like me, waffling between trying to make it work and giving up entirely. Knowing my mother, the choice to leave had probably been an easy one. She held grudges, she didn't forgive, and when life got too hard, she bailed.

But I wasn't like my mother, not anymore. So instead of finding the taxi driver and blowing what was left of my babysitting money on cab fare, I found a fast food joint and ordered the biggest, greasiest cheeseburger on the menu. Then, feeling fuller than I had in days, I went back to my father.

Chapter Twenty-two

On Sunday night, after the kids had gone to bed and I was watching TV alone, I received a text from Shelby.

> Piper Olivia was born at 6:25 this evening. 6 pounds, 14 oz. Healthy & perfect. We're both doing fine. Miss you. Call me when you get home.

Relieved and teary-eyed, I sent her my congratulations and promised to visit them when I got back. A few minutes later, she answered with a picture. Their very first family portrait. Shelby and Evan, both looking like they hadn't slept in weeks, smiled into the camera as baby Piper lay in her mother's arms, fast asleep. The three of them together seemed untouchable, like the only thing ahead of them was joy.

But that was the tricky thing with pictures—those images, those captured memories, were incomplete and fleeting.

I shut off the TV and headed for bed. But instead of going into the guest room, I continued down the hallway and stopped outside the door right next to it. My father's music room.

He'd been shut up in there for the past hour, strumming his guitar and reliving his band days. I didn't know much about guitar or bass or any instrument, really, but he sounded pretty good for an old guy. During a pause in riffs, I knocked on the door.

"Come in," he said, and I peeked inside to find him sitting on a leather stool with a bright red guitar in his arms. He brightened when he saw me, then leaned over to turn off the amp at his feet. The room instantly became quiet. "I wasn't keeping you awake, was I?"

I shook my head and stepped farther into his sanctuary. I hadn't been in there since the day I arrived, and at the time I'd been too overwhelmed to give the room more than a cursory inspection. Now, I took the time to really look.

"Are all these yours?" I asked, taking in his collection of guitars. I'd never seen this many strings outside a music store. Two guitars hung on the wall behind him, and three more—two bass guitars and another six-string—rested in stands on the floor. "What else can you play?"

"I can handle a simple beat on the drums, but mostly I stick to guitar and bass. Can't sing to save my life, either."

Something else we had in common. Dogs howled whenever I tried to sing. I turned away from the guitars and approached the opposite wall. Every inch of it was covered in autographed pictures of bands I'd never heard of and a few old, wrinkled flyers promoting a band called Rust, which I *had* heard of. It was Eric's old band, the one he'd played bass for in his twenties, when he was with my mother. He'd told me a bit about them over the phone a few weeks ago. They were together for eight years, during which they played in bars and small arenas in cities and towns all over this side of the country. "We even did a few shows in Seattle," he'd told me proudly. I had no idea why this was a big deal, but I'd tried to act impressed.

"I was pretty skinny, huh?" Eric said as I leaned in to study one of the flyers, which showed Rust on stage in mid-song. My father wore baggy shorts, black combat boots, and no shirt, his hair hanging in his eyes as he pounded on the bass. And yes, he was practically emaciated. I glanced back at the present-time him, bright-eyed and healthy.

"Was that when . . . " I let the sentence trail off. What was I supposed to say? *Was that when you were a hopeless junkie?*

"Yeah," he said, gently placing the guitar back on its stand. "That was the worst of it."

I looked back at the picture and noticed the date of the concert being promoted. Three years after I was born. So unless the picture on the flyer was an old one, he'd had a little daughter at the time, not to mention a girlfriend. But instead of going back to them after the show, he'd probably spent the rest of the night searching for the perfect high, the kind that had let him forget all about who was waiting for him at home.

Or so I assumed. Eric spoke often about his memories of me as a baby and toddler, but we never ventured any deeper than that. In the past few days, I'd learned a lot about him, little things like he went jogging every morning at six a.m., was allergic to cats, and had a weakness for mint chocolate chip ice cream. I knew some more significant things, too. He'd relapsed twice before finally getting clean, and he'd gotten my name, Lexi Claire, tattooed across his rib cage the week after I was born. I knew a lot of things, good and bad, but after dozens of emails, almost as many phone calls, and four full days together—we still hadn't discussed his side of the story. Even though my need to hear it was the reason I'd contacted him in the first place.

It would mean a lot to me if you'd give me the opportunity to explain my side someday, he'd said during that very first phone call. *Not today, but someday.*

It was after ten and Renee and the kids were all upstairs. For the first time all week, it was just me and my father, alone with nothing to do and nowhere to go. Tonight, right now, was his opportunity. *Someday* had arrived.

Moving away from the wall, I grabbed one of the folding chairs in the corner, set it up a couple feet in front of Eric, and sat down in it, facing him. "Tell me how bad it was."

Myriad emotions crossed his face—fear, shame, resignation—and he said, "What do you want to know, exactly?"

"You told me things had gotten really bad the year before Mom and I moved," I reminded him. "I want to know your definition of *bad*. Mom said . . . well, she told me a few things about you."

His back stiffened as if he was bracing for a hit. "Like what?"

"She said you spent all our money on drugs and that you drove drunk with me in the backseat. Did you?"

"I did a lot of things," he muttered. Then he sighed, rubbing a hand over his face. "Look, Lexi. These past few days have been more than I could have ever hoped for. Having you here, getting to know you and seeing how incredible you turned out. Watching you with Willow and Jonah." He looked at me, eyes pleading. "I don't want to ruin it by resurrecting the past."

It was if he'd slapped me. I'd worked up the nerve to email him, then talk to him, then *see* him, and he wasn't even brave enough to tell me the truth? "But it's *my* past too," I said, that constant, familiar resentment emerging. "It's why I contacted you. Why I came here. I deserve to know, Eric. You said you wanted to explain your side."

"Yeah? Well, my side is totally fu—" He stopped when he realized he'd raised his voice and was about to swear in front of me. A habit from having young children around.

"Fucked up," I finished for him. "I know. You think my

side isn't?" My voice shook as I continued. "I don't know what my mother was like when you knew her, but growing up with her wasn't exactly a picnic. My friend Nolan's parents practically raised me because she was always either too drunk or too busy with one of her asshole boyfriends to bother. She didn't even go to my *graduation*. Know why? Because she thinks it's my fault her boyfriend couldn't keep his damn hands to himself."

Eric's face turned pale under his tan. "I didn't know. . . . I mean, every time I called she seemed fine. I was—"

"What?" I cut in. My heart was racing. "What do you mean, every time you called? You never called. After we left, you forgot I even existed."

"No," he said firmly. "No, I never forgot, not for one second. Jesus," he muttered to himself. "You really don't know."

"Know what?"

He leaned forward on the stool, elbows on his knees and eyes back on me. "After I got out of rehab, I used to call your mother several times a year. Most of the time she hung up on me or avoided my calls, but I kept trying. Eventually, she changed the number and made it private so I couldn't call anymore. You can ask Renee if you don't believe me," he said when I shook my head, unconvinced. "Every single year I sent you birthday and Christmas cards. I sent pictures. I never stopped trying to contact you, even after Stacey told me you hated me and pretended I was dead. The last thing she said to me before she took you away was that she'd make sure you grew up hating me as much as she did. That's why I was so shocked when I saw your email. All these years, she let me believe you wanted nothing to do with me."

The room was spinning, the colorful array of guitars bleeding together and then separating again, shifting sharply into focus. If my mother had been standing in front of me right then, I would have bludgeoned her with one. "How could she have kept that from me?" I asked, and then I thought, *Of course she kept it from me.* She kept everything from me . . . her love, my past, the truth, right down to the fact that my own father was alive, sober, and ready to be my father again.

"She wanted to protect you."

Teresa had said the same thing, but I wasn't buying it. Not anymore. "My mother has never protected me from anything. She hates me. I probably would have been better off with you."

"No," Eric said, leaning back. "You wouldn't have been better off with me. Not back then."

"We were close. I know we were. I have this memory of us, walking in the woods together . . . " I blinked back tears and looked away, toward the paper-covered wall. "That was real, wasn't it?"

"Yes, it was real. There was a path in the woods behind my parents' house. We used to walk there all the time, just the two of us. You loved it."

I thought again about how safe and happy I'd felt with him there, under a canopy of trees. It wasn't just the walk I'd loved—it was him. "I see how you are with your kids," I said, tearing up again. I let them come. "You're a good dad. You've always been a good dad for them. Why couldn't you do the same for me? I mean, was it my fault? What the hell is wrong with me?"

I felt his hand close over mine and then he squeezed it, willing me to look at him. When I did, his face was drawn with pain. "There's nothing wrong with you, Lexi, and I'm sorry I made you feel that way," he said, his voice breaking. "You know how long it took me to learn to be a good dad? There's ten years between you and Willow. That's how long it took. I wasn't a good dad to you, Lexi.

Not even close. Good dads don't smoke crack in front of their three-year-olds. Good dads don't leave syringes lying around the house for their babies to find. I did that. I drove drunk with you and exposed you to other addicts and bought eight balls instead of diapers. I put you in danger every single day, even when I knew CPS could intervene at any time and remove you from the house. And I'll never forgive myself for that. Never." He grasped my hand again, his warm palm enveloping my fingers just like I remembered. "Your mother *did* protect you, Lexi. She took you away so you could be safe and I didn't try to fight it. You deserved better than me, so I let you go. I was a horrible excuse for a father, but I loved you so much it hurt. I always have."

Tears rolled down our faces. I'd come to get his side of the story, and now that I had it, I realized how skewed and incomplete the other side actually was. On the outside, my father's life looked perfect. Normal. But on the inside, underneath the thriving business and expensive house and beautiful family, was a rotting core of guilt, shame, and regret. I knew because I had the same rotting core inside me, and the same layer of armor on the outside, hiding it from view.

"Why didn't you come back to Alton?" I asked him a while later after we were sufficiently cried out and he was once again plucking on his guitar. The air between us felt clear, lighter. "After rehab, I mean. Why did you stay away?"

He glanced up at me, his fingers still and resting against the strings. "People, places, and things. It's a recovery thing. Avoid people and places and things you associate with drugs and drinking. Alton was my place."

"But you came back to run the business."

He started strumming again. "Yes, and it wasn't easy. It

still isn't. There are a lot of people in this town who remember the old me very clearly, and some of them assume I'm still the same troublemaking punk I was back then."

I looked over at his picture wall and caught another glimpse of the younger, much thinner Eric. "Obviously you're not," I said, turning back to him. "I mean, they should be able to tell that just by looking at you."

"True," he said with a shrug. "But I guess I understand where they're coming from. Sometimes you get an image of someone stuck in your head and then you can't let go of it, even after they show you they've changed. All you can see is that one side of them."

I nodded. I was guilty of that very thing myself. As a child, I'd known only one version of him, only a part of the story. But now I saw the full picture. There were two sides to everything and everyone, and somewhere in the middle was the truth.

Chapter Twenty-three

The sky was just starting to turn light as I stood in the driveway next to my father's truck, my suitcase sitting upright at my feet. Eric picked it up and stowed it in the back of the truck while I gazed up at the dark, quiet house. Renee, Willow, and Jonah were still sound asleep inside, having said their good-byes the night before.

"Ready?" Eric asked me. "We'd better get on the road if we're going to make it to the airport by eight."

"Yeah," I said, and climbed into the truck. When I was buckled in, I looked at the house one last time. When I first got here a week ago, I'd been so sure leaving would be easy. But the ache in my chest when we pulled away suggested otherwise.

Before we hit the highway, Eric pulled into a gas station on Alton's main street and got out to fill the tank. While he was inside paying, I gazed out my window at the various storefronts, thinking about my mother and Teresa and how they'd hung out together on this very street once, so many years ago. I pictured the two of them as teenagers, girls my age. Best friends on diverging paths in life, one leading east and one beginning and ending right in Alton. Then meeting again in Oakfield a few years later, only to split apart even wider.

"How did you and my mother meet?" I asked Eric once

we'd left the town behind. Mom never shared any of her happy memories of my father. Their good times, however few, would have to be recounted by him.

He accelerated, gradually inching over the speed limit. "She was waitressing at Ziggy's Diner, that grease pit on the corner of Pike Street," he said, eyes on the road. "Back then, the band always rehearsed in our buddy Lyle's garage, and afterward we'd all go to Ziggy's. It was the only place open at three or four in the morning and the food tasted damn good when you'd been drunk since the night before." He smiled, remembering. "Your mom did the night shift, so she was usually the one who had the unfortunate experience of waiting on us. All the guys tried to date her, of course, but it was me she ended up choosing. I knew she was too good for me, but I couldn't help myself. She was the prettiest girl I'd ever seen, but it wasn't just that. She was smart and funny and feisty as hell."

Feisty, I could see. And she'd been undeniably beautiful back then, before time and misfortune had hardened her features. But smart? Funny? Those qualities had gotten lost along the way, drowned in a bottle of wine or trampled by men like Keith Langley. The only quality she'd held on to, it seemed, was her weakness for guys like Keith and Jesse and, initially, my father. Guys with easy charm and killer smiles and an irresistible element of danger. It was the same weakness that infected me and ultimately drew me to Tyler. Hopefully, our relationship, wherever it stood, wouldn't turn out like any of hers.

We arrived at the airport with little time to spare. Eric and I didn't speak as we maneuvered through the crowds, both of us intent on getting me through security as soon as possible. My flight left in less than an hour and the lineup was long.

"Well," Eric said, stopping near the security area and placing my suitcase on the floor. We stood there looking at each other much as we'd done the same time a week ago, after I'd first stepped out of the gate. We weren't the same, though. Not even close. "I guess you should get going before the plane takes off without you."

"Yeah," I said, swallowing hard. Panic flared in my chest. I needed to say so much more, but all I could manage was, "I'm glad I came." It wasn't enough, but it would have to be.

"I'm glad too," he said, and the next thing I knew my face was pressed into his shoulder as he hugged the breath out of me. "Thank you for coming here, Lexi. For giving me a second chance. I'll never let you go again, okay? That's a promise."

He said those words with so much gratitude and sincerity, I couldn't help but believe them. The panic faded and I hugged him back, breathing in the scent of Irish Spring and motor oil that would always remind me of this trip. Of him. "I'll come back," I promised him.

"You're welcome anytime. We'll always have a room for you. Remember that."

He let me go and I shifted my attention to gathering my suitcase, giving us each time to blink the moisture out of our eyes before facing each other again. "I should go," I said, giving him a tremulous smile.

"Text me when you land, okay?" He leaned down and kissed my forehead, a fatherly gesture I'd never experienced. "I love you, Lexi."

I nodded, not trusting myself to speak, and then quickly got in line before I changed my mind and went back to Alton with him. By the time both pieces of my luggage had passed through the scanner, he was gone.

Teresa and Nolan were waiting for me when I landed, just as I knew they would be. Just as they'd done almost fourteen years ago, when Mom and I arrived at this very airport, tired but hopeful. It must have been scary for us, leaving everything we knew and starting over in a strange, unfamiliar place. Now, in spite of what had brought us here, it was home.

"Lexi!" Teresa folded me in her arms and squeezed. "Oh, sweetie, I know you were only gone for a week, but we missed you!"

As we hugged, I looked over her shoulder at Nolan, who grinned back at me. Would he sketch my face like this? Lit up with the sheer joy of being near them again? We didn't share the same blood, but they'd always been my family.

"So how'd it go?" he asked as we left baggage claim and rounded the corner to the exit.

I glanced up at him, unsure of what he meant. The trip? The flight? The good-bye with my father? So I answered for all three. "Better than I'd expected."

When we pulled into the Bruces' driveway an hour later, I glanced across the street at my house. It was dark and quiet, our Ford nowhere to be seen. Either Mom was working until nine or she was avoiding my homecoming.

"Um, I have a few things to take care of," I told Nolan, who was unloading my luggage from the trunk. "I'll be over later on."

"Sure," he said, eyes teasing. On the way home, he'd caught me sending a quick text to Tyler, alerting him to my return. He knew exactly why I wanted to go over to my house. "See you later."

The house was warm and slightly stuffy when I walked in. Instead of turning on the central air, I cracked open all the windows, letting in the humid breeze. The kitchen and living room looked as neat as they did the day I left, as if they hadn't even been used. The only thing different about the kitchen was that the note I'd written Mom had disappeared from the counter.

Downstairs, the first thing I did was check on Trevor. My bedroom was as dark and stuffy as the rest of the house, but Trevor liked the dark. I wasn't sure if it was possible for snakes to miss people, but he seemed extra lively when I lifted him out of his tank. He twisted his body around my wrist as I wandered around my room, opening the window and unpacking my suitcase. As I was separating dirty clothes from clean, my phone dinged with a text.

i'm here

I dropped my phone and the bra I was holding, put Trevor back in his tank, and went to the window.

Within seconds, Tyler dropped to his stomach on the grass, his face suddenly inches from mine. "Hi." His smile, which was somehow still bright after several years of smoking, looked even more brilliant against his sun-bronzed skin.

My entire body fluttered, like the butterflies weren't satisfied with just my stomach and decided to branch out.

Just as I was about to pop my screen and yank him inside, a car door slammed out front. We both looked toward the sound. *Shit.* My mother. Tyler rolled away from my window and disappeared, just in case she decided to venture around the corner of the house. I listened as she walked up the driveway and entered the house, her footsteps heavy in the thick, comfortable shoes she wore for work.

"She's inside," I whispered out the window, and Tyler appeared again, crouching this time. "You probably shouldn't come in right now."

"So you come out."

I glanced up at the ceiling. Mom was plodding around the kitchen, presumably noticing the open windows and my house keys on the table. *I'm not ready,* I thought. *I can't face her right now. Not yet.* Tyler, recognizing the anxious, deer-in-headlights look on my face, gestured for me to crawl out the window.

"I haven't done this since I was fourteen," I told him, removing the screen and tossing my flip-flops outside.

"Well, I've been doing it for the last ten months. It's not too bad."

Backing up a few feet, I made a running start toward the window, using the wall and the grip of my bare feet for leverage as I hoisted myself up and out.

"Easy, right?" Tyler said when I landed beside him on the grass, panting. He grabbed my hands and pulled me to standing. As I slipped into my flip-flops, he said, "We have to check and make sure none of the neighbors are looking, then we haul ass to the street and walk at a normal pace, like we're taking a leisurely stroll."

I laughed. "You really have done this a lot."

He took my hand again and led me to the edge of the house. When the coast was clear, we crossed the front lawn and turned left.

"Where are we going?" I asked, amused by how proficient he was at making a clean getaway. I'd never done anything like this with him. Our relationship had always been confined to the four walls of my bedroom. We'd never walked together, down my street or anywhere else in public, and I liked it. I liked seeing a different side of him.

"For a drive. My car is parked at the store."

Sure enough, it was. We got in and Tyler started the engine, then squealed out of the parking lot like we were still eluding detection. I scrambled for my seatbelt and clicked it in. Sitting with him in his car felt even stranger than walking with him, and not in a bad way. His old Impala was surprisingly comfortable, and despite the fact that he drove like a maniac, being there seemed *right*, somehow. I thought about Ben's brand new Acura, how carefully he drove it and how proud I'd been to finally claim its coveted passenger seat. But nice as that car was, I'd always felt like an imposter sitting in it. Like I didn't belong. Not once had I ever relaxed against the seat, feet up on the dash and right arm out the window, slicing through the wind. Not once had I thrown my head back and laughed or watched the muscles flex in the forearm of the boy next to me as he shifted gears. Not once had I felt like me.

After driving for fifteen minutes, Tyler turned down the road that ran alongside Donovan Lake and parked against the curb. Without a word, we got out of the car and made our way toward one of the weathered picnic tables that sat along the edge of the lake. We sat down, facing the water with our backs against the table. Donovan Lake was huge, and just looking at it gave me a sense of peace.

"You mentioned once that you missed the water," Tyler said, picking a rock off the ground and lobbing it into the lake. "When you were gone."

I *had* missed it—the only body of water I'd encountered in Alton was the chlorinated one in my father's backyard. But I didn't recall ever mentioning this to Tyler, unless it was during one of our dreamy, semiconscious conversations in the dark. Now that I was next to him, those moments no longer felt real.

But this one did. I shifted closer, taking my place against the perfect fit of his body. "I did miss it. I missed it a lot."

Our hands collided and then joined, the movement fluid and effortless. It felt good to be home.

Chapter Twenty-four

I had yet to lay eyes on my mother since I got home, and she'd certainly never swallow her pride and walk over to the Bruces' house to talk to me. She nursed grudges like bottles of wine and never owned up to her mistakes. After everything Eric told me about her, the phone calls she'd ignored and the cards I'd never received, plus everything she'd said in the kitchen after the altercation with Jesse, I was holding a bit of a grudge myself. She'd have to make the first move.

On Saturday, I put all that aside for a couple hours and went to visit Shelby. She and Piper had been home for a few days, but between my trip and everything else going on, I still hadn't seen them. So that afternoon, I borrowed Teresa's car and drove across town to her house.

Shelby was expecting me and answered the door herself. When I saw her, I almost gasped. She looked exhausted and disheveled, but she was *thin* again. Or at least, the giant bump had turned into a smaller, softer one.

"What?" she said, peering down at her oversized T-shirt, which had several wet stains down the front. "Come on, now. Did you expect me to just bounce back? I carried a seven pound human in there."

"No," I said, stepping inside. "You look great."

"Right." She rolled her eyes, then laughed and pulled

me in for a tight hug. "It's good to see you. It's good to see *anyone* who's not my mother or a sadistic breastfeeding consultant."

I laughed and handed her the gift bag I'd brought. A present for Piper.

"Thanks. Come on in. She's sleeping in her car seat in the living room. Excuse the mess."

I followed her through the house, which was nowhere near messy. Shelby's mother was one of those obsessive, neat-freak types who ironed towels and alphabetized the food in the pantry. Even though Shelby's parents had eventually gotten used to the idea of a granddaughter, it must have killed her mom to suddenly have a baby around, sullying her pristine house with dirty diapers and spit-up.

"Here she is," Shelby said when we reached the living room, where Piper's car seat—with her in it—rested on the floor beside the couch. I knelt down to admire her while Shelby opened the gift. "Oh!" she said, holding up the tiny denim jacket I'd picked out at the mall yesterday. "This is adorable. Thank you."

"You're welcome." My eyes were on Piper, sound asleep in a pink onesie with a pacifier affixed to her mouth like a plug. She looked just like her picture, except maybe a little plumper, and her skin had a yellowish tinge.

"She has a touch of jaundice," Shelby explained before I could ask. "It'll go away."

Joining her on the couch, I asked, "So how was your labor?"

"Long," she replied, grimacing as she folded the jacket and put it back in the bag. "But not too bad. I was numb for most of it, and I didn't need a C-section so that was a plus. Pushing her out took forever, though."

Hearing this, my legs crossed automatically. "Was Evan there through the whole thing?"

"Yeah. He was awesome. Counted through the pushes and even cut the cord when she came out." She glanced down at Piper, who was beginning to stir. "He's been good all week, actually. He comes over every evening after work to help me with her, and he buys diapers and wipes and stuff. I told you about his new lifeguard job, right? He started right after graduation."

I nodded. "That's great."

Piper was full-on fussing. Shelby bent down and scooped her up, settling her against her shoulder. The baby looked impossibly small, like one of those lifelike dolls in the see-through plastic boxes in the toy section at Wal-Mart.

"You want to hold her?" Shelby asked.

"I . . . she's probably . . . isn't she hungry?"

She laughed at my panicked stammering. "I just fed her and changed her diaper like a half hour ago. She just wants to be in someone's arms. Here." She cradled the baby, one hand under her head, and placed her in my arms. "See? She stopped fussing."

Piper may have looked like a doll, but she didn't feel like one. She was warm and solid and smelled like baby powder and something indefinable, a sweet, new-baby smell. Her eyes opened for a second and then closed again, the pacifier popping out as she drifted into a deeper sleep.

While the baby napped in my arms, Shelby and I talked about my trip and her first few days as a mom and our plans for the rest of the summer. But of course, all this talk was just perfunctory, a necessary hurdle to cross before we could move on to what she *really* wanted to discuss.

She grinned wickedly at me. "So. You and Tyler Flynn, huh?"

Stifling a smile, I dropped my gaze to Piper's tiny face. "Shocking, I know."

"Not really. I always thought Ben was too stuffy for you."

"Emily thinks it's shocking," I reminded her.

"Emily thinks most things are shocking. She lives on a safe little island of conformity and expects all her friends to do the same. Then, the minute you step off your designated spot, she freaks out. She didn't speak to me for two months after Ben dumped me, remember? She's not exactly open-minded, but unlike Ben, she does forgive."

Piper started to squirm and grunt, so I handed her back to Shelby. "I don't know. She thinks Tyler's a loser. And I lied to you guys."

"You didn't lie, exactly, you just hid stuff from us. To be honest, I think Emily's more hurt that you didn't tell us about your father. *I* get it, but unlike her I'm not a black-and-white kind of person." Shelby grabbed the pacifier from the couch cushion, examined it for lint, then nudged it into the baby's mouth. "As for Tyler . . . he's changed, right? Since he's with you, I'm assuming he's over his man-whoring phase, and you said he stopped selling drugs, too. That's progress, at least."

I had to agree. Not only had he stopped selling, he'd recently gotten a one-hundred-percent legal, legitimate job. A friend of his parents owned a house painting company and had hired him on full-time for the summer. In fact, it was his first day. It may not have paid as well as his last job, but he probably wouldn't get arrested for this one.

"All those rumors about him," I said, "most of them were either exaggerated or made up. He's not as bad as everyone thinks."

She shrugged. "Hey, it's not like I have room to judge. Look at who *I* chose for a boyfriend. Sure, he's on his best behavior right now, but you know what Evan's like . . . here one minute and gone the next. And I'll be dealing with him for the rest of my *life*." She let out a loud yawn, as if the mere prospect of it exhausted her, and then gazed down at her sleeping daughter. "I really hope he sticks around this time. If not for me, then for her. She needs her dad."

"True," I said, looking down at Piper. She was quiet and content again, her little fist clutching Shelby's finger as if to assure her that yes, she needed her dad, but she needed her mother just as much.

When I got back from visiting Shelby and Piper, I headed over to my empty house to clean Trevor's tank and feed him the mouse I'd defrosted earlier (I would have taken him over to the Bruces', but I was afraid Gus would mistake him for a chew toy and eat him). With that done, I returned to the kitchen to check my stock of rodent coffins and sort through the mail, which I'd noticed was piling up on the kitchen table. For once, there were no overdue bills or collection agency threats. My mom had actually paid them all this month, even without my reminders.

As I stood there staring at a zero-balance credit card statement and contemplating this sudden display of responsibility, a car door shut out front, followed by footsteps. I froze. My mother already? Usually she worked late on Saturdays, so I thought I'd be safe at five. *Apparently not*, I thought as a key slid into a lock that was already open and she entered the house, oblivious. There was nothing I could do but stay where I was and face her, head-on. It had to happen eventually, and it was as good a time as any.

She reached the threshold to the kitchen and paused, her eyes locking onto mine as I stood by the table, credit card statement still in my hand. Her features vacillated between surprise and dread and anger before finally settling into her most familiar expression—contempt.

"Oh, so you finally decided to come over and talk to me?" she said, dropping her purse on the counter. "You've only been back, what, three days?" She glanced at the table, taking in the stack of ripped-open mail, then spotted the paper in my hand. "Yes, I did pay the bills last month. Every one of them. Believe it or not, I *can* manage without you and your constant nagging."

I looked away, tears stinging my eyes. Maybe it wasn't the time. Obviously she hadn't changed her mind about blaming me for the Jesse thing, and in her eyes, my running away to Alton only confirmed my culpability. Not that we'd ever lived in peace, but I wondered if my mother and I would be able to co-exist in this house—or anywhere—ever again.

"I just came over to feed Trevor." I tossed the statement on the table on top of the other mail. "I'll leave."

"No, no, wait," she said, leaning against the counter toward me like a friend eager for gossip. But her flat, cold eyes told a different story. "I want to hear all about your wonderful trip to Alton."

She was playing with me, circling and jabbing like Trevor did with his motionless prey. Only I wasn't doomed like those mice or unable to fight back. I was alive and capable, and the decision to run or stay was on me. I was through running. "It was great," I said, looking straight at her. "I learned a lot."

She scoffed. "Oh, I'm sure. I bet you heard hundreds of stories about what a cold, irrational bitch I was, taking a child away from the father she adored. That's why you've been avoiding me, right? Because he filled your head with lies about me?"

"No, he didn't fill my head with lies. In fact, the only time he ever talked about you was when I brought it up, and most of his stories were good ones. He's not the same guy he was back then, you know. People grow up. They mature." I raised my eyebrows at her as if to say *present company excluded.*

"Unlike me, right?" she said wryly. "Well, look in the mirror, honey. You may have gotten his pretty blue eyes, but the rest is all me."

Not if I can help it, I thought, shifting my gaze to the wall by the door. It wasn't noticeable, but if you stood really close or ran your hand along the paint, you could make out a slight, circular indentation, the result of a head slamming against the wall at full force. A memento of the night that had pushed Tyler over the edge and me along with him. The tipping point that had sent me running to Alton and my father and then, ultimately, to this moment.

"This avoidance thing goes both ways," I told her, getting back to the subject at hand. "And it has nothing to do with anything my father said to me. It has to do with Jesse."

Her cheeks turned red and she straightened up, crossing her arms over her chest. "*What,* Lexi?" she barked. "He left. He's never coming back. What else do you want from me?"

As usual, her delusion simply astounded me. "Well, just for starters, how about an apology for blaming me for something I didn't do? How about a mother who takes her daughter's word over her creepy asshole boyfriend's? How about that?"

She turned her head to the side, her jaw twitching as she struggled to contain her emotions.

Which emotions, I had no clue.

"I was drunk that night," she said. "I didn't know what was happening."

"You knew *exactly* what was happening," I yelled at her. "That excuse doesn't work on me anymore, Mom. I'm not five years old. You knew what he did and you didn't care. You told me it was my fault. Mothers are supposed to protect their kids from being hurt, not blame them for it."

"Yeah, well, clearly I'm a horrible mother," she said, flinging her arms out. "You think so, and I know for damn sure Teresa thinks so. She's always made that abundantly clear."

"How would you know? You haven't spoken to her in over five years, all because she was brave enough to tell you what you needed to hear. Who do you think took care of me when you were passed out on the bathroom floor or couldn't get out of bed in the morning?"

"Right, she's mother of the year. Believe me, I'm well aware. When you were little and you got hurt or felt sad, who did you run to? Not me. You went right to Teresa, every time. Jesus, you even called her Mommy for a while. And she did nothing to stop it. 'Just let her adjust,' she'd say. Right. She taught you to believe she was the only one who could comfort you and take care of you. Me? I was worthless."

"She took care of me because you didn't," I said. My body was shaking with pure frustration. How could she not see what kind of mother she'd been to me? "Teresa didn't have a choice. You can't resent her for stepping in any more than you can resent me for getting attached to her."

"And I knew it, too," she continued as if I hadn't even spoken. "I knew I was worthless as a mother. Why else would I have kept you in Alton for so long?" She glanced at me, her face tired and slack. "Let me guess. He didn't tell you all *those* stories, right? About how bad he'd gotten before we left?"

"He told me the truth." To prove it, I listed off every appalling offense he'd confessed to, from doing drugs in front of me right down to his lack of resistance when she took me away.

With each word, my mother drifted further into her own memories and sins.

"He thinks you were right to take me away," I finished. "And you were. I get that. I wasn't safe there. Who knows what would have happened if we'd stayed. I probably would have been taken away and put into foster care, or worse. What I *don't* get is why you refused to take his calls after we moved, and why you kept all his birthday and Christmas cards from me."

Her head jerked up and she stared at me, surprised. I hadn't included this little tidbit in my index of Eric's confessions.

"He told me everything," I emphasized. "You think Teresa turned me against you? Well, that's nothing compared to how you turned me against him. You told me he was probably dead when you knew very well he wasn't. You told me he didn't give a shit about us. About me. It was Teresa who told me he was living in Alton again. She was the one who gave me his information in case I wanted to contact him. Want to resent her for that, too? Go right ahead. Unlike you, she thought I deserved the truth."

In all my years of fighting with my mother and telling her off and avoiding her bad moods and verbal blows, I'd never seen her look like she did at that moment. Like my words had totally gutted her, striking against something deep inside. Like what I'd said, and the feelings behind it, actually mattered. While I watched, wary and amazed, she shuffled over to the table and sank down into a chair, burying her face in her hands. She mumbled something, but with the heels of her hands over her mouth all I could make out was "I wanted."

"What?" I said, gingerly sitting in the chair across from her.

Her hands dropped from her face, revealing a red nose and wet cheeks. "I wanted to do it on my own. Raise you, I mean. Without him or anyone else. But I couldn't. I had no idea what I was doing. I was too scared. I needed

Teresa, even after I'd saved enough money to leave their house. That's why we moved across the street instead of to another town or city or whatever. I couldn't take you away from the people you loved. Not again. And I trusted Teresa to raise you right."

My mother looked so small, curled up into herself like Piper had been earlier when she lay in my arms. Keeping me near the Bruces was probably one of the most caring things my mother had ever done for me, aside from removing me from a drug house.

"Teresa misses you," I said quietly. "She wants to be your friend again."

Mom grabbed a napkin from the holder on the table and wiped her nose. "What Teresa wants, she already has."

Me, I thought. *She means me.* It was crazy how many ways a situation or intention could be perceived. To Mom, it was like Teresa had hatched an evil plan to steal me away and undermine her as my mother. But the way I saw it, she'd simply been there for me, providing the love she knew I lacked.

I focused on my mother's face, which had been wiped clear of all her artfully applied makeup. Without it, she looked every bit her age. "If that's what you really think," I said, "then get your act together and fight for me like my dad did."

I wasn't sure what shocked me more, that I'd challenged my mother to be my mother or that I'd used the *d* word in reference to Eric. In any case, my legs felt weak with tension as I stood up and started toward the door. "You know where to find me."

I walked out the door and back across the street.

Chapter Twenty-five

Since I'd come home from Alton, Tyler and I had been spending every spare minute together. In the evenings, after his various painting jobs, he would drive over to see me at the Bruces' house. At first, I worried he and Nolan wouldn't get along, that Tyler would see him the same way Ben had and things would get weird. But when I broached the subject to Tyler one night, he simply shrugged.

"If we can't trust each other, then what's the point?" He knew what Nolan meant to me and accepted our friendship. He understood.

And once Nolan realized that Tyler didn't feel threatened by him, they got along just fine.

The only thing we were lacking was time alone. My room at the Bruces' house had a window, but just the thought of sneaking Tyler in felt disrespectful and wrong. Instead, I kept my ears and eyes open whenever I was at my own house, hoping I could somehow nail down a time after six o'clock when the house would be empty.

One Saturday in mid-July, I got my chance. When I went over at around seven to feed Trevor, my mother was all glammed up and gabbing on the phone to one of her girlfriends about their forthcoming night on the town. *Jackpot.*

I didn't even bother going back across the street after she left. I texted Tyler, who came straight over. And not to my bedroom window, either. For the first time ever, he entered my house through the front door.

As I led him down the stairs to my room, I wondered—just for a moment—if the sexual chemistry between us would suffer now that our relationship was out in the open and he'd lost some of his mystery and danger. But I shouldn't have wondered. If anything, it intensified.

"Tyler," I said much later as we lay twisted together on my bed, half asleep.

"Hmm?"

"I need to talk to you about something."

His chest rose and fell under my cheek. "Okay."

I swallowed. How did I bring this up without sounding all girlfriend-like and presumptuous? But I had to. The farther we got into summer, the more I started thinking about college and what would happen to us when I left. I'd be hours away, only coming home for major holidays. Would he be okay with that? Would *I*? Could I really ask him to wait for me? No, I couldn't, at least not right this second.

He was waiting for me to say something, so I did. "Promise me you'll never do drugs."

"Uh," he said, confused by the random request. "I'm afraid that ship has already sailed. You've even sailed with me a few times, remember?"

"I'm not talking about a bit of weed here and there. I mean the heavier stuff."

"Ah." He rolled to the side and pulled me against his warm skin. For a moment, I forgot what we were discussing, then he said, "In that case, you don't need to worry. That stuff scares the shit out of me. I've seen *Intervention*."

I gave him a half-hearted smack. "I'm being serious."

"So am I," he said, moving on top of me and nibbling my earlobe. "Very serious."

For a minute, I just closed my eyes and let him distract me. Then, just like that night in Dustin Sweeney's yard, I snapped out of it and pushed him away, only gently and without the kick to the shin.

He opened his mouth to protest, but I cut him off. "I have to say something else."

"What is it?" he asked, sensing my apprehension.

I sighed. "I'm leaving for college soon."

Tyler looked at me, waiting.

"In six weeks," I went on.

"Yeah . . ."

"And I don't plan on coming home very often."

He blinked and looked away, finally getting it. "Right. I figured."

I touched his forearm, running my fingertips over the faded splotches of paint that clung to his skin no matter how hard he scrubbed. "I'll understand if it's . . . too much."

"Too much what? Time apart?"

I nodded.

"Lexi," he said, holding my chin so I'd look at him. Not forcefully like Jesse had held it that awful night in the kitchen, but soft and light, so if I wanted to—which I didn't—I could easily break free. "It's okay. I mean, it sucks that I'll hardly ever get to see you, but I know how much you want to get away. It doesn't matter what I think or what anybody else thinks. Just go. Start fresh."

All I could do was stare at him in amazement. Back in September, when I'd seduced him for my own selfish reasons, I'd barely given a thought to how he felt or who he really was. All I'd seen was the image he projected to the world—the petty criminal, drug-dealing badass who slept around. But the more I got to know the real Tyler, the more that old image became distorted, evolving and changing until finally, a brand new one took its place. This new one never ceased to surprise me.

I bit my lip. "So, you'll be here when I come home?"

"I'm not going anywhere."

"That's not what I mean."

He dropped a kiss on the bridge of my nose where my freckles were the most concentrated. "I know exactly what you mean. Like I said, I'm not going anywhere."

I smiled. Somehow, in spite of our unconventional beginning, Tyler Flynn had become something more. I wasn't a normal girl in a normal relationship with the boy everyone loved, but then again, I never had been.

An hour later, we got dressed and I walked Tyler outside. When we reached his car, which was parked in my driveway for the first time ever, I turned and leaned my backside against the hood. My cheeks burned, and I was suddenly grateful for the darkness obscuring my face. "Tyler, when did you realize you had, um . . . deeper feelings for me?"

He moved in front of me, so close I could feel the lingering warmth from my bed radiating off his skin. "You mean when did I fall in love with you?"

Since breath was necessary for speech and I'd just lost both, all I could do was nod idiotically.

"December," he said.

I studied the shadowy outline of his face, trying to remember something significant that had happened between us last December. Nothing. In fact, we'd barely seen each other that month. All the holiday parties had kept him pretty busy.

"It was the last day before Christmas break," he continued, running his fingers over my bare shoulder and down my arm, making me shiver. "I remember because everyone was in a good mood, even the teachers, and they let us leave twenty minutes early. On my way out, I saw you standing by the library with your friends. You were wearing that dark blue sweater that makes your eyes look almost purple and I couldn't stop myself from watching you. Anyway, that ass-wipe Ben was talking to someone at the other end of the hallway and you were gazing at him like you were starstruck or something. Like there was no one else in the world but him. And all I could think was I wish she looked at me like that."

Some kind of insect was draining the blood from my left ankle, but I barely noticed. My brain was too focused on the realization that Tyler Flynn had his own layer of armor and it was just as brittle as mine. "You never said anything."

"Of course I didn't. Can you blame me?"

No. I couldn't. After all, I'd made my intentions pretty clear from the start. Avoid each other in public, keep our secret, and most important, do not get attached. Obviously, my *Lexi Rules* were all null and void at that point. "If you felt that way about me, why did you stop caring when I started dating Ben? Why did you give up?"

"I didn't give up. I backed off. There's a difference. And I never stopped caring. . . . I just thought you'd be happier with someone like him. He was better for you."

"But he wasn't."

"Yeah, I realize that now."

For a moment, all I could hear was the rustle of the leaves in the lilac bush and the occasional car on the road beside us. I was sure people were looking at us, intrigued by the teenage couple embracing in public for all to see, but I no longer cared about who might be watching or what they might think of me. For once, I was exactly where I was supposed to be.

"So," Tyler said in a lighter, slightly teasing voice. "When did you fall in love with me?"

Another car rolled past, its headlights illuminating his face and giving me a clear view of the devious, cocky smile I somehow knew would be there.

I grinned right back. "Just now."

On the first day of August, the doorbell rang while Teresa and I were cleaning up the kitchen after dinner.

"That's Tyler," I said, bolting out of the kitchen and down the stairs to the front door. When I swung it open, my smile froze and then melted away. It wasn't Tyler on the other side . . . it was my mother.

"I just came over to give you these," she said, handing me a shopping bag filled with what looked like unopened mail. "They're not all there, but it's most of them, I think. Everything I managed to save."

I reached into the bag and brought out a square blue envelope. My name and address was scrawled across the front in a handwriting I vaguely recognized. Then I looked at the return address. My father. That was when it hit me—these were the cards he'd sent over the years, the ones my mother had kept from me. "Oh my God." I looked back at her.

She was standing nervously on the steps, staring at the house like it was haunted.

"Um," I said. "Are you coming in?"

She shook her head quickly. "Not quite ready for that yet."

Fair enough, I thought, and stepped outside, letting the door close behind me. I sat down on the top step and tore open the blue envelope. A Christmas card, going by the winter scene on the front. When I opened it, two pictures and a check fell out onto my lap. The check, made out to me for a hundred dollars, was dated three years ago. The pictures were of Willow and Jonah, their names and ages written on the back. They'd been there all along, hidden away like treasures, begging me to find them. If only I'd known to look.

Mom sat down next to me as I ripped through the rest. There were about twenty cards, each with a check for a hundred dollars, some with pictures and some not, all signed by my father.

"Thanks," I said, putting them back in the bag.

"Better late than never, right?"

I could feel the tension in her body as she sat there, like she was bracing herself for another fight. For a moment, I felt like giving her one, blasting her right off the steps for keeping it all from me, keeping my family from me, but for some reason I held back. Yes, it was her fault for letting me believe my father had abandoned me, but maybe I should have pushed harder. Maybe I shouldn't have been so quick to believe I was easy to forget.

"So," she said, biting her lip the same way I did. "Do you think you'll move out there someday?"

To *Alton*? A town so small and secluded it only had one traffic light and the nearest college was a zillion miles away? I stifled a laugh. "No. My home is here."

Her slight smirk told me she knew exactly what I was thinking. After all, she'd never gone back, and she never once mentioned missing it. "Is that old dive on Pike Street still open? Ziggy's?"

"Yeah. Eric told me you used to work there. He said that's where you met."

When she smiled, the lines on her face disappeared completely and I could see what Eric meant when he'd said, "She was the prettiest girl I'd ever seen."

She nodded. "Yep. I never could resist those bad boys."

As if he was just waiting in the wings for the perfect opening, Tyler drove up then in his dusty black Impala, music blaring and cigarette dangling from his lips, the personification of every parent's nightmare. He cut the engine, ditched the cigarette, and got out, exhaling smoke into the evening air. When he saw me sitting with my mother on the steps, he barely even flinched. He just kept going, across the walk and up the steps, nodding at me as he passed as if to say *I'll be inside if you need me.*

My mother followed his movements until he was in the house, then she turned to me and said, "Isn't that the boy who tried to strangle Jesse?"

The casual way she said it, along with the absurdity of that whole situation, made me burst out laughing. I couldn't help it. "Yeah. That's Tyler. He's not perfect, but he loves me."

"Well." She stood up and brushed the dirt off her shorts, glancing back at the house again like she might actually make it inside one day. "That's all any of us can hope for, right?" With that, she clomped down the steps and headed for home. She hadn't exactly come over to fight for me, but she *had* come over. It was a start.

Later that night, after Tyler left and I was sure my mother had gone out, I went over to my house to grab some extra clothes. It took all of five minutes, but afterward I lingered in my room, not quite ready to move back in but not quite ready to leave either. There was something I needed to do.

Corn Snakes: An Owner's Guide was still exactly how I'd left it a couple months ago, the last time I'd added an item to my bursting collection of secrets. I sat down on my bed and opened the book to the middle, then watched as the contents dropped in unison to my quilt. The scrap of paper—my father's contact information—I no longer needed, so I crumpled it up and tossed it in my garbage can. All that was left were the pictures—my parents young and in love, my father holding two-year-old me, and Nolan's sketch of Tyler as he crouched outside my window, waiting for me to appear. A sketch so candid, so amazingly detailed, it didn't deserve to be hidden away in a drawer.

I taped the old photos on the mirror above my dresser, right below the new one I'd acquired in Alton—a shot of all five of us in front of the pool, taken the day before I left. Eric had immediately printed two copies, one for each of us.

"I finally have a family picture that's complete," he'd said when he first saw his copy.

It was hard to stay bitter when he said things like that.

Next, I emptied the shopping bag of cards Mom had given me and added the shots of Willow and Jonah to my mirror collage, arranging them so they slightly overlapped the picture I'd stuck on my mirror way back in tenth grade—Shelby, Emily, and me, arms around each others' shoulders and beaming into the camera like we were untouchable. I thought of the still-unanswered texts I'd sent to Emily a few days ago. If she responded, great, and if she didn't, that was okay too. Having the "right" friends didn't seem so important anymore; I much preferred to focus on my real ones.

When all the pictures were displayed, crookedly but thoroughly, I finally picked up the sketch of Tyler. This one wouldn't go on my mirror. For one thing, there wasn't room, and for another, he didn't belong there.

He belongs with me, I thought as I approached the series of sketches on my wall, my face as seen through Nolan's eyes. Carefully, I taped the drawing of Tyler underneath the very first sketch, which was yellowed and curling at the edges.

As I moved back near Trevor to admire the new row I'd started, something inside his tank caught my eye. At first, I thought he'd produced another snake, but seeing as Trevor was male and confined, that made no sense at all. When I looked a little closer, it suddenly clicked. Of course. After all, the process had been ongoing for days. First his color faded. Then, gradually but steadily, his thin outer layer of scales loosened and peeled away until finally, he emerged on the other side, fresh and bright and all the more beautiful.

Trevor had shed his skin.

Read on for a sneak peek at ANY OTHER GIRL by Rebecca Phillips, coming next February!

I didn't set out to flirt with someone else's boyfriend at Miranda Lipton's party. But I did it like I did a lot of things—without even thinking about it, as spontaneous and subconscious as breathing. The incident itself probably would've gone virtually unnoticed if the boyfriend in question had been anyone other than Braden Myers, and if the "someone else" had been anyone other than my best friend.

"I'm gonna miss you," Shay said, squeezing me into an impulsive, coconut-scented hug. We were standing in Miranda's main floor bathroom, primping in front of the mirror above the double sinks. Our second-to-last week of school had ended just three hours before, and since then we'd hit Starbucks for Frappuccinos, gorged on deep-dish pizza at Mario's, and then walked to Miranda's house in the warm June sun to help her set up for the party. Most of the junior class planned to end up there, eager to take a one-night break from studying and blow off some steam before final exams started on Monday. But for now, it was just us girls.

"I'll miss you too," I said, hugging her back. "It's just for a couple months, you know. I'll be back before school starts again."

"I know." She pulled back and took a swig from her

bottle of vodka cooler, one of several currently sitting in Miranda's fridge. Her parents had left this morning for an out-of-town wedding. "Summer's boring without you around, though."

I laughed and sipped at my own cooler. She'd said the same thing last summer, and the summer before that. She always acted sentimental in the week or so before my parents and I left to spend the season at our cottage on the lake. Shay and I had only been best friends for two years, but we'd been inseparable since the day we'd met in the spring of freshman year, when we both turned up in Mrs. Lockhart's after-school study group for math. There, we'd bonded over our mutual failure to comprehend polynomials.

"What do you think?" I stepped back from the mirror and turned from side to side, inspecting myself from each angle. I didn't have much of a tan yet, so my white off-the-shoulder dress didn't set off my skin tone as much as I'd hoped. "Does this make me look washed out?"

Shay glanced at me through the mirror as she brushed her glossy black hair. "You look like Marilyn Monroe with those fake eyelashes on. Only you're thinner. And not blond."

I smiled, pleased. *Seven Year Itch* was one of the first classic movies I'd ever seen, and I often went for the Marilyn look—wavy hair, parted on the left. Curve-hugging dress. Thick eyelashes. I liked to stand out.

"My God, Kat," Cassidy Boveri said when Shay and I joined her and Miranda in the kitchen. "This isn't a nightclub."

I just laughed and slid up on the counter, bare legs dangling off the edge. Cassidy used to bother me back in freshman year, when my reputation made me basically friendless, but all that changed when I started hanging around with Shay. Everyone liked her, which meant they had to like me, too. Or at least tolerate me like Cassidy tried to do, even though it pained her. She still hadn't let go of the grudge she'd been holding against me since the eighth grade, when her boyfriend dumped her at the Halloween dance so he could start going out with me.

"I think she looks hot," Shay said, grabbing a Cheeto from the bowl on the counter and popping it into her mouth.

"We all do," Miranda said, ever the neutral peacemaker. "And speaking of hot," she added, a grin unfurling on her freckled face. "Is Man Candy coming tonight, Shay?"

Shay washed her Cheeto down with a gulp of cooler, trying to appear nonchalant. But I knew her well enough to see past the act. Braden Myers was more than just man candy to her. They'd been dating for about a month. Not long enough to become serious, but it was obvious how much she liked him. Braden was a senior at Nicholson, a huge high school across the city from ours, and she'd met him at a basketball game. The rest of us had only seen him once, when we all went to the movies together a couple weekends ago, but once was enough to stick him with the "Man Candy" nickname. He was a lean, muscular jock, like Shay, but whereas she was short and dark, Braden was tall, blond, and fair. And pretty damn hot.

"Yeah, he'll be here," Shay said, and then she shot me a private look, reminding me of what we'd discussed earlier. About how if the mood struck her, she planned to lure Braden into an empty bedroom so they could advance their relationship to the next level. Not the *final* level, but at least the one that came after kissing. For Shay, this was a big deal.

Several bottles of vodka cooler and bags of munchies later, the party was in full swing. I stuck close to Shay until Braden showed up around ten, then I headed off to circulate. The house was packed and stuffy, the music deafening. In the dining room, I paused to join a group of guys playing quarters at the table. All the chairs were taken, so one of the guys—Chris Newbury—pulled me down on his lap. I wrapped my arm around his shoulders and made myself comfortable, only vaguely aware of the judgmental stares coming from a cluster of girls sitting in the attached living room. Let them stare. I felt buzzed and happy and carefree, immune to rumors and whispers.

"You want to go somewhere?" Chris breathed wetly in my ear after losing his fifth consecutive round of quarters.

"Oh look!" I said, craning my neck toward the kitchen. "There's Shay. I'd better go say hi."

I hadn't actually seen Shay, but I needed some kind of diversion. I was good at making diversions.

"Wait," Chris said as I slid off his lap and shouldered my way out of the dining room. He said something else, but I didn't quite catch it over the music.

I could guess, though. The word *tease* was attributed to me often, along with various other unflattering terms.

The house was an oven, the mass of bodies blocking any breeze the open windows may have created. I could feel my dress sticking to the sweat on my back. *Gross.* Craving fresh air, I made my way through the kitchen and outside to the deck, where half a dozen people were gathered around on the patio furniture, smoking. So much for fresh air.

"Kat."

I turned at the sound of my name and saw Braden "Man Candy" Myers leaning against the deck railing, alone. I walked over to him, relishing the feel of the light breeze against my skin. "What are you doing out here all by yourself?" I leaned next to him, peering out at the tiny backyard and the distant downtown lights beyond.

"Have you seen Shay? She went inside to use the wash-room and never came back."

I presented him with one of my toothy, full-watt smiles. "There's a big line in there."

He smiled back, and I felt myself light up inside the way I always did when a guy responded to my attention.

"Mostly girls, right? You girls take forever in the bath-room."

I let out a big gasp, pretending to be offended, and he laughed. The sound of it made the light inside me glow even brighter. "That's because we actually take the time to wash our hands afterward," I teased.

"Hey, I wash mine." He held up his hands, which were big and powerful-looking.

I playfully swatted them back down, and an uneasy ex-pression flickered across his face in response to the contact. He shifted away from me and glanced toward the door like he was wishing for Shay to appear.

Undeterred, I continued to tease him. "I bet you spend just as much time in front of a mirror as any girl. You don't just roll out of bed looking like that."

"Yeah, well . . ." He scratched the back of his neck, which looked flushed in the dim light coming from the kitchen window.

"Stop being so modest. I'm sure you hear compliments like that all the time." I turned and leaned my back against the railing, aware of the way the moonlight played on the bare skin of my shoulders and cleavage. "Shay is a very lucky girl."

He laughed nervously. "So, uh, are you ready for exams next week?"

I threw back my head and laughed, even though his question wasn't even remotely humorous. Vodka coolers and warm summer nights made me giddy. "Oh, come on, Braden." I sidled closer to him and poked him in the shoulder with my finger. "This is a party. It's almost summer. Exams are *so* not what I want to be thinking about right now."

His throat moved as he gulped, like he was imagining what, exactly, I *did* want to be thinking about. I peered up at him through my fake eyelashes and grinned, slow and mysterious. If he were any other guy, he probably would have drawn closer, intrigued by the endless possibilities in my smile and eager for more.

But not Braden. Uncomfortable, he shifted again and started backing away. "Well, I'm going to go, um, find Shay."

"Okay," I said, confused. What was his problem? Why was he acting so eager to get away from me? I rewound our short conversation in my head, trying to pinpoint something I'd said or done to offend him. Nothing. I'd just acted like my typical bubbly self. Then again, Braden didn't know me very well—in fact, it was the first time we'd ever spoken to each other for longer than a second—so he wasn't exactly familiar with my effusive personality. The guys (and girls) I went to school with and saw on a regular basis were all used to it. No one took me too seriously.

But going by the scandalized look on his face as he walked away from me, Braden wasn't accustomed to assertive girls who modeled their appearance after retro actresses and liked to stand out in a crowd. Shay, after all, was none of these things.

Shay. For whatever reason, I felt a sudden, intense need to go look for her. Call it intuition, or premonition, or whatever the hell people called it when they were struck with that ominous sense of foreboding. I just knew I had to find her, and soon.

The kitchen was even more congested, and it took me a few minutes to get through. As I maneuvered around the bodies, Cassidy Boveri's strident voice rang out from somewhere behind me. "Classy, Kat. Real classy."

Distracted, I didn't bother to look back and ask what she meant.

In the dining room, the guys were still playing quarters at the table, though their coordination had decreased significantly since I'd left. As I passed, Chris Newbury made a grab for my arm, but I dodged him and headed for Miranda, who was mopping up a spill on the living room hardwood.

"Where's Shay?" I asked when she straightened up, wad of paper towels in hand.

"She just left with Braden," Miranda told me.

"Left? I thought we were spending the night."

She shrugged. "I thought so too."

I dug out my phone to see if Shay had texted me. She hadn't, so I sent her a text, asking where she was and what was going on. What had Braden said to her to make her ditch me without explanation? What exactly did he think had happened between us out there on that deck?

Shay never did text me back.

I wasn't used to being invisible. Especially not in the loud, crowded hallways of Brighton High. The cacophony of voices, footsteps, and bursts of laughter seemed almost subdued today, the first day of final exams.

No one paid any attention to me as I walked away from Mr. Porter's English class, my wrist sore from the three-hour exam I'd just written. Cassidy brushed past me like I didn't exist. I knew where she was going—to meet up with Shay outside the main doors. From there, they'd probably hit Starbucks and then maybe study together for their next exam. That was what Shay and *I* would've done, anyway, if last Friday night hadn't happened and she was still my best friend.

Friday night. It had been three days, but knots still formed in my stomach whenever I thought about the uneasy look on Braden's face and Shay's disappearance, and the fact that she'd ignored my texts and phone calls all weekend. Worst of all, it was due to one giant misunderstanding, which she refused to give me a chance to explain away.

I had every intention of heading to my locker next, but instead of turning left at the end of the hall, I turned right and followed Cassidy. Intent as she was on escaping, she didn't notice me skulking a few feet behind her. I trailed her all the way down the stairs, across the lobby, and out into the hot sun, where Shay waited on a small patch of grass near the sidewalk.

"Shay," I said, but my voice was lost in the roar of a passing transit bus. Brighton High was located in one of the busiest areas of the city, surrounded by restaurants and coffee shops. It came in handy for fast-food runs during lunch hour, something else Shay and I used to do together. "Shay," I repeated, louder.

She glanced up. Immediately, the welcoming smile she'd had for Cassidy dropped into a scowl at the sight of me. "Seriously, Kat?" she said, shaking her head like she couldn't quite believe I had the nerve to seek her out after she'd avoided me all weekend. "You seriously want to do this right now? Here?"

I glanced around. Students were still teeming out of the main doors like ants, squinting as the afternoon sun hit their faces. Several eyed us with interest. A lot of people had been at that party Friday night, had heard what I had done to Shay, my supposed best friend. My *only* true friend, really. They'd waited a long time for a confrontation like this. Waited to see me, Kat Henley, shameless flirt and supposed boyfriend stealer, get what was coming to her, at last.

"Please, just listen to me," I said, reaching out to touch Shay's arm.

She stepped back, closer to Cassidy, who leaned toward her in support and gave me the same look she'd been giving me since Shay had brought me into their group, the one that said *I'm a much better friend than you.* She was loving this more than anyone.

Suddenly, I remembered what she'd said to me at the party. *Real classy.* She'd seen me, I realized. Seen me talking to Braden outside. Maybe he hadn't been the one to tell on me, after all. "You have it all wrong, Shay."

She folded her bare, caramel-colored arms over her chest and smirked at me. "Oh, *do* I? Tell me, then, Kat. What exactly do I have wrong?"

I opened my mouth to speak then closed it again, unable to come up with an acceptable answer. Maybe there wasn't one. To me, the way I'd acted with Braden wasn't any different from the way I'd acted with Chris Newbury in Miranda's dining room or the rest of the boys at school—just harmless, playful flirting. Shay knew how I was, knew about my reputation when it came to boys, but she'd always accepted me at face value. She'd believed in me . . . until I gave her a reason not to.

"We were just talking." Frustrated tears throbbed at the backs of my eyes. "It wasn't anything more than that, I swear. You *know* me, Shay. I act like that with all the guys. It's no big deal."

Shay wasn't like me—she didn't relish the weight of many sets of eyes on her. She didn't seek attention or enjoy an audience. I knew her anger at me had completely taken over when she thrust a finger in my face and started yelling at me in front of everyone.

"No big deal? Braden isn't just some random guy at a party, Kat. He's my boyfriend. *My boyfriend.*" She turned her face to the side and blinked a few times. Shay hated crying. "I can't believe I was actually stupid enough to trust you."

"You *can* trust me," I said quickly. Pleadingly. "I'm your friend, Shay. You know I'd never—"

"Even after hearing what everyone said about you, I gave you a chance. And this is how you pay me back for two years of friendship? By flirting with my boyfriend the minute I turn my back? Screw you, Kat."

She turned and stormed away, leaving me there on the grass, the center of everyone's attention just like I always craved. Only this time, their gazes made me feel ashamed. Naked.

"You know," Cassidy said as we both stared after Shay, who was disappearing quickly down the sidewalk, her black ponytail swinging behind her. "I'm glad you're going to be at your cottage for the summer, Kat. I think we all need a break from you."

With that, she turned and went after Shay, catching up to her at the crosswalk. Together, they crossed the busy street and headed toward the Starbucks on the corner, arm in arm.

I watched them go as the crowd milled around me, already back to whatever it was they'd been doing before the drama started. They gave me a wide berth as I stood half in shock and unable to move. Like I was some kind of disease. Like my very presence was stressful and exhausting and something from which people needed a vacation.

Summer couldn't get here fast enough.